Albert Virgil Goodpasture, William Henry Goodpasture

Life of Jefferson Dillard Goodpasture

Albert Virgil Goodpasture, William Henry Goodpasture

Life of Jefferson Dillard Goodpasture

ISBN/EAN: 9783337333836

Printed in Europe, USA, Canada, Australia, Japan

Cover: Foto ©Raphael Reischuk / pixelio.de

More available books at **www.hansebooks.com**

LIFE OF

Jefferson Dillard Goodpasture;

TO WHICH IS APPENDED

A GENEALOGY OF THE FAMILY OF JAMES GOODPASTURE.

BY HIS SONS

A. V. AND W. H. GOODPASTURE.

NASHVILLE, TENN.:
CUMBERLAND PRESBYTERIAN PUBLISHING HOUSE.
1897.

PREFACE.

This book was not written, primarily, for the benefit of the public, but as a loving tribute to a venerated father, and for the pleasure and encouragement it may be to his family. Many things might otherwise have been omitted and others elaborated, but the authors have kept steadily in view the objects sough to be attained.

It makes no pretentions; if it meets the expectation and approval of those who knew and loved him, it will have achieved their fullest aspirations.

NASHVILLE, October 1, 1897.

CHAPTER I.

The country commonly called the Mountain District of Middle Tennessee may be said, in general terms, to extend northeastwardly, between the Cumberland Mountains and the Cumberland and Caney Fork Rivers, from a line drawn lengthwise through the center of the State, to the Kentucky line, embracing the counties of Overton, White, Jackson, Putnam, Fentress, Clay and Pickett. It is possibly the most imperfectly known and least appreciated portion of the State, owing to its inaccessibility, the rest of the country being many years in advance of it in matter of transportation. The child born there fifty years ago, was taught to expect a railroad through the Mountain District before he reached his majority, and in his turn held out the same delusive hope to his own children. Many of its ambitious young men sought honor and wealth in more inviting fields, and those who remained, finding little opportunity for individual enterprise and development, spent sufficient effort in acquiring a competency, to have made them eminent in a more favored community. Still the country possessess great natural advantages, especially to the manufacturer, on account of its vast mineral deposits, and unsurpassed water power, and will one day reach a degree of prosperity for which life has hitherto been too short to wait.

The Mountain District is distinguished as well for the beauty and variety as for the bold and rugged character of its topographical features. Its towering hills wall in picturesque coves; and its beautiful valleys are furrowed by impetuous streams, often forming magnificent cascades, like those on the Caney Fork, Calfkiller and Roaring Rivers and their tributaries, whose water powers cannot be excelled.

Roaring River. In 1802, F. A. Michaux, the great French naturalist, after describing the many falls of Roaring River, following each other in rapid succession, and making the confused noise that suggested its name; the great height of its banks, rising, as he declares, from eighty to a hundred feet; its immense caverns, some of which were celebrated for the dyestone they contained; the large rivulets that terminated their windings at its steep banks, whence they fell murmuring into its bed, forming beautiful cascades, several fathoms wide; the many varieties of trees and shrubs skirting its margin, especially the wild magnolia, so celebrated for the beauty of its flower and foliage, declared that, "All these circumstances give the banks of Roaring River a cool and pleasing aspect, which I have never witnessed before, on the banks of other rivers."

It was on the head waters of this beautiful stream that the "Long Hunters," who spent eight or nine months of the years 1769-1770, in the Cumberland Valley, buried one of their party—the first white man killed in Middle Tennessee. They had proceeded down the Cumberland River from their camp in Wayne County, Kentucky, till they reached Obeds River, which received its name from Obediah Terrill, a member of their party. They then came to Roaring River, and while hunting on Matthews Creek, one of its tributaries, Robert Crockett was ambushed and killed by a party of seven or eight Indians, who were traveling North on the war trace leading from the Cherokee nation towards the Shawnee tribe.

Overton County Established. All the Mountain District was not opened for settlement at the same time. By the treaty of Holston, in 1791, the Indian line was made to begin at a point on Cumberland River, from which a southwest line would strike the ridge that divides the waters of Cumberland from those of Duck River, forty miles above Nashville. This line ran two miles and a half east of Livingston, and divided the Mountain District into two almost equal parts. The west was open to settlement, but the east was reserved to the Cherokee nation, and was commonly called the wilderness.

By an act of the General Assembly, in 1798, the line of the Indian reservation was made the eastern boundary of Sumner County, which, in 1799, was reduced to its constitutional limits, and the new counties of Smith and Wilson established out of its eastern territory. Two years later, Smith County was reduced, and the county of Jackson erected, extending to the wilderness. By the treaty of Tellico, in 1805, the Indian title to the wilderness was extinguished, and from that time the whole of the Mountain District was open to settlement.

The next year Overton County was established. It lay on both sides of the Indian line, and included, besides its present limits, all of the counties of Fentress and Pickett, and parts of Clay, Putnam, Cumberland, Morgan and Scott. It was named for Judge John Overton (1766-1833), a native of Virginia, who early emigrated to Tennessee, and under appointment of the Legislature, negotiated the compact with North Carolina, by which the State of Tennessee was authorized to perfect titles to lands reserved under the act of cession, which had just been ratified by Congress, and finally settled the hot dispute between North Carolina, Tennessee and the United States, respecting the public lands in this State. At this time he was one of the judges of the Superior Court of Law and Equity, having been appointed in 1804, to fill the vacancy occasioned by the resignation of Andrew Jackson.

The Goodpasture Family. From the best information now to be had, there appears to have been six brothers and two sisters, namely, James, John, Abraham, Isaac, Cornelius, Solomon, Elizabeth and Martha Goodpasture, who emigrated from the region of Wolf's Hill, in Virginia, sometime in the latter part of the eighteenth century. They seem to have come first to Tennessee, whence most of them moved to Kentucky, and settled near Owingsville, in Bath County. Cornelius died in that county, and Solomon volunteered in the war of 1812, and was probably killed, as he was never heard of afterwards. Of the two sisters, Elizabeth married and moved to Missouri, and Martha raised a family near Owingsville. John did not remain long in Kentucky, but moved to Warren County, Ohio. Isaac married and left children, but their location is not known to the writer. Abraham, who is said to have reached Bath County about the year

1795, made it his permanent home, and became the ancestor of the large and influential family of Goodpastures in and around Owingsville.

James Goodpasture. James Goodpasture, with whose family we are more intimately concerned, was well advanced in years when he came to Tennessee. His oldest son. William, had already married, and remained in Virginia, where he has many worthy descendants. He first located in the neighborhood, as neighbors were then counted, of Southwest Point, a Federal fort, at the junction of Clinch and Holston Rivers, on the eastern border of the Indian reservation. The place was then in Knox County, about a mile from Kingston, now the county site of Roane County. One of his last acts while a citizen of Knox County was to sign a petition to the Legislature, praying the erection of a new county. As it is the only paper to which the writer has found his name attached, it is here given in full.

"To the General Assembly of the State of Tennessee:

"We, the subscribers, living in Knox County, below the mouth of Turkey Creek, or north of Clinch, petition that Knox County may be divided, so as to leave the same a constitutional county, and that a new county be formed, so as to contain therein a part of the tract of country lying between the river Holston and Clinch, and above Southwest Point, and a part of that tract of country lying north of Clinch, and we, as in duty bound, will ever pray. July 15, 1799."

This petition was signed in fair and legible hands, by James Goodpasture and Jno. Goodpaster, and by Jacob

Gardenhire, John Gilliland, John Eldridge, James Copeland, and many others, who afterwards became leading citizens of Overton and adjoining counties. The curious fact will be noted, that James spelled the final syllable of his name "ture," while his son, John, spelled it "ter." Afterwards, John and all his family adopted his father's orthography, but the descendants of his uncle, Abraham, of Bath County, Kentucky, and perhaps other branches of the family, adhere to the final "ter." Such small difference in orthography is not remarkable, however, in an age and country which took such astonishing liberty with men's names as to call Chapin, Chapel; Barksdale, Basel; Christian, Christy; Chowning, Tunin; and Howard. Hoard.

The Walton Road. The General Assembly did not grant the prayer of the petitioners. But, as we have seen, it established the new county of Smith out of the eastern territory of Sumner, extending to the line of the Indian reservation, and the Goodpastures and some of their neighbors determined to move to this new county. It lay directly across the wilderness from their home near Southwest Point. There had long been a trace across the mountain from Southwest Point to the Cumberland settlements. Francis Baily traveled it in 1796, and has left an interesting account of his journey. But at the time the Goodpastures crossed the mountain a wagon road had been recently marked out, under authority of the General Assembly, between Southwest Point and the mouth of Caney Fork River, where Carthage was afterwards established. The work was the enterprise of Capt. William Walton (1760-1816), a native of Birtie County, North Carolina, who had enlisted at the age of seventeen, as a private in the Revolutionary war, and served till its close in 1783, coming out with the rank of captain. He emigrated to the Cumberland settlement in 1785, and located his military land warrant on the north bank of the Cumberland River, at its confluence with Caney Fork, in 1786. The road, which still bears his name, was about a hundred miles in length, and contained four "stands" for the accommodation of travelers. Coming west, the first of these was at Kimbrough's, on the eastern foot of the mountain; the second, at Crab Orchard, a once famous place on the mountain plateau, in Cumberland County; the third, at White Plains, in Putnam County, on the western foot of the mountain; and the fourth, near Pekin, also in Putnam County. The road was completed in 1801. In the fall of 1802, Michaux writes of this road:

"The road that crosses this part of the Indian territory cuts through the mountains in Cumberland; it is as broad and commodious as those in the environs of Philadelphia, in consequence of the amazing number of emigrants that travel through it, to go and settle in the western country. It is, notwithstanding, in some places very rugged, but nothing near so much as the one that leads from Strasburg to Bedford in Pennsylvania. About forty miles from Nashville we met an emigrant family in a carriage, followed by their negroes on foot, that had performed their journey without accident. Little boards, painted black and nailed upon trees, indicate to travelers the distance they have to go."

In the year 1800, when the Goodpastures crossed the wilderness, the road was neither so good nor so safe as it was when Michaux traveled it, although, even then, it was not considered prudent to travel it, except in parties, on account of roving bands of Indians, one of which he met before he reached Southwest Point.

John Goodpasture. John Goodpasture first intended to settle in Hickory Valley, White County, but the title to his land proving bad he located on Buffalo Creek, near the present village of Hilham, in Overton County. There were then few settlers in this section of country. His nearest neighbor, for a time, was one Anderson, who lived eight miles distant. A wandering Indian was sometimes seen, and a few buffalo were still to be found. The country was wild and beautiful. Its surface was rough and broken, but the valleys were covered with luxuriant cane brakes, and the hills bore so abundantly the wild pea vine, that stock would fatten in the woods. He did not have to feed his stock, winter or summer. Besides, there were the other two important points always considered by the pioneer, namely, wood and water. There was no finer timbered country in the Mountain District than the region around Hilham. Buffalo Creek was a beautiful little stream, fed by many of the never failing springs, so much sought after by the first settlers. It should be remembered that the river bottoms were quite unhealthy when the country was new, and for this reason the pioneers were deterred from occupying them.

Not long after the immigration of the Goodpastures, came also William Bryan, a native of Virginia, who, with his family, settled at the Hiram Allen place, on Flat Creek, in the same neighborhood. Here, in 1803, John Goodpasture was married to his daughter, Margery. They began life poor, but by industry and economy they

Residence of John Goodpasture (1778-1864), Hilham, Overton County, Tenn., as it Appeared August 23, 1894.

were enabled to make a comfortable living, and to give each of their children a common school education, such as the country afforded. They raised a family of fifteen children, fourteen of their own, and a nephew, Jefferson, the son of James Goodpasture, deceased, all of whom survived them, except Andrew, who died in the State of Illionis after he had reached his majority, and left the parental roof. They had first lived in a log cabin, such as was common among pioneers, but in 1804, Mr. Goodpasture built a two story, weatherboarded, hewn log house, with a kitchen in the rear, connected with the main part of the house by an enclosed hallway, which served them as a dining room. In this house they lived, without intermission, from that time until their deaths, which both occurred in 1864.

Plain and unpretentious as it was this humble dwelling saw more of the bright sunshine of a happy home, and less of the dark shadows of sorrow and distress, than many more imposing structures—even of the present day. Under its roof, seven little boys and seven little girls were born into the world. Never in want and never idle, the years rolled on, and they grew to be seven honest, self-supporting, Christian men, and seven virtuous, domestic, pious women. There was never a death in that old house from the day it was built until the master and mistress, whom it had sheltered for sixty years, in ripe old age—eighty-six and seventy-nine—within two months of each other, were gathered to their fathers, and left it tenantless; for no one of the fifteen children any longer called it home.

John Goodpasture was a man of strong, positive character. Firm and just, he was at the same time so conservative and liberal that he never had a lawsuit in his life, and maintained at all times the utmost respect and confidence of his neighbors, among whom he was regarded as a leader. For half a century, he took two newspapers—a political paper supporting the Democratic party, with which he always affiliated, and the organ of the Cumberland Presbyterian Church, of which, for fifty-five years, he was a member. Temperate in all things, he never used tobacco in any form, and for the last fifty years of his life totally abstained from intoxicants. Regular and domestic in his habits and taste, he never spent but eight nights from home after his marriage. Faithful to his public duties, he voted at every election held in his district. And with a powerful constitution and an orderly manner of life, he never had a serious spell of sickness, except that of which he died.

CHAPTER II.

Jefferson Dillard Goodpasture, the twelfth child of John and Margery (Bryan) Goodpasture, was born on Buffalo Creek, one of the many beautiful little streams tributary to Roaring River, near the classic village of Hilham, in Overton County, Tennessee, on the third day of August, 1824. The older members of the family were then growing up. His oldest sister was in her twentieth year, and before he was a year old had married and emigrated to Illinois. He was only four when his third sister married and moved to the same State. The community was excellent, having not only much intelligence, but considerable learning. There is undoubtedly much in environment. A boy cannot well resist the atmosphere by which he is surrounded. The example and influence of one leading man has often been known to affect the character of a whole neighborhood, long after he has passed away. There is an inspiration in the life of every man, whose character, achievements or learning have been so conspicuous as to attract the notice of his fellows, that pervades the entire circle of his acquaintance. It is this silent, perhaps unconscious, influence, that causes one section of the country to send out more successful and influential men, than another with equal apparent advantages. Among their nearest neighbors when Judge Goodpasture was growing up,

Captain Arnold. Capt. Jesse Arnold was a native of Providence, R. I. He was an only child and his father died when he was quite young. At the age of sixteen he ran away from school, with a view to adopting the life of a sailor. He obtained employment on an outward bound vessel, and his career was commenced. He rose in his profession, until he found himself the commander of an American merchantman. When the war of 1812 came on, in which the American navy won such brilliant laurels, he entered the service as the captain of a privateer, which he commanded until peace was established. After the war he left the navy, and drifted to White Plains, Tennessee, about the year 1817, and engaged in the mercantile business with William Burton, whose daughter he subsequently married. In the meantime, he purchased a small farm at Hilham, whither he was attracted by the prominent New England people it contained. After his marriage he moved to Hilham, and continued the mercantile business there, until his death, which occurred in 1846, on the very day his son, Jesse, now President of the Bank of Cookeville, was born. Capt. Arnold had two daughters, Avo and Ova, the latter of whom married Judge Goodpasture's brother, Dr. J. M. Goodpasture, and still survives him.

The Tottens. Daniel Brown married a sister of Benjamin Totten, the first County Court Clerk of Overton County. The courts of the county were organized at Totten's house, on Eagle Creek, and continued to be held there until the General Assembly passed an act providing that after the first day of June, 1810, the courts of the county should be held at the town of Monroe. He was the father of James L. Totten, who practiced law at Livingston until sometime in the thirties, when he moved to Trenton, was elected to the Legislature in 1835, and soon afterwards moved to Mississippi, where he became a circuit judge; Benjamin C. Totten, of Huntingdon, who was on the circuit bench from 1837 to 1845; and Archibald W. O. Totten, who began the practice at Troy, and moved thence to Jackson, and was on the supreme bench from 1850 to 1855.

The Hindses. Capt. Simeon Hinds was a sturdy old veteran who raised an honorable family. His son, John, became a distinguished Cumberland Presbyterian preacher, and was the father of Prof. J. I. D. Hinds, of Cumberland University. It was with John Hinds that Abraham H. Goodpasture went to Alabama, where he professed religion and himself entered the ministry of the Cumberland Presbyterian Church, in which he labored faithfully and earnestly until his death, which occurred at Petersburg, Illinois, in 1885, a period of fifty years. Elizabeth B. Goodpasture married Claiborne, another son, and moved with him to Guntown, Mississippi, where she died on the first day of January of this year. Simeon, a third son, became a prominent physician. He did not originally intend to enter the medical profession, having first thought to devote himself to the law. Indeed he did obtain a license to practice law, but abandoned the profession on account of impaired eyesight. His eyes failed him while he was reading law, but he was a bright, intelligent, ambitious fellow, and determined to prosecute his studies notwithstanding his misfortune. Accordingly he employed a young man in the neighborhood, named Parker-Lane, to read to him. This arrangement was kept up for a year or more, and when Hinds applied for his license, Lane said he thought he would get one too; and he did, after which he moved to Texas, where he became a distinguished lawyer, and and died in his young manhood.

Moses Fisk.　Moses Fisk (1759-1843), originally from Grafton, Massachusetts, was a man of great prominence in the early history of this State. He was a graduate of Dartmouth College, and had been for seven years a tutor in that famous institution, where he had taught with much success. One of his pupils, Gen. E. W. Ripley, a man of national reputation, writing him in 1817, pays him this high tribute: "If it has been my lot to acquire distinction or reputation: if I have served the interests of my country in any manner however limited, the cause of it may be traced to the admonitions and precepts of three respectable benefactors: yourself, Capt. Dunham and Wm. Woodard."

He came to Tennessee in 1796, the year of its admission to the Union. At Philadelphia, he met William Blount, just lately elected one of the first United States Senators from Tennessee, and carried a letter from him to Governor Sevier, at Knoxville. From that time he became a warm friend of the Blounts, the younger of whom addressed him as "chum." He did not, however, remain long in Knoxville, having early made his way to Cumberland, where he was connected with many public enterprises. He studied law and was admitted to the bar, at the suggestion of William Blount, through whom,

also, he was tendered the presidency of the University
of North Carolina, which he declined. Being a great
mathematician. in 1802 he was appointed by Governor
Roane one of the Commissioners on the part of Tennessee to settle and locate the true boundary line between
this State and Virginia, and as such assisted in running
the line lately upheld by the Supreme Court of the
United States; and for the same reason, in 1817, he was
urged by Governor McMinn to accept the place of
mathematician, to aid in the adjustment of the difference
between Tennessee and Kentucky. His business as a
surveyor was quite lucrative. bringing him large bodies
of valuable land, mostly in the Mountain District.

He found time, however, for much literary labor.
In 1803, he was appointed by the General Assembly, in
connection with Willie Blount, to compile the laws of
the State, which work he undertook alone, and reported
to the Legislature in 1805, when he was paid for the
work done, and the matter was referred back to him for
completion. But Haywood's Revisal. covering the same
ground, having appeared before he was ready to report,
his work was never published. His correspondence with
distinguished individuals. and with antiquarian and historical sicieties. was very great. Valuable contributions
from his pen will be found in the first volume of the
Transactions of the American Antiquarian Society, and
the seventh volume (second series) of the Massachusetts
Historical Society Papers.

Following the tide of immigration back east, from
Nashville. we find him acting as pro tem. clerk. when
Smith County was organized. in 1799. In 1801, he was
Chairman of the County Court of Smith County, and

when Jackson County was organized, under an act of
that year, it was he whom the Legislature named to ad-
minister the oath of office to its first justices.   In 1802,
he was living at Fort Blount, for some years called Wi-
liamsburg, with the old Indian fighter, Sampson Williams, one of the daring men who came to Cumberland
with James Robertson, in 1780, and who was Sheriff of
Davidson County as early as 1790, and subsequently a
member of the State Senate, first from Sumner County,
then from Smith and Jackson, and still later from a
larger district.   Judge Goodpasture remembered to have
seen the old pioneer in his youth, but was impressed
by nothing about him so much as the immense size of
his ears.

We next find Mr. Fisk laying off the town of Hilham,
about the year 1805.   He staked his fortune on the
success of Hilham.   He spent much money in laying out
and undertaking to construct a system of turnpikes, all
centering there.   But his first care was to provide it
with suitable institutions of learning.   He was a trustee
of Davidson Academy, of Overton Academy and of Fisk
Female Academy.   The latter institution was endowed
by the gift of one thousand acres of land, each, by Mr.
Fisk and his old friend Sampson Williams, and established by legislative authority, in 1806, "at a place called
Hilham, on the eastern part of Magnolia River, in the
county of Overton."   This was the first distinctively
female school chartered in the South, and one of the first
in America.   The name of the stream on which it was
located was no doubt that by which Mr. Fisk called
Roaring River, as he was the traveling companion of
Michaux, when he raved so over the wild magnolias

found on its banks. Although so ambitious an enterprise as Fisk Female Academy was not destined to succeed, still Mr. Fisk made it a prime object to see that good schools were maintained at Hilham, and for many years it was done under his own direction and control. He induced many young New Englanders to come to his neighborhood, generally as teachers. Notable among these was Judge Leonard, who taught successfully at Hilham, married Mr. Fisk's daughter and moved to Missouri, where he became an eminent jurist. Another was Sidney H. Little, who taught at Monroe, and afterwards became a distinguished lawyer in the State of Illinois.

John Dickinson. Under his inspiration other intelligent and educated New Englanders came to the West, such as John Dickinson (1781-1815), who graduated at Dartmouth in 1797; taught a while in Knoxville; became a distinguished lawyer in Nashville; fought a duel with one of the Overtons (using Fisk's dueling pistols); and died in the very opening of what promised to be an unusually brilliant career.

Moses Madison Fisk. Another was a kinsman, Moses Madison Fisk (1780-1804), who graduated at Dartmouth in 1802, and died in Nashville two years later. This amusing college story is told to illustrate the brightness of his intellect: Professor Woodard was maintaining the identity of the person, in despite of bodily changes. He illustrated his position by a ship, whose parts have all been renewed, leaving it still the same ship. Young Fisk held out a penknife and asked, "If I lose the blade and get another, is it the same knife?" The Professor answered,

"Yes." "If I next lose the handle and get another, is it still the same?" "Yes." "But my chum finds both the lost blade and handle, and puts them together—what knife is that?"

Dr. T. T. Barton. One other should be mentioned, his neighbor, Dr. Titus Theodore Barton (1766-1827), a graduate of Dartmouth College, an ordained minister of the Congregationalist Church, and a doctor of medicine, who reached Hilham November 28, 1817, and practiced medicine there until 1827, when he left for Jacksonville, Illinois, and died en route.

The Goodpastures and Fisks were good friends during all the long years they lived neighbors. John Goodpasture, the father, who was a Justice of the Peace at the time, performed the marriage ceremony, when, sometime about 1815, Mr. Fisk, then more than fifty years of age, found himself a wife; and when, many years afterwards, they failed to agree, by their request, he fixed the allowance to be made her, upon their separation. She lived thenceforth in a house of her own, in the same yard, and both parties carried out their agreement faithfully as long as they lived.

Judge Goodpasture used to tell some interesting anecdotes, illustrating the character of Mr. Fisk. He said he was a man of marked peculiarities—eccentric, unapproachable, and, as he recollected him, awe-inspiring. He was postmaster when the Judge was a small boy, and when he went for the mail, as it was his business to do, it was always with considerable trepidation. On one of these occasions, there was almost an open rupture between them. The Judge was only ten or twelve years old at the time, and wore a brown jeans cap his mother had made him. When he walked into the room he laid his cap beside him on the floor, and took a seat to wait the pleasure of the learned old postmaster, who was not accustomed to hurry himself for the accommodation of even more important personages. When he discovered the boy's cap on the floor, he told him, in a manner that was construed to be a command, to put it on the table. The boy rebelled at once, and made some remark to the effect that it would do very well down there. "Sir," shouted Mr. Fisk, "I say take your hat off of my floor;" which, seeming reasonable, he did, compromising with his humiliation by placing it on his head.

Speaking of having to wait Mr. Fisk's pleasure brings to mind another anecdote. He was a Justice of the Peace as well as postmaster, and on a certain occasion Capt. Hinds had some business with him. When he walked in Mr. Fisk was reading a newspaper, and paid not the least attention to his salutation, which was repeated a second, and perhaps a third time. When he had finished the paragraph he was upon, he raised his eyes from the paper.

"Good morning, Capt. Hinds, be seated," he said.

"Sir," said Hinds, in high dudgeon, "I had some business with you, but I will see you another time," and turning upon his heels walked out.

Capt. Hinds kept a mill, but in addition he was a cobbler, and when, not long afterwards, Mr. Fisk called on him, he chanced to be engaged mending a shoe, drawing his threads with both hands, as the manner was.

"Good morning," said Mr. Fisk.

But the threads came through again and again, and

his eyes were never raised from his work, until he had completed his seam.

"Good morning, Squire Fisk, come in."

Mr. Fisk said not a word, but taking in the situation, turned and left in as great a miff as Capt. Hinds himself had shown on the former occasion.

The Seviers. This account of these near neighbors has been thought necessary, as illustrating the strong, sturdy stock of men who settled this part of the country, and as accounting, in some measure, for the intellectual atmosphere that surrounded Hilham, stimulating the ambition and elevating the aspirations of its young men, many of whom have won honorable names among their countrymen. Besides these, there were representatives of many illustrious families in other parts of the county. Governor Sevier located two grants for something over 57,000 acres of land in Overton County, now Overton and Clay. On this vast domain many members of his family settled. After his death in 1815, his widow, the celebrated "Bonnie Kate," moved to "The Dale," now known as the Clark place, in Clay County. It was in a romantic and secluded spot, upon a high bench, among the hills of Obeds River. Around her, but not with her, were her brother, brothers-in-law, sisters-in-law, sons and daughters. Mrs. Matlock, a sister of Governor Sevier, was the mother of Valentine Matlock, one time Sheriff of Overton County; and Geo. W. Sevier, a son, was Circut Court Clerk. Her brother, John Sherill, lived near the mouth of Wolf River, as did also her son, Dr. Sam Sevier, who afterwards removed with her to Alabama. Of the Governor's brothers, Abram lived about ten miles north of Livingston, and Joseph near the mouth of Ashburn's Creek. Among his sons and daughters, there was Catherine Campbell, whose second husband was Archibald Ray; Joanna Windle and Valentine Sevier, who lived on Irons Creek; Mary Overstreet, who lived on Obeds River; George W. Sevier, who lived on Sulphur Creek, and afterwards moved to Nashville; Sarah Brown, who lived at the James McMillin old place; and Ann Corlin, who lived on Ashburn's creek.

The Women. Not only did they have the heroic deeds of such men as the Seviers to excite their emulation, and the learning of Fisk and his Dartmouth coterie to direct and discipline their minds, but there was a wonderful concord and fellowship among the pioneer settlers, that strengthened the home ties and inspired the deepest patriotic sentiments. The log-rolling, the corn-shucking and the quilting have been too often described to be repeated here. Each neighbor was always ready to lend a helping hand to the others. The women of the household never lost an opportunity to do little acts of kindness towards each other, not generally valuable in themselves, but sufficient to manifest a neighborly feeling, and on occasion, to relieve the wants of any who might be in distress. The very earliest recollection of Judge Goodpasture related to a visit he made to Mrs. Robert Mitchell, who lived not far from his father's place. When he was ready to leave, Mrs. Mitchell gave him a pint cup of butter, which he was requested to carry to his mother. The thing that impressed the incident upon his mind was the circumstance that, though he took the butter in good faith, in playing along the road he let the cup fall, causing the butter and sand to become so mixed that he thought it not worth while to deliver it.

On another occasion about the same time, his father needed a trowel, and sent him to borrow one of John Ashworth, who lived about a quarter of a mile away. Not comprehending fully what it was that was wanted, he asked the loan of a towel. Mrs. Ashworth seemed to have some misgivings as to the accuracy of so singular a request, but she did not hesitate to comply. Taking a nice, clean towel, she wrapped up a mess of dried-pumpkins in it, as if in token of her entire willingness to be obliging, and asked him to deliver them to his mother.

Enters School. Such were the surroundings when Judge Goodpasture began to reach an age at which he was to enter school. He could hardly have been over five years old when he suffered that terrible ordeal. The teacher was John Smeltser. Smeltser married a daughter of their neighbor, Daniel Brown, and his grandson, John Smeltser Brown and Judge Goodpasture were, for many years, the warmest of friends. But he was in such mortal terror of John Smeltser, that as the first day of his school approached he hid his shoes, thinking, as it was then bitter cold weather, they could not be so cruel as to make him go without them. After diligent search, however, some one found his shoes, and there was no longer any excuse left him. He found the master so much less dangerous than he had anticipated that, as he used to relate, he was not at all times as obedient as he ought to have been to his reasonable rules. It was not long before he had to stand up before the school with the little girl whose only fault was to reciprocate his youthful affections. But he must have borne it heroically, as we find the master changing his tactics on his next offense. The school was being held in an old dwelling, and under one corner of the room there was a potato cellar, with a trap door leading down to it. He raised this door and let the culprit down into the cellar. But hardly had he reached the bottom when he discovered a light coming through a rent made by removing a stone from the underpinning. His plans were formed in an instant. He made for that hole, and in an incredibly short time was safe at home. However, according to his account, he did not feel at all safe until the whole of the next day had passed without the matter having been referred to by the master.

Works on the Farm. Judge Goodpasture—and the same was measurably true of all his neighbors—was only able to go to school in the winter months, his services being required at home during the cropping season. At that time every member of the household was required to work. Even the carding, spinning, weaving, knitting and sewing necessary to clothe the family was done at home. The writer has seen a beautiful sample of silk, from a dress of Judge Goodpasture's sister, Hettie, who raised the cocoons, reeled the silk, dyed it, wove the cloth, and made it into the dress herself. As a very small boy it was his daily task to pace around the field, whooping and shouting, making all the noise he could, in order to protect the corn against the myriad of squirrels that committed such depredations upon it as to seriously endanger the crop. Then the same process had to be enacted in the orchard, where the parrakeets collected in such numbers as to strip the trees of their fruit in an incredibly short time if they were not frightened away.

A little later he grew to the stature of what was called in those days a "plow boy," which was usually reached at the age of about ten years. From this time he made a regular hand in the field. The work was divided up, some running the plows, and others the hoes. He and the negro, Bob, did most of the plowing, in which he attained a proficiency of which he was proud even in his mature life. He thought, no doubt with good reason, that few men could run a straighter furrow than he. And he never forgot old "Grog," for many years the companion of his toil; so many, in fact, that he came to understand the summons of the dinner horn as well as his master, and persisted in going to the gap when it sounded, without regard to his wishes in the matter. When his sister, Betsy, married Claiborne Hinds, old Grog was given to her and was put in the wagon that moved them to Mississippi. It was thought that he ought to be shod in anticipation of so long a journey. He was now quite old and had never worn a shoe, so the smith found great difficulty in shoeing him. In fact, he only succeeded in getting one shoe on, and was not able to clinch the nails in that, and so, old Grog made the long journey to Mississippi without lameness, with but a single shoe half put on.

Sees a Governor. One day in the summer of 1839 he was informed that Governor Cannon and Colonel Polk, the candidates for Governor, who were stumping the State together, would pass the field where he was plowing. He had never seen a Governor, and his curiosity was greatly excited. At the proper hour, he stationed himself on the fence to see them go by, like the small boy now watches for the circus. Governor Cannon rode an immense iron grey horse, with more trappings than he had ever seen before, and received much more of his attention than his opponent and traveling companion. The next day, however, he was permitted to go to the speaking. It made a lasting impression on his mind, the superiority of Colonel Polk's address, in his estimation, more than counterbalancing the splendid trappings of Governor Cannon's horse. In the next canvass, Governor Polk, who had defeated Cannon, and a few years later, Governor Aaron V. Brown, each spent a night with his father.

Goes Into Business.

It was during these years that Judge Goodpasture made his first business venture. One evening a traveler was entertained at his father's, and when the stranger had departed next morning, he found a silver ninepence in the room he had occupied. This was his first capital. He had his mother make him a purse to put it in, while he was looking out for an investment. He soon bought two beautiful, blue pullets from a neighbor, and entered the chicken business. The arrangement he had with his mother was this: He was allowed to keep all the pullets, and one rooster to every dozen of them. The excess of roosters she killed as they were needed for family consumption. He succeeded so well that it was not long until he had a flock of two hundred for sale. These he sold to John Barksdale for $25.00. When he received the money he loaned it to his neighbor, George Christian, a son-in-law of Moses Fisk, who was a good citizen and an upright man, with whom he maintained the warmest friendship up to the day of his death. The writer saw Mr. Christian in 1888, who was hale and hearty, in the eighty-seventh year of his age, and carried a cane, made of coffee wood, which Judge Goodpasture had brought him from Mexico, and which he prized above its value on that account. Christian gave him his note, which he held until the interest more than equalled the principal.

Rescues His Pigs. Judge Goodpasture gave close attention to business, even in his early childhood. Many anecdotes are told of him, illustrating this trait. One will suffice. He had a sow and pigs. In order that they might get water, the pen was made so as to enclose a part of Buffalo Creek. In the night there came up a sudden storm. The rain fell in torrents. The boy knew it would flood his pen and drown his pigs, unless they were released. The night was dark, and the pen some distance from the house. He asked an older brother to go with him to the rescue. His brother declining, he went alone, and found the sow standing in the water, and the little pigs swimming in great distress around her. He tore away the fence, and had the pleasure of seeing them find a place of safety and lie down in perfect contentment.

CHAPTER III.

In the meantime, he continued at school in the fall and winter, where he was enabled to acquire the rudiments of an education. Old Union, less than a mile from his father's, was a famous meeting house, in those days. In its quiet, shady old church yard, the remains of his father and mother have reposed in peace, these thirty odd years, under the modest marble slabs his filial love erected over them. The house was sometimes also used for school purposes, and it was here that William Hall once taught a prosperous school of more than sixty students, in which Judge Goodpasture was a pupil. He next entered Judge Leonard's school at Hilham. Then he recited privately to Dr. Simeon Hinds. The last school he attended was taught by Judge Gardenhire.

While he was growing up the boys organized a debating society at Old Union, which attracted the attention of the country for miles around. The value of such societies for the purpose of drawing out and developing the latent talent of young men, can hardly be over-estimated. In this society, Judge Goodpasture manifested considerable skill as a debater, and received not a little rustic applause. Always precocious, and ever self-reliant, he began to mark out his own career, and assume the responsibility of his future destiny, long before he had reached majority. His first step was a

bold one. Stimulated by his success in the debating
society, at the age of seventeen, he determined to adopt
the profession of the law. The daring character of this
resolution can be appreciated when it is understood that
among all his ancestors, so far back as tradition reached,
none had ever tested the field of the law. When he
mentioned to his father his purpose to read law, the old
gentleman readily consented, with the observation, that
had at once occurred to his strong, conservative mind,
that "it would do him no harm."

Studies Law. Accordingly, when he had made up
his mind to be a lawyer, without a
disturbing doubt as to his ultimate success, he at once
began teaching school, at $12.00 per month, in order
that he might be able to put a hand in his place on the
farm, while he gave more time to the prosecution of his
studies. When he was ready to begin reading law, at
about the age of twenty, he rode over to the house of
his father's personal and political friend, Judge Alvin
Cullom, who from that day became his own devoted and
intimate friend, while he lived, and at his death be-
queathed him his extensive political library, as a token
of his warm esteem. Judge Cullom was then just back
from serving his first term in Congress, and was regarded
by his young friend with much awe and great admiration.
He loaned him a volume of Blackstone's Commentaries,
and gave him such advice as he thought might be useful
to him, in entering upon its study.

The Culloms. His association with the Culloms was
so long and intimate that a short
sketch of the family will not be considered out of place.
They were of Scotch descent, tracing their lineage back

to the clan MacCullom. The grandfather, George Cullom, was a Maryland tobacco planter, and William, the father, was a small farmer in the Elk Spring Valley, near Monticello, in Wayne County, Kentucky, where all his eleven children were born. Two sons, Edward N. and Alvin, and two daughters, Elizabeth, the wife of Dr. Spencer McHenry, and Lucinda, wife of the late John Hart, who was for many years County Court Clerk, at Livingston, came to Overton County early in the twenties, and settled near Monroe, then the county site. The father and most of the others followed them about 1830. Richard N., the third son, moved to Illinois, where his son, Shelby M., became Governor of the State, and at present represents it in the United States Senate. The only one of the boys who never figured in public life, was James N., who married a daughter of Benjamin Totten. William Cullom, Sr., was a devout Christian man, and for forty-six years a class leader in the Methodist Church. Rev. T. F. Bates describes him, after he came to this State, as having a patriarchal appearance that reminded him of the pictures he had seen of John Wesley. He died in 1838, and was buried at Monroe. Edward N. Cullom was Judge Goodpasture's immediate predecessor in the office of Clerk and Master, at Livingston. But the two members of the family best known in this State, and most intimately connected with Judge Goodpasture, were Alvin and his brother William.

Judge Alvin Cullom.
Alvin Cullom (1793-1877), to whom young Goodpasture went for advice and assistance, when he was ready to take up the study of the law, is described by Rev. T. F. Bates, who knew him well, as large of frame, portly and

rugged, and every inch a man. He was fully identified
with all the best interests of the country, and never be-
trayed a trust, nor was guilty of a dishonorable act.
Brave as Julius Caesar, he was yet as tender of heart
and gentle as a woman. Whether acting as legal counsel
at the bar, wearing the ermine of judicial authority on
the bench, or looking after the interests of his constitu-
ency as a representative in Congress, he was still the
refined gentleman, to whom you could commit your
dearest interests without the slightest apprehension of
betrayal. He threw the weight of his influence uniformly in the scale of right, peace and justice, and lived
in harmony with these great principles. He was not
inflated with vanity by success, and could not be cajoled
into improper measures by flattery.

Judge Cullom did not adopt the legal profession until
the mature years of his life. When a young man he
seems to have raised a small crop of wild oats. Judge
Goodpasture used to repeat this sentence from a speech
of Hon. Thomas L. Bransford, who was Judge Cullom's
competitor in his race for Congress, in 1843: "Little
did I think, fellow citizens, twenty years ago, when I
was riding a mule and carrying the mail from Gainesboro to Monticello, and my distinguished competitor was
keeping a saloon in Old Monroe, that we would ever be
opposing candidates for a seat in the Congress of the
United States." The habits of the young men of
Monroe do not seem to have been the best about 1823.
It was in that year that Andrew J. Marchbanks, afterwards so distinguished on the circuit bench, went to
that village to study law under his brother-in-law, Major
H. H. Atkinson, but in the course of a year, discovering

that he had become quite idle, and was doing no good,
like a wise young man, he returned to his father.

But when Judge Cullom did take up the law, he left
all idle habits behind him. There was another young
man who came to the Monroe bar about the same time.
But the sprightly, buoyant young Edward Cross (1798-
1887), whether for the same reason that moved Judge
Marchbanks, or not, for some reason, determined to leave
old Monroe and emigrate to the State of Arkansas.
When he parted from Judge Cullom, his leave taking
proved a prophecy. "By the gods. Cullom. I am going
to Arkansas, and when I next meet you I expect it to be
in the Congress of the United States." When Judge
Cullom went to Congress, in 1843, he met, for the first
time since their parting, Judge Cross, then the only
representative from the State of Arkansas.

Adam Huntsman. Monroe seems to have been on the
wane, even at that early period.
Adam Huntsman had been their leading lawyer, and
represented them in the State Senate from 1815 to 1821,
but he too left about the same time, and moved to
Jackson, where he was again elected to the Senate, in
1827, and subsequently served two terms in Congress.
In 1835, with the help of the Jackson administration,
he defeated the amiable and inimitable Davy Crockett,
who was so chagrined at his defeat that he left the State,
and found a glorious death at the Alamo, in the Texas
war of independence. Judge Goodpasture met Huntsman once, when he was visiting among his old friends.
He was a one legged man, and was then much advanced
in years, but he was still sprightly and animated, and
when an early friend asked if he knew him, he replied:

"I think I used to know an old sinner about your size."

In his profession, Judge Cullom made rapid progress. He had not been at the bar long when a leading citizen —perhaps one of the Armstrongs—was indicted for murder. Felix Grundy was retained to defend him. Cullom assisted him. The defendant was acquitted, and Judge Grundy received a valuable negro for his fee. Before leaving he said to the assembled crowd: "Gentlemen, it will not be necessary for you to send for me in the future. You have a man here," pointing to Cullom, "who can serve you as well as I."

Judge Cullom soon drifted into politics, as nearly all lawyers did in his day. One of the most exciting elections ever held for representative in the county occurred in 1835, between him and Jonathan Douglass, who had been a member of the Legislature in 1826. It may be that it was the more bitter on account of the asperities growing out of the contest which resulted in the removal of the county site from Monroe to Livingston, a result which was never wholly acquiesced in until the adoption of the constitution of 1834, that made a two thirds vote necessary to remove a county site. It was a hot and bitter campaign. Jacob Dillen, who came to the bar with Judge Cullom and Ed. Cross, in 1823, and whom Judge Cullom told the writer, in 1876, he regarded as the most brilliant young lawyer he had ever known, took the stump for him, and though he saw his friend elected by a small majority, he contracted a cold in the canvass, which soon afterwards resulted in his death. At the time of that unhappy event, he had a little daughter, only three months old, who, when she had grown up, became the wife of Judge Goodpasture.

After that Judge Cullom was a member of Congress from 1843 to 1847; Circuit Judge from 1850 to 1852; and one of the delegates elected by the Legislature to the Southern Conference in 1861. He lived to be eighty-four years of age. Rev. J. W. Cullom preached his funeral, at a little church he had erected near his home, five miles south of Livingston.

Gen. William Cullom. In 1835 a handsome young stranger of twenty-five, walked into the leading hotel in McMinnville. He stood full six feet three inches tall, and as straight as an Indian, with a profusion of raven black hair. His presence was handsome and intelligent, and his manners courtly and self-satisfied. When he came in, a quiet old gentleman, a Mr. Ramsey, the father Judge Goodpasture's valued friend, Chis Ramsey, of McMinnville, was nodding in the office, perhaps just a little in his cups. As the handsome young man strode back and forth across the office, with the air and mien of a lord, the quiet old gentleman, who was himself something of a character in his country, began to interrogate him.

"Young man, what might be your name?"

"William Cullom, sir. I am the newly elected Attorney-General of this circuit."

"Yes. Where are you from, young man?"

"Gainesboro, sir."

"Yes. Gainesboro, on Doe Creek! I believe the principal products of Doe Creek are babies and dried pumpkins."

Such was the introduction of William Cullom (1810-1896), when he went to attend the first court after his election to the office of Attorney-General of the Sixth

Judicial Circuit. He had begun his career by serving two years as Deputy Sheriff of Overton County, after which he took the law course in Transylvania University, at Lexington, Kentucky. He commenced the practice at Gainesboro, was soon afterwards elected Attorney-General, and, in 1839, moved to Carthage. As soon as his time had expired, in 1843, he was elected to the State Senate, and re-elected in 1845. Judge Alvin was an uncompromising Democrat, but Gen. William was a Whig. He was a Taylor elector in 1848, a member of Congress from 1851 to 1855, and Clerk of the National House of Representatives in 1856-7. After the war, he moved to Livingston, and was appointed and afterwards elected Attorney-General of the Sixteenth Circuit, and held the office from 1873 to 1876, when he resigned to accept an appointment as Circuit Judge in the same circuit. While Attorney-General he moved to Clinton, on the other side of the mountain, where he died in December, 1896, at the advanced age of eighty-six years.

Judge Goodpasture thought he had the greatest mind ever developed in the Mountain District. He was little acquainted with books, not more, perhaps, with law books than those of a literary character. Yet, he was a successful practitioner, and, at times, a powerful advocate. He relied wholly on the inspiration of the moment and the occasion. The writer has often heard him say that his great Kossuth speech, by which he electrified Congress, in his first appearance before that body, was a pure inspiration. He did not know when he arose what he would say, and when he had concluded he was quite as ignorant of the language he had employed. It was for this reason that he supposed he had made an unfortunate break when General Breckenridge asked him: "Have you any friend in this House?" And for the same reason he was ready to believe he had made an unusually felicitous effort, when he added: "If you have he ought to kill you at once, while you are at the zenith of a reputation some representatives have sought in vain on this floor for thirty years." Perhaps his greatest Congressional speech, however, was that in opposition to the Kansas-Nebraska bill, which cost him his seat in the next House, but undoubtedly made him clerk of that body.

Judge E. L. Gardenhire. After Judge Goodpasture had been reading law a short while, in 1845 he entered the law office of Judge E. L. Gardenhire (1815———), who had moved to Livingston in 1844, and pursued his studies under his direction. Judge Gardenhire was a grandson of Jacob Gardenhire, whose name we have seen attached, along with those of James and John Goodpasture, to a petition for the division of Knox County. He had the good fortune to receive a better education than fell to the lot of most of the aspiring young men of the Mountain District, having spent the last two years of his school life in a classical institution, called Clinton College, in Smith County. At this time he was just entering on a large and lucrative practice, which he has been able to hold for more than half a century. He was well grounded in the law, as well as in history and belles-letters. Judge Goodpasture always thought he would have made a famous teacher in one of our great law schools. In one of his letters he says: "I feel confident that as a teacher, Gardenhire has not a superior in the State. In addition to his fine legal attainments. his literary taste and acquirements are of the very best, and his vigorous, systematic, orderly manner of studying is unsurpassed."

The writer himself read law with Judge Gardenhire some thirty years after his father had entered his office, and desires to bear witness to the elevated conception he had of the profession, and the wise counsel and valuable instruction he was able to impress upon his pupils. After magnifying the fundamental principles of the law, and discussing their practical application to the infinite variety of human activities, he never failed to urge upon the student the importance of giving a "painful" investigation to the facts of each particular case.

The lawyer who rode the circuit in the Mountain District had to travel long distances, not unfrequently without a companion. In order to utilize these weary hours, Judge Gardenhire early adopted the plan of keeping commonplace books, in which he copied such passages from classic literature as he deemed might be useful, on occasions, either by way of illustration or ornament. These delightful pieces he would commit to memory, as he rode along the tiresome way, thus accomplishing the double purpose of relieving the tedium of the journey and fixing in his mind the choice language in which our great authors have clothed their brightest thoughts. The writer remembers many such passages now. Some were from the Psalms, of which he was particularly fond. Shakespeare also was a favorite author, and Junius was another. Irving's Sketch Book was liberally used, and occasional lines were taken from Dr. Holmes. Hon. Benton McMillin, a nephew of his wife, had studied law with him, and, he

said, had adopted this plan, which he had found quite
useful.   It may be added, that Judge Gardenhire pre-
dicted a bright future for Mr. McMillin, though he had
not then offered for the seat in Congress, which he has
now occupied for twenty years.

Judge Gardenhire was not wholly exempt from the
prevailing disposition to enter politics.   In 1849-50,
he was a member of the State Senate, and in 1858 was
elected Circuit Judge.   The war coming on, in 1861,
he was a member of the Confederate Congress.   He was
a member of the lower House of the General Assembly,
in 1875, a member of the Arbitration Court, in 1877,
and a member of the Court of Referees, in 1883.

Early in his career, Judge Gardenhire greatly distinguished himself by the able manner in which he conducted the defense of Mary Copeland, indicted for the
murder of Ruth Daugherty.   The masterly opinion of
the Supreme Court in the case was delivered by Judge
Turley, and is reported in Seventh Humphrey's Reports.

CHAPTER IV.

Judge Goodpasture had as a chum, in his law studies at Livingston, Daniel McMillin, of whom he always retained the most pleasant recollections. After his admission to the bar, McMillin went to Texas, where he made a distinguished lawyer. The field of his own future activity was not for a time entirely clear to him. He made a tour of the Southern counties of Middle Tennessee and North Alabama, as far as Huntsville, "singing geography," as well with a view of replenishing his now almost exhausted means, as for the purpose of prospecting for a location in which to practice his profession. Perhaps some reader may not be familiar with this character of instruction. It was a primitive method of fixing geographical names and localities in the mind. The teacher would lead, and the pupils would follow in concert. For instance, if they were learning the capitals of the States, they would sing out: "Maine, Augusta; Maine, Augusta—New Hampshire, Concord; New Hampshire, Concord," and so on. After returning from his tour, singing geography, he enlisted as a volunteer in Captain Richardson Copeland's company for service in the Mexican war. The company was not accepted, but President Polk made a place for their gallant commander, in the Quartermaster's department, with the rank of captain. By this time he had definitely determined to make Livingston his home, and accordingly opened an office for the practice of his profession.

Ridley-Marchbanks. He had not been long at the bar before he attracted the kindly notice of Chancellor Bromfield L. Ridley, one of the most distinguished jurists and accomplished gentlemen that have adorned the bench of this State. The year 1825 saw two notable additions to the McMinnville bar. Andrew J. Marchbanks (1804-1865), who found old Monroe not a profitable place in which to prosecute his law studies, in 1823 returned home, and in 1825 located at McMinnville, where he was afterwards twenty-five years on the circuit bench. In the same year, Bromfield L. Ridley (1804-1869), a native of North Carolina, and a graduate of Chapel Hill, emigrating to Tennessee, also settled at McMinnville, and was subsequently twenty years Chancellor of his division. There was only three months difference in their ages, and they had an even start for their remarkably parallel careers. Ridley was the more accomplished, by reason of his superior mental training and education; but Marchbanks' rugged manner only made his unbending integrity the more conspicuous. Ridley commenced an entire stranger with rather limited means; Marchbanks with no acquaintance and without any means. But they each had in abundance the one thing that has contributed more than any other to the success of men, namely, a fixed determination to succeed in his profession. Chancellor Ridley was always prompt, active, energetic and laborious, and these characteristics he had in common with Judge Goodpasture. He was an elder in the Cumberland Presbyterian Church, and a noble

Christian gentleman, who grappled many hearts to him with hooks of steel. Judge Goodpasture always cherished his memory with the deepest veneration.

Clerk and Master. Perhaps Chancellor Ridley, who was uniformily kind to the young men just commencing the practice, was touched by the hard struggle that was manifestly before young Goodpasture, as well as attracted by his sturdy virtues. At any rate, when Edward N. Cullom's term as Clerk and Master expired, in 1847, without his knowledge or solicitation, Chancellor Ridley announced his purpose to appoint him to the vacancy. During all his life Judge Goodpasture had the rare faculty of attracting the notice and inspiring the confidence of all with whom he was associated. Just before his first term as Clerk and Master expired, he chanced to be in Smithville, where Chancellor Ridley was holding court. While there Chancellor Ridley approached him in this manner: "Mr. Goodpasture, is it not about time you were renewing your bond?" He answered that his term would expire before the next sitting of the Chancery Court at Livingston, but added that he was not acquainted in Smithville, and would not be able to give bond there. "I will arrange that," said Chancellor Ridley, and when the bond was written up, himself procured the necessary sureties, and gave him an order to be entered on his minutes, re-appointing him for a second term.

At Lebanon Law School. Judge Goodpasture realized his imperfect equipment for the practice of his profession, and determined as soon as he should realize from his office sufficient fees

for that purpose, to attend the law school, then just
established at Lebanon by Judge Abraham Caruthers.
Accordingly he entered the law class of 1848-9, the
second taught in Cumberland University. Judge
Caruthers had then associated with him, as additional
professors, Judge Nathan Green, late of the Supreme
Court and Chancellor Bromfield L. Ridley. It was a
class of fifty-six magnificent young men, many of whom
have achieved more than a local reputation. There was
Judge Abram L. Demoss, the near neighbor and intimate
friend of Judge Goodpasture, in Nashville, who saw him
laid to rest in Mount Olivet; Nathan Green, Jr., the
present Chancellor of Cumberland University, who succeeded his father as one of the professors of law; Robert
Hatton, the brilliant Congressman and gallant Confederate General; Col. John F. House, the orator and
statesman, who represented the Hermitage district in
Congress in a manner not unworthy of Bell and
Grundy; Judge Wm. S. McLemore, of the circuit bench;
Gov. James D. Porter, who was first assistant Secretary
of State, under President Cleveland's first administration; Chancellors John Somers and B. J. Tarver, and
many others who took the highest rank in their
profession.

Judge Abraham Caruthers. While at Lebanon, Mr. Goodpasture
boarded with Judge Caruthers, who
became much attached to him.
When he was about to leave Judge Caruthers declined
to receive any compensation for his entertainment until
assured that its payment would be the cause of no
embarrassment to him. Judge Abraham Caruthers
(1803-1862) was a native of Smith County, Tennessee.

He studied law and commenced the practice in Columbia, but returned to Carthage, and became Circuit Judge, at the age of thirty, under appointment of Governor Carroll, and continued to hold the position until he resigned in 1847, to enter upon the work of establishing a law school in Lebanon. He discarded the old plan of lectures, and assigned as the daily lesson a given portion of the text, upon which the students were rigidly examined. This he followed by a system of moot courts. For this purpose he found no text book exactly suited to his use, and to meet the want, he prepared a pamphlet of forty pages, which he modestly called his "primer." The catalogue of 1848-9 announces that "two tracts have been prepared by one of the professors, the first containing the History of a Law-Suit, in the Circuit Court of Tennessee, noting incidentally the jurisdiction and mode of proceeding in all the other courts." . . . Such was the humble beginning of Caruthers' History of a Law-Suit, now a standard text-book found in the library of every Tennessee lawyer.

Hon. John M. Bright has paid this beautiful tribute to Judge Caruthers: "He was modest as he was meritorious, consistent as he was conscientious, useful as he was laborious, exalted in principle as he was liberal in spirit, profound as he was accurate, sound as a lawyer, able as a jurist, popular as a professor, successful as an author, irreproachable as a citizen, exemplary as a Christian."

Joseph Bates. Among the first business entrusted to Judge Goodpasture, after he came to the bar, was his employment to write the will of Joseph Bates (1777-1849), who lived in Bates' Cove, near Monroe, on the Livingston road. He was a man of strong intellect. of fair education and well posted on current events. In religion he was a Cumberland Presbyterian, and in politics a Democrat. He was a prosperous man of good, sound judgment; proud of Bates' Cove, on which he built one of the first, if not the very first, brick house in the county. He owned many negroes, whom he treated well, but made profitable. He was the father of the late Rev. Thos. F. Bates, and a cousin of Mrs. Harvey M. Watterson, the mother of Henry Watterson, and of Rev. Joseph H. Bates, who married a sister of Judge Goodpasture. Mr. Bates died in April, 1849, while Judge Goodpasture was at Lebanon, and he was called home to prove his will, which he had witnessed as well as written. Afterwards the will was contested and he defended it through all the courts. and at last had the pleasure of seeing it sustained in the Supreme Court.

Elijah Garrett. One of the highest evidences of the trust and confidence reposed in Judge Goodpasture, was the great number of wills he was called upon to write. He wrote the will of the original old pioneer "Big" Joe Copeland, a perfect giant, who is said to have cracked walnuts with his teeth, and who was often known to reach over the fence and lift two hundred pound porkers out of the pen, and put them in the scales. He took great interest in relating the circumstances under which he wrote the will of Elijah Garrett. It was a bitter cold day. with a light snow falling. But being informed that the occasion was urgent, he proceeded without delay, though it was then nearly night, and Mr. Garrett lived on Wolf River, some twelve or fifteen miles away. He found the old man apparently in a very low state, so feeble, indeed, that he began to doubt whether he had not arrived too late after all. Upon invitation he took a chair by the fire, thinking to warm himself before he should begin his work. After a little, Mr. Garrett roused up and began to talk. Presently his neighbor, Cope, was mentioned, and he began to tell of his numerous fights with Cope. He had whipped him, he said, many times before they left Virginia, but he was so persistent and stubborn, that he had to repeat it frequently after their arrival in Tennessee. As he talked he became excited, got out of bed, ate a hearty supper, and continued his animated discourse, until Judge Goodpasture expressed a wish to retire, it being too late to undertake the work in hand. A bed was prepared for him in the room, and being tired he slept soundly. In the morning Mr. Garrett again commenced on Cope, but Judge Goodpasture suggesting that if there was a will to be written they had better be at it, he called one of his sons to go for brother West and brother Matheny, two good men of the neighborhood, who were to witness his will. When they parted he said "My son, you will never see me again in the flesh," which proved entirely true, the old man having died a few days afterwards.

Elijah Garrett was a good man, a devout Christian and a useful citizen. He was a faithful minister in the Primitive Baptist Church, as were also three of his sons, and one of his negroes. While they were waiting for brother West and brother Matheny, he said to Judge Goodpasture: "Right there, standing in that door, last Sunday week, I heard my son, John Garrett, preach the ablest sermon I ever heard fall from the lips of a man. I imagined he was very much such a preacher as the apostle Paul." "Well," replied the Judge, "Paul was a man of considerable reputation in his day."

Now John Garrett had been rather wild in his youth, so that, it was said, his brothers expressed some little incredulity when he made a profession of religion. Judge Goodpasture, some years later, made the first speech delivered in the Mountain District against Know-Nothingism. It was in the Wolf River country, and all the Garretts were present. The pass word of the Know-Nothings was said to have been, "Have you seen Sam?" The applicant who was able to answer this question satisfactorily, was permitted to enter the lodge. Referring to this Know-Nothing pass word, Judge Goodpasture told the story of John Garrett's admission to the church, as he said he had heard it. He said Elijah Garrett, his brother, asked him many searching questions, and turned him over to his brother, William. By this time the old man, who had John's conversion much at heart, was getting very nervous, and as William proceeded he became more so. Finally, Bob, the negro, began to ask him a few.

"Wait," said the old man who could stand it no longer, "let me ask him a question."

"Johnny, my son, did you hear a voice?"

"Daddy, I did."

"Not another word, boys, I'll eat hell if he ain't all right."

The Garretts took no offense, but laughed as heartily as any at the pointed thrust.

State vs. Troxdale. When Judge Goodpasture was appointed Clerk and Master, he had never made an argument in a lawsuit. His first appearance was in the case of the State against Brit Collins, while he was in the law school at Lebanon. He had, however, soon after his admission to the bar, as Attorney-General pro tem. drawn the indictment in the celebrated case of the State against Troxdale, reported in Ninth Humphreys. Patsy Troxdale was a young, buxom girl of about twenty, who lived with her father, Edward O'Neal, on his little mountain farm in the eastern part of Overton County. The other members of her family were her mother, and her five brothers and sisters, the oldest of whom was Jackson, a lad of twelve. Patsy having commenced to keep the company of certain dissolute young men, her father was very indignant, and threatened to exclude her from his home. On the evening of Friday, September 15, 1846, she entertained Nicholas Stephens and William Upton, who were afterwards indicted jointly with her. Saturday morning a peculiar smoke was observed in the direction of the O'Neal farm. On Monday the horrible truth appeared. O'Neal, his wife and their five little children had been murdered with an axe, their bodies piled together, and the house burned down over them. The defendants were convicted. In the Supreme Court the judgment was reversed, but not on account of any defect in the indictment, which was drawn in strict conformity to the technical pleadings of that day.

State vs. Logston. Many years afterwards, by appointment of the court, and without hope of reward, Judge Goodpasture defended a prisoner charged with a similar butchery, who greatly enlisted his sympathy, and in whose behalf he made a strong and earnest effort. Just after the war, there lived in Fentress County a family consisting of the grandmother, her daughter and three little grandchildren; James, the oldest of whom was not over eight. One day in November, 1868, the two women and the second child were found dead in their house, having been murdered the day before, with an axe. James' head was badly crushed, but he finally recovered. The youngest child, an infant, was not hurt.

Calvin Logston, a young Kentuckian, of rather good appearance, and Jane and Eliza Brown, were indicted in the Circuit Court of Fentress County for the murder. Logston was tried and convicted, and the sentence of death pronounced against him. He appealed to the Supreme Court. Judge Goodpasture appeared as his counsel, and at his request, in view of the extreme penalty involved, the court, then sitting in sections, heard this case in full bench. A report of the proceedings, published at the time, says: "We do not recollect ever witnessing a trial that produced so marked an effect upon the court and bar. There was not a stir in the court room; at the bar stood the prisoner, whose life depended upon the result. The court and counsel seemed to feel the responsibility resting upon them. There was a solemn earnestness in the proceedings. The argument of the counsel for the prisoner was able. He discussed the questions of law arising upon the record with great force and clearness. The argument of the Attorney-General in behalf of the State, exhibited great ability, candor and fairness."

The court reversed the judgment and remanded the cause for a new trial. Judge Goodpasture followed the case back to the Circuit Court of Fentress County. The venue was then changed from Jamestown to Livingston, and a new trial had, again resulting in a conviction, mainly on the testimony of the little boy, James, which he thought was too questionable to allow so important a verdict to rest upon it. He again appealed for Logston, and again appeared as his counsel in the Supreme Court, but his earnest effort proved impotent to save his poor client, who soon afterwards suffered the death penalty at the hands of the Sheriff of Fentress County.

As a Trader. From the time Judge Goodpasture entered the practice, he was a very busy man. Always prompt and accurate in the discharge of his duties as Clerk and Master, he was at the same time building up a practice in the Circuit Court of the county. In addition to his official and professional duties, he was also beginning to exercise and develop his remarkable talent for trading. There has rarely been a more successful trader. His forte lay in an unusually sound judgment, upon which he was able to rest with absolute satisfaction, without regard to the opinions of others; the rapid, almost instantaneous process by which he reached his conclusions, and the unhesitating, undaunted, tireless, sleepless manner in which he prosecuted every purpose he had matured. He was bold to a degree, but, to use his own expression, there was a streak of caution in his nature that deterred him from risking much, where the result appeared to depend in any considerable measure on chance, rather than judgment. He traded in anything and everything in which his watchful eye could see a profit. But he never overtraded himself. During all his life he was never so involved as to imperil his solvency. Even in the panic of 1893. which broke so many brilliant financiers of Nashville, though he was and had been for twelve or fourteen years trading largely in real estate, and notwithstanding the loss of eight or ten thousand dollars. through the failures of the Commercial National Bank and the Southern Iron Company, it was never necessary for him to sell a foot of land at a sacrifice; but. on the contrary. he was always able to buy when a great bargain offered.

He also ventured. to a limited degree. into commercial fields. The reader will bear in mind that three years previous to this time he was well-nigh penniless. and his efforts were greatly paralyzed for the want of means, and he was now trying every avenue, and bending every energy to put himself in independent financial condition. On March 4. 1850. he entered into a four years partnership with his friend, Thomas F. Bates, and his brother, James M. Goodpasture. for the sale of general merchandise in Livingston.

Rev. Thos. F. Bates. Thomas F. Bates (1822-1897). was a son of Joseph Bates. heretofore mentioned. He had received a classical education at Alpine Institute, on the mountain near his father's, a school that had been established by Dr. John L. Dillard (1793-1881), one of the fathers of the Cumberland Presbyterian Church, and bore a high reputation for many years. Dr. Dillard rode the Overton circuit as early as 1815. Judge Goodpasture was named for him, and under his ministration, in his youth. be-

came a member, and, many years afterward, an elder in
the Cumberland Presbyterian Church.   While Mr. Bates
was there, the school was being taught by John L.
Beveridge, afterwards Governor of Illinois, J. L. Hough
and Rev. Wm. M. Dillard.   He studied for the ministry and became a well known Cumberland Presbyterian
preacher.   After his father's death, he lived for a time
at the farm, in Bates' Cove, but finally settled at Shel-
byville.   Judge Goodpasture wrote of him a few years
ago: "Fletcher Bates, as we always called him, is a fine
preacher, and one of the best men I ever knew.   He is
patriotic—loves his country and friends, and has a great
attachment for the old county where he was born and
reared.   Nothing gratifies him more than to hear of
the success of an Overton County man.   I don't think
he preaches much now, but is living quietly at home,
where he takes great interest in his garden, his flowers
and small fruits of which he has a great abundance.   He
is well to do, has plenty of everything he needs, and
seems to be living a peaceful and happy life.   He is
now seventy-three years old."

Dr. J. M. Goodpasture.   Dr. James McDonnold Goodpasture
(1827-1876), was three years younger
than the Judge, and was his favorite
brother.   When a lad, he had a disease in one of his
limbs, which necessitated its amputation, when he was
only thirteen years old.   He had a warm heart, and was
a man of unusually fine feeling and sentiment.   He
studied medicine and was a successful physician, at
Cookeville, where he was in active practice, until he
died, at the age of forty-nine years.   During one term
of six years, he held the office of Clerk and Master.

He was a devout Christian and an elder in the Cumberland Presbyterian Church.

By the terms of their partnership agreement, Judge Goodpasture was not to give his personal attention to the business.

CHAPTER V.

One can hardly conceive the restless energy that characterized Judge Goodpasture during this period of his life. Discharging with care and diligence his official duties; prosecuting with energy and success the practice of his profession; trading in everything that promised a profit; engaging, though not extensively in the mercantile business—yet, within the first five years of his career, he found time to make an active canvass of the eight counties of the Mountain district, as a Democratic candidate for Congress.

He was not a man of many books—he did not have time to read them. His first great enemy was poverty, which, he thought, had virtually cost him several years of his life. Poverty had denied him the finished education he believed necessary to the attainment of the highest eminence, and which, in after life, it was his chief care to provide for his children. It was the gaunt figure of poverty that interposed itself between him and every exalted aspiration and every ambitious hope of his early life. No wonder then, that the first struggle of his young manhood should have been with this blighting foe. He entered the contest with a courage and determination only equaled by his absolute confidence in the result. If he pursued it further than the demands of a learned and exacting profesison would justify, it is matter of little surprise. And that he should have entered the domain of politics, was only in keeping with the universal practice of the lawyers of the Mountain District, who esteemed political position as one of the fruits of the legal profession.

Col. John H. Savage. His competitor in this canvass was Col. John H. Savage (1815-—), a chivalrous gentleman, a true friend of the people, a gallant soldier and an eminent statesman. Coming home from the Mexican war with the rank of Lieutenant-Colonel, and bearing upon his person the scars received while gallantly leading an assault upon the Mexican stronghold at Molino-del-Rey, he was easily elected to Congress in 1849, though opposed by such popular men as Sam Turney and John B. Rodgers. In Congress he had been hardly less distinguished than in the army. It was in 1850 he made the eloquent speech on the Union, inserted in Field's Scrap Book, which closes with this sentiment: "I have ever hoped that our ship of state, self-poised upon the billows, would gather the tempest in her sails and fly with lightning speed to the home of transcendent national glory amid the plaudits of an admiring world. And for this I shall still be ready to make any sacrifice except my honor and my right to be free and equal on every foot of land beneath the stars and stripes."

This was in 1851. Both candidates were of the same political party, and Judge Goodpasture was unable to overcome the advantage that Colonel Savage's distinguished services had given him, but he made an honorable race, and one that did him great credit, and some service in the way of a favorable introduction to the people of the district.

Congressional Conventions. Judge Goodpasture was never elected to Congress. Some twenty-five years afterwards his name was presented, with a multitude of others, before a number of Democratic conventions assembled in rapid succession, during the period in which two members-elect of the Forty-Fourth Congress from the fourth district of Tennessee, died before taking their seats; and while he always showed much, sometimes more, positive strength than any of his competitors, it was his misfortune to live in a sparsely settled mountain county, and the nomination uniformly went to one of the rich and populous counties on the other side of the district. He soon found that though he might, and did in more than one convention, receive a majority of the votes cast, it was impossible for any of the mountain counties to effect a combination that would bring to its man the two-thirds vote necessary to a nomination.

Marries. Colonel Savage admits that he received at least one surprise in the contest between him and Judge Goodpasture. He expected a large majority in the Olympus district of Overton County. When the returns came in, the vote was found to be practically unanimous against him. The explanation he received was, that Judge Goodpasture's fiancee lived in that district, and had taken an active interest in his behalf. The reference was to Sarah Jane, the youngest daughter of Jacob and Jane C. (Marchbanks) Dillen, whom Judge Goodpasture married the following spring, namely: on the 16th day of May, 1852. The ceremony occurred at the home of her brother-in-law and guardian, H. R. Ryan, in Albany,

Kentucky, the Rev. Josiah G. Harris, of the Cumberland Presbyterian Church, officiating.

Jacob Dillen. Jacob Dillen was born in Henry County, Virginia, December 11, 1795, and moved with his father, Henry Dillen, an old Revolutionary soldier, to the Wolf River section of Overton County, Tennessee, about 1810. He adopted the legal profession, and though he died on the 21st day of August, 1835, in the very prime of life, so successful had he been that he left each of his four children a patrimony of several thousand dollars. Sarah Jane, the youngest of these, was born on Wolf River, May 4, 1835, and was, consequently, only three months old when her father died.

The Marchbankses. Her mother, Jane Caroline, was the daughter of William Marchbanks, a native of Scotland, who came from South Carolina to Tennessee, and settled near the present village of Algood, in Putnam County, where she was born, November 23, 1807. Her mother was Jane Young, a sister of James Young (1787-1860), fourteen years sheriff of Jackson County and twice a representative in the State Legislature. He was grandfather of the late J. Howard Young, of Dixon Springs, and of Oliver F. Young, of Simpson's Mills. Andrew J. Marchbanks, the distinguished lawyer and jurist of McMinnville, was her brother. Her sister, Sallie, married Maj. Henry H. Atkinson, a lawyer of some prominence in Overton County. Sometime in the twenties, Major Atkinson was elected Circuit Court Clerk, at Monroe. He had as his deputy Jacob Dillen, who also studied law in his office. It was on a visit to her sister, that Jane C. Marchbanks first met young Dillen, whom she married on the 3rd day of February, 1828. Mrs. Dillen survived her husband only ten years. After his death, she was married a second time, to Richard Poteet, and lived at Netherland, on Spring Creek, where, on September 19, 1845, she was thrown from a horse in a rocky branch near her home and instantly killed.

Charleston Commercial Convention. Being now in fairly comfortable financial condition, he took a still more active interest in public affairs. He was a delegate to the Commercial Convention of the Southern and Western States, which was held in the city of Charleston during the week commencing on the 10th of April, 1854. This convention was a revelation, as well as a great object lesson to him. It was one of the most intellectual bodies ever assembled in America. Fifteen states were represented. The delegation embraced many of the most brilliant and widely known men of the South and West. It was presided over by Hon. Wm. C. Dawson, of Georgia, and included among its delegates, such men as Matthew F. Maury, Clement C. Clay, Sr., Leslie Combs, James C. Jones, John H. Reagan and Albert Pike. Judge Goodpasture took great interest in the proceedings. He was particularly captivated by General Pike.

Albert Pike's Address. General Pike had introduced a series of resolutions favoring a confederation of the Southern States, for the purpose of building the Southern Pacific Railroad, and made a powerful speech in advocacy of them. He so charmed the Convention, that in the evening session he was called out again. He was a man of splendid presence, faultlessly attired, wearing neatly fitting kid gloves on the outside of which a brilliant diamond sparkled in the gas light. When he appeared in his perfect self-possession, and paid his beautiful tribute to the ladies, Judge Goodpasture thought he was the personification of grace and gallantry.

"Only a week or two ago," he said, "I was among the snows of the North. Even when I left Washington there were no leaves on the trees. But when I arrived here, I found the trees in leaf and the flowers in bloom. Sir, there is an Eastern fable which tells us of a lady of such benignancy and grace, that when the light of her eyes strikes the trees, or glances upon the flowers, the trees are instantly in leaf and the flowers in bloom; and I know now, after seeing the fair forms and bright eyes, which grace and enlighten those boxes, why it is that the trees are in leaf and the flowers in bloom in Charleston."

Judge Goodpasture, in his youth and younger manhood, had great ambition to be a speaker, and the impression made upon him by the grace and beauty and power of General Pike's oratory can hardly be over-estimated. The writer has reason to know something of the effect it produced, as he has, for these forty years, borne the General's first name, as a direct result of his magnetic eloquence.

Feeding Buzzards.

It was in Charleston Judge Goodpasture first met the late Judge Nathaniel Baxter. Walking out on the beach one day he saw an innumerable multitude of buzzards, collecting from the four quarters of the heavens, and fighting and scrambling over some object he could not see. It turned out that Judge Baxter had been to the market and bought a lot of haslets, which he was throwing out on the beach, in order to see the remarkable spectacle of hundreds of perfectly gentle buzzards falling in a black, scrambling, fighting, ravenous mass, two or three feet deep, and rising almost instantly, without leaving a vestige, not even a throttle, to mark the place where the object of their greed had been.

National Democratic Convention. In 1856, he was a delegate to the National Democratic Convention, which met in Cincinnati, June 2-6, and nominated James Buchanan for the Presidency. He took his wife and baby with him, traveling through the country in a buggy as far as Lexington, Kentucky. The beautiful blue grass region had on its richest verdure, and its lovely landscapes made their journey very enjoyable. While at the Convention he called on Hon. Thomas H. Benton, who was himself aspiring to the Presidency, and who assured him that he was "sound, sir, both in mind and body." He had a contesting delegation from Missouri. Not having been assigned seats upon the floor, immediately after the election of the President pro tem. they forcibly thrust the doorkeeper aside and rushed into the hall, taking possession of the vacant seats assigned to New York, whose delegates were all excluded pending a contest. Their leader mounted a seat and addressed the Convention, amid cries of "Order! order!" Great excitement prevailed, until an agreement was reached, and the contestants retired. The bold leader of this contesting delegation was the Hon. B. Gratz Brown, whom Judge Goodpasture, as elector for the Fourth Congressional District, supported for Vice President on the ticket with Horace Greeley, in 1873.

State Senator. In 1857, he resigned the office of Clerk and Master, and was elected to the State Senate, defeating John Bowles, who had been a member of the House of Representatives, in 1851, and a member of the Senate from 1853 to 1857. Bowles afterwards achieved great local notoriety during the reconstruction period in Tennessee.

In his legislative career Judge Goodpasture manifested the same accurate judgment of public affairs, and the same firm and energetic manner of dealing with them that characterized the whole of his private and professional life. He opposed the bill providing for a conventional rate of interest in a speech of strong, practical sense, which affords some insight into the financial maxims by which his private business was influenced. "I hold," he said, "that a man is none the better off by having his pocket full of money, if his notes are out for it, bearing even six per cent. interest; but if he is paying ten per cent. interest, it would be better for that man to drain him of his money at once and relieve him of his debt."

"Speculation, however," he says in another connection, "never did and never will increase the real wealth of the country; whilst one speculator is getting rich, another is becoming bankrupt. . . . It is to labor that we are indebted for all our prosperity."

He introduced a resolution proposing an amendment to the constitution, providing for the election of Governor and members of the General Assembly once in four years, and for quadrennial sessions of the Legislature, which he supported in an able speech. The resolution provoked wide discussion in the press of the State, drawing out strong editorials from such papers as the Brownsville Journal, McMinnville New Era and Athens Post. The Union and American, the leading Democratic daily at the capital, declared that the urgent necessity for such an amendment was patent to the most casual thinker, and expressed a confidence that if the proposition were referred to the people it would be adopted by an overwhelming majority. The resolution passed the Senate, but was defeated in the House by a narrow margin.

His chief service to the State, however, was in connection with a resolution, which he introduced on the 18th of March, 1858, just before the final adjournment of the session, providing for the appointment of a joint select committee to investigate the manner in which the securities of the several free banks had been managed in the office of the comptroller, and whether any interest had been improperly paid on the State coupon bonds. They were directed to report on or before the first day of the succeeding October, and were empowered to send for persons and papers. The committee appointed under this resolution, of which Judge Goodpasture was chairman, sat all summer making a thorough investigation of the matter referred to them. They detected the frauds of the Exchange Bank; the embezzlement by the Secretary of State to the amount of fifty thousand dollars; and the over payment of interest to about the same amount. Their report, making a volume of several hundred pages, was made to

Governor Harris, and showed great skill in the management of the investigation. A thousand copies were printed for the information of the public.

Meets the Grey-eyed Man of Destiny. While in Nashville Judge Goodpasture had the pleasure of meeting Gen. William Walker (1824-1860), the "grey-eyed man of destiny," who was then just back from his brilliant career in Nicarauga. He was at that time under indictment in the United States District Court of Louisiana for beginning in the territory of the United States. a military enterprise to be carried on from there against the State of Nicarauga. His father lived in Nashville, where he himself was raised and educated, and on this occasion gave a dinner in honor of his distinguished son, to which many prominent people were invited.

5

CHAPTER VI.

A Trial For Witchcraft.

At the expiration of his term in the Senate, Judge Goodpasture declined to be a candidate for re-election, and determined to devote his time wholly to the practice of his profession. The Mountain District, extending from the fertile valleys along the Cumberland River, to the sterile plateau on top of the mountain, at that time contained every shade of character and every degree of civilization to be found in the country. Less than ten years before Judge Goodpasture came to the bar, there occurred, in Fentress County, the only trial for witchcraft ever had in the State. He knew all the parties connected with it well. Judge Abraham Caruthers was on the bench and John B. McCormick was Attorney-General. The resident lawyers at Jamestown then, were John M. Clemens, the father of Mark Twain and Wm. B. Richardson.

Subsequently, Clemens' law library came into the possession of Judge Goodpasture, and a few years ago he sent Mark Twain his father's copy of Tidd's Practice. He acknowledged its receipt in a characteristic letter. He expressed an appreciation of the books, on account of his father's signature, which he recognized; but referring to their contents, he expressed regret that some book other than a law book should not have been found, as he was the one man most incapable of understanding the law, unless it were his elder brother, who practiced in the West.

The celebrated mountain lands, of which Mark Twain writes in the Gilded Age, lie in Fentress County; and the picturesque village he describes under the name of Obedstown is none other than its county site. The court-house, on the fence surrounding which the male population of the village were sitting, chewing tobacco and spitting at bumble-bees and such other objects of interest as appeared within their wide range, while they waited the arrival of the mail; and to which one of them referred, when he observed that, "if the judge is a gwine to hold cote," he reckoned he would have to "roust" his sow and pigs out of the court-house, was the same in which this singular case was tried.

It seems that an old man by the name of Stout, who lived on Obeds River, was arrested for bewitching the beautiful daughter of a certain man, named Taylor, who lived on the mountain. The defendant was treated with much rigor, and his person abused by the various experiments to which he was subjected, for the purpose of establishing his guilt. The guards had taken the precaution to remove the lead from their guns, and to load them with silver, which was considered the only metal to which a wizard is not impalpable.

The accused was carried before Esquire Joshua Owens, a leading magistrate of the county, whom Judge Goodpasture knew intimately for many years afterwards. The prosecutor and many of his neighbors were introduced as witnesses on behalf of the State, and proved, in addition to the particular facts charged, that the defendant had frequently been seen to escape out of houses through the key holes in the doors; and that he had on divers occasions not only operated on the bodies and minds of human beings, and that at a distance of ten or fifteen miles, but also on horses, cattle and other stock.

On this evidence the defendant was found guilty and bound over to the next term of the Circuit Court. When the grand jury met, General McCormick being of opinion the prosecution could not be sustained, refused to prefer a bill of indictment. The defendant was accordingly discharged amid great excitement, some of the mountaineers boldly declaring that it would be better to live without laws, if such offenders could escape with impunity.

Stout, on the other hand, went before the grand jury and indicted a number of persons concerned in his arrest, for assault and battery. When these cases came on to be heard before Judge Caruthers and a jury of the county, the defendants admitted the assault and battery and justified on the ground that it was committed in arresting a felon, relying on the statutes of Henry VIII. and James I., making witchcraft a felony, which they declared had never been repealed in this State. The enlightened Judge, however, charged the jury that they were "destructive of, repugnant to, or inconsistent with the freedom and independence of this State, and form of government," and were never in force here by virtue of the act of 1778, and the defendants were accordingly convicted.

Sam Turney. The bar that practiced at Livingston during this period was one of the strongest in the State. On account of Judge Goodpasture's interest in him, particular mention will be made of Sam Turney, who was not only a successful lawyer and politician, but one of the most unique characters this State has produced. He was a warm friend of Judge Goodpasture, who used to relate many anecdotes illustrating his eccentricities and peculiarities. He was born in Smith County, on the farm now owned by Hon. Sam Young, near Dixon's Springs. In his youth he lived for a time with Moses Fisk, at Hilham, working on the farm to pay for the instruction he received at the hands of that eminent educator. When Judge Goodpasture was a boy, he was shown large piles of stumps on Fisk's farm that were said to have been dug up and hauled there by Turney. After he came to the bar he moved to Sparta and made that his home until his death, which occurred about the close of the civil war. He was a member of the State Senate from 1839 to 1847. In 1841, he was Speaker of that body, and one of the "immortal thirteen," who prevented the election of United States Senators by the Twenty-Fourth General Assembly, in which the Whigs had a majority of one. Turney was not a partisan. He did not care anything about party. In 1856, when he was a candidate for Congress, and Judge Gardenhire was spoken of as his competitor, he said to Judge Goodpasture: "I can beat Mr. Gardenhire, and I'll give him choice of sides; if he wants the Democrat side, I'll take the Know-Nothing side; or if he wants the Know-Nothing side, I'll take t'other side." But the Democrats nominated his brother, Hopkins L. Turney, and it was in his interest that he was induced to join such partisan Democrats as Samuel H. Laughlin and Andrew Johnson in their determined effort to defeat the election of two Whig Senators.

Turney was very careless of his personal appearance. It was not at all unusual, as he rode into town, to see a shirt sleeve or a drawers leg hanging out of his saddle bags. On one occasion Judge Goodpasture had spent the night with him, and as they came in next morning, he left a heavy blue blanket with a tailor to be made into an overcoat. When he had gone a short distance the tailor hailed him and asked him to return, stating that he had not taken his measure.

"No difference," said Mr. Turney, "just put it all in, Mr. Gibbons, just put it all in."

This indifference to personal appearance was not confined to his apparel. At a certain court in Jamestown, Turney, Goodpasture and James Snodgrass occupied the same room. Turney was a great reader, and seemed to have no choice of books, except he liked old books—the older the better. On this occasion, after Goodpasture and Snodgrass had retired, he found one that had long since lost its backs, and was soon absorbed in its contents. The tallow candle was about two inches long, and he read until it was quite consumed, when the room became perfectly dark. Presently he began a queer little whick-a-whack noise, which was kept up for sometime. Snodgrass grew quite restless and nervous and finally asked:

"Sam, what in the blank are you doing?"

"Trimming my hair," was the response.

Next morning, after inspecting the job in a glass, Turney said: "God-a-mighty, Jim, if it ain't cut as well as if a barber had done it."

This profanity would not have been allowed to go to print, had it not been desired to make it the occasion for recording the fact that Mr. Turney abandoned the habit many years before his death. Early in his political career, he had been charged with being a deist, and in answering the charge, he went no further than to declare that he believed it right to do right, and appealed to his constituents to judge his conduct by that rule. Sometime in the fifties, however, while he was attending the sittings of the Supreme Court, at Nashville, he became greatly interested in the meetings then being held there by Alexander Campbell, and in the end joined the church and was baptized. He was stopping at the Sewanee Hotel, and rooming with Judge Goodpasture and Maj. A. A. Swope. The important will case of Peterman against Cope, was pending in the Supreme Court, but had not been heard. Turney and Swope were together in the case. The evening of his baptism, while he was sitting before the fire drying his socks, resting the heel of one foot on the toe of the other, and occasionally reversing the position, the Cope will case was mentioned.

"Major Swope, have you a brief in that case," asked Turney.

The Major assured him he had.

"Read it, Major, please."

Major Swope read until he came to a point that struck Mr. Turney with unusual force.

"Swope, read that again, please."

Swope read it again.

"God-a-mighty dam, Swope, if we can't win on that." Not another word was spoken for a full minute, when he

added, "but a man ought not to swear." Though, to
use his own expression, the process of his religion was
"gradual," he soon entirely abandoned the habit and
became quite religious, sometimes lecturing on the
Scriptures.

Builds in the Country. Judge Goodpasture practiced his profession with such vigor that he soon built up a clientage not inferior to that of any of the distinguished lawyers with whom he was associated. He first lived in a frame house on the west side of the square in Livingston, where three of his children were born. In 1860, he built a splendid brick residence in the country, two miles west of Livingston, and moved into it just at the beginning of the civil war, and continued to live there until he moved to Nashville, in 1879.

When the war came on Judge Goodpasture gave his allegiance to his State, but never entered the army. Although he had led an exceedingly active life, the philosophy by which he lived had made him few enemies and many friends. He was only giving the rule of his own conduct when he wrote to one of his sons: "Make it a point from which you must never vary, always to do right; treat everybody kindly, rich and poor alike, and especially the unfortunate and neglected; permit no consideration to influence you to, in the smallest degree, slight any on account of poverty or position in society; avoid, as much as possible, the society of the wicked and dissipated, but at all times treat them politely and kindly; and be strictly moral and upright in all your conduct and deportment."

A Mysterious Horseman. The result was, he experienced a singular freedom from fear in those perilous times, though he was sometimes in imminent danger. With no firearms in his house, his doors were never locked, day or night, and he never refused to answer a call. One evening a horseman rode rapidly up to his front gate. When Judge Goodpasture had answered his summons, he stated that a man had been thrown from his horse and dangerously hurt at the lawn gate, some three hundred yards distant, and asked him to bring a light and come to his assistance. The horseman then turned and rode back to his companion. It so chanced that two of his wife's kinsmen, William and Young Marchbanks, were spending the night with Judge Goodpasture. They were men of great courage and armed to the teeth. They asked the privilege of accompanying him and to guard against treachery, which was suspected, they carried their pistols in their hands. When they arrived at the lawn gate, no one was visible, and the only sign of life was the sound of retreating horse hoofs heard in the distance.

Writes a Pass. About this time he experienced a remarkable evidence of the confidence his neighbors reposed in him. Old man Jewett, who lived in the upper part of the county, came to his house one day, to ask Judge Goodpasture to write him a pass to Union City, in West Tennessee. He said one of his sons, who was in the Confederate army, was reported to be dying there and he wanted to go to his bedside. Judge Goodpasture at first undertook to show him the absurdity of the request, but Mr. Jewett still insisted upon his writing the pass. As he had ridden twenty miles to get it, Judge Goodpasture was unwilling to disappoint him, and accordingly wrote an order, addressed to "All Officers and Soldiers of the United States Army, and of the Army of the Confederate States," and directing them to permit the bearer to pass without molestation or hinderance to the place of his destination; explaining that he was a non-combatant, a good citizen and an honest man; and stating the sad mission that carried him from home. To this he affixed his own signature. The remarkable part of the incident is, that Mr. Jewett passed safely through the lines of both armies with no other authority than this request of Judge Goodpasture.

Death of His Mother. Perhaps the sadest event of this period was the death of his mother, in May, 1864, while he was a prisoner in the hands of the Thirteenth Kentucky (Federal) Cavalry. It was a source of great sorrow to him that he was deprived of being present at her last moments. He always regretted that in his busy, active, pressing life he had not been more thoughtful of his parents. In a letter to one of his sons, in 1880, he writes: "I am getting along a little in years. I have just been thinking of what occurred to my mind after the death of your grandfather and mother. They were good people and dearly loved their children, and felt a deep interest in their welfare. In their old days nothing did them more good than a letter or a visit from one of their children. I did not think much about it then. I lived only a short distance from them and could and ought to have visited them every week or two. I am sorry I did not. I have regretted it ever since. It was not a want of affection for my parents, but I did not realize the deep interest they felt in me. So, as time rolls on and cares increase, don't forget to write your father frequently and visit him occasionally."

Tinker Dave Beaty. The most desperate set of Federal guerillas in the Mountain District was the company commanded by Tinker Dave Beaty, of Fentress County. Before the war Judge Goodpasture had defended Beaty in the Circuit Court at Jamestown, on an indictment for a very grave offense. This circumstance gained him immunity from the bloody raids of his men during the war, as it also gave him a sort of protection during the equally dangerous time just succeeding that demoralizing struggle. About the close of the war, Judge Goodpasture met Tinker Dave for the first time after hostilities had commenced. He was somewhat embarrassed as he did not know how he would be received. After passing the compliments of the day he enquired for the news. "Nothing new," said Tinker, but after a moment he added, "Well, I believe our men did kill a lot of the Hammock gang this morning." In the course of the conversation Judge Goodpasture observed that Beaty had never been at his house. "No, sir," he replied, "I had no business with you."

The Courts Open Again. This last statement he took as an assurance that Tinker still remembered his former services, and with his characteristic ability to turn an advantage to account he determined to make Tinker's friendship useful to him. When the war closed there was a great accumulation of business awaiting the opening of the courts. He had a number of bills ready when the first court met at Jamestown, which he determined to file. It was considered as much as his life was worth to attend this court, and would be if he failed to receive Tinker Dave Beaty's protection. No other lawyer ventured to appear. The evening before the court met, Judge Goodpasture rode directly to Beaty's house, about twenty-five miles over the rough mountain roads, where he was received in a friendly spirit, and spent the night. In the morning Beaty rode with him into Jamestown, and after he had dispatched the business in hand, brought him back to his house. Next day, when Judge Goodpasture was ready to depart, Beaty told him it would not be safe for him to go alone, and sent his brother, Flem, with him, as far as old man Hill's, at the foot of the mountain, whence he reached home in safety. From that day, Judge Goodpasture never missed a court at Jamestown, until he left the Mountain District, and in one year did business in that county to the value of seven thousand dollars.

From 1865 to 1875, his business was phenomenal and the amount of work he did was enormous. In a letter dated June 20, 1869, he says: "I rode home from Jamestown last night—reached home at 3 o'clock this morning." He lived about thirty miles from Jamestown, and the way was the very worst of mountain roads. He frequently rode home from Cookeville, some twenty miles distant, after court adjourned in the afternoon. So, he was at Livingston, Jamestown, Sparta, Cookeville, Gainesboro, Celina and Nashville—always going and ever full of business.

Hidden Treasure. A circumstance occurred in 1870, that will illustrate how completely he was absorbed in his practice at this time. During the war, he had three or four hundred dollars in gold, which he concealed under the parlor hearth. As soon as the courts were open, he plunged into a flood of new business, without giving the hidden treasure a thought. In the winter of 1867-8, his wife was sick and thought she would be more comfortable in the parlor. She was moved in and occupied it during the remainder of the winter and spring. One day, some five years after the war, for the first time, the circumstance of the hidden gold suddenly flashed into his mind. He removed the hearth and found every piece of the money safe, though much blackened by the constant fire that had burned above it during his wife's sickness.

Family Afflictions. On the 8th day of June, 1867, he lost his favorite son, Harvey Dillard, then a bright little boy of two short summers, from the bite of a venomous reptile, which was never discovered. Not long afterwards, February 20, 1868, Jacob Dillen, his infant son, died. And within the year, on the 21st day of April, 1868, he suffered the greatest of all bereavments in the death of his beloved wife. Mrs. Goodpasture was a noble little woman. She was as bright, vivacious and intelligent, as she was kind, gentle and charitable; and being the best of company, she was a universal favorite. Many bright stories of her wit and social charms are still told in the neighborhood. These were the only deaths that ever occurred in his family during his lifetime. So true it seems, that "misfortunes come not singly, but as if they watched and waited." No wonder he should have felt "that the real happiness of this life is hardly worth a thought."

After the death of his wife, his household was in a desolate condition. His family now consisted of three boys. Two of them were sent off to school, first at Cookeville and then at New Middleton. The third was too young to leave home. He employed a housekeeper, but his necessary absence from home, sometimes for a considerable period, together with the fact already noted, that he never locked a door, had the effect to strip his house of nearly everything of a movable nature it had contained.

Marries Again. On the 17th of June, 1869, he was married a second time, to Nannie Young, daughter of Austin C. and Lucette Young, who lived near Sparta, Tennessee, his old friend Jesse Hickman performing the ceremony.

Uncle Jesse Hickman. Rev. J. E. Hickman (1805-1888), was one of the most consecrated men in the pulpit of the Cumberland Presbyterian Church. Born in the Pendleton district, South Carolina, he came to Tennessee in his childhood, and was brought up to the saddler's trade. Yielding to an impression to preach, he joined the Madison Presbytery, in West Tennessee, but moved to Cherry Creek, in White County, in 1837, and was one of the charter members of the Sparta Presbytery, in which he labored fifty-three years, and where he died at the age of eighty-three.

Judge Goodpasture called in person to request that he officiate at his marriage. When he arrived, Uncle

Jesse ordered his cook to "put the big pot in the little one," and so overwhelmed him with polite attentions, that he had spent the whole of the day before he found an opportunity to mention the subject of his visit, though he thought he was in a great hurry. But Uncle Jesse was hospitable to a degree little met with in these days. Many years later, after Judge Goodpasture's oldest son had entered the ministry of the Cumberland Presbyterian Church, he chanced to pass through Uncle Jesse's country, and called to pay his respects. The old man made him welcome to the best his home afforded, and when he was ready to take his departure, ordered his own horse and rode with him to the very uttermost limit of his neighborhood; and as they passed along the road, from house to house, he would call out his friends: "This is Brother Goodpasture, one of our young preachers." "Brother Goodpasture, this is one of my elders. I was unwilling you should leave the neighborhood without making his acquaintance." And so on.

Takes His Boys To College. From the time his children began to be old enough to go to school, Judge Goodpasture took the liveliest interest in their education. In 1871, the two older boys, after attending preparatory schools at Cookeville and New Middleton, were entered in the University of Tennessee, at Knoxville, where they graduated in 1875. He took them across the mountain from Livingston to Knoxville on horseback, accomplishing the journey in three days. After he saw them properly located, he returned the same way, leading the two extra horses. It was his theory that a boy should be taught to use his own judgment and act on his own responsibility. He

advised them. moralized on current events, counseled
them out of his ripe experience, stimulated every worthy
ambition, but in the end made each take the responsibility of his own actions.   Some of his letters are worthy
of preservation.   The one that follows was written to
his two older sons just as they were completing the law
course in Vanderbilt University:

"Livingston, Tenn., May 27, 1877.
"Ridley and Albert:

**Letter To
His Sons.**
"Dear Sons:—I received a letter from
Willie yesterday. He says his examination [at Burritt College] begins
on the 11th and ends on the 13th of July. If you
remain at home that long, as I suppose you will, I want
you to go over. I will try to go myself.

This is Sunday, and I have nothing to do but meditate,
and as usual, a large amount of my thoughts is upon the
welfare of my children. The days of my youth are as
fresh in my memory as they were twenty years ago. I remember well the difficulties that were then in my way.
I was ambitious, but I had no one to advise me upon the
questions that most troubled me. My ambition led me
to new fields, about which my own family had no
knowledge or experience. I longed to be a speaker, and
thought if I could be a lawyer the measure of my ambition would be filled. But I never had been in a court-
house, and I knew that my best friends regarded the idea
as ridiculous. So, without consulting a human being
on earth, at the age of twenty, I took up 'Blackstone.'
But my greatest trouble was to stick to it. My pros-
pects looked so gloomy, it required all the nerve I had

to keep me from quitting it, and taking up something more flattering. What little money I had, I had made by raising chickens and teaching school at $12.00 per month, $5.00 per month of which I paid for a hand to work in my place on father's farm. To spend this hard earned money, distressed me. To pay $1.25 per week for board, looked like utter ruin. To do without good Sunday clothes troubled me, but to spend my money for them seemed equally bad. I could not sleep of nights. I could not study to advantage. But I felt determined and never doubted that at some time in the future I would have plenty and endeavored to submit patiently to present privations, looking to that time. But enough on this subject. I will add, however, that on account of these adverse circumstances, I virtually lost several years of my life.

"Now, you are differently situated. I would here say, it is a very great mistake to suppose, that in order to succeed a man must be surrounded with all these difficulties. It is not so. True, it is an evidence that a man possesses some of the elements of greatness to succeed at all under such circumstances; but, on the other hand, to be able to weigh, appreciate and utilize the advantages that education and property give, is also evidence of greatness. There is one thing certain, no man, I care not what his native intellect is, can reach the very highest type of greatness without a thorough education. The true metal may be there, but it is the polish that glitters and charms the world. But there is one thing every young man should learn, namely, that it takes time to accomplish any great thing; therefore he should be patient. It is better that he should grow slowly; let him build a firm foundation, and as he rises he can feel and know that it is substantial. It were better if he could keep a little ahead of his reputation; then there is no danger of a fall.

"You should start out determined at any cost to understand thoroughly everything you undertake, and never think of stopping short of the first ranks of your profession. You may expect to spend several years of hard labor, without much return. You will often be disheartened, I care not how great a philosopher you are; you can't help it. You will think fees come in slowly, but you must remember that the closest observer cannot see the young tree grow, yet we know that in a few years it grows from a small bush to a large tree. So it is with the professional man.

"I would assure you of this, that there is not a lawyer in the State who has qualified himself properly, and been an honest, upright, sober, industrious man who has not, sooner or later, succeeded. Every man who deserves success, succeeds. It has always been so and always will be so. The great difficulty is in doing what one knows to be right; it requires more determination, firmness and courage than most men have. Yet, it is within the power of any young man, with strong, discriminating intellect and good education; firm, resolute, unshaken morals and strict integrity; fair power of endurance and a reasonable amount of patience; never flagging industry, and an exalted ambition, to reach any point of eminence open to the proofession. And after all, it takes but little more labor than to plod along in the crowded middle or lower ranks. Besides, the pleasure is much greater.

"Now, I know as well as I know anything that does not admit of mathematical demonstration, that if you and Willie should all keep your health and follow strictly through life the advice I am going to give you, you can stand at the very head of the bar in the State. I do not pretend to give details.

"1. Be Christian gentlemen.

"2. In everything you do in life, let the first inquiry be, is it right?

"3. Make as few promises as you well can, and keep strictly all you make.

"4. Be prompt in all your undertakings.

"5. Never go in debt.

"6. Never go security.

"7. Be strictly temperate.

"8. Have a good library.

"9. Have a good office and keep it neat and clean.

"10. Give your whole time to your profession.

"11. Examine every lawsuit you have thoroughly, and make a brief in every case.

"12. Never speak on any subject you do not perfectly understand.

"13. Be polite to everyone, good and bad, but associate with none but the very best society.

"14. Dress well; be neat and clean.

"15. Read the newspapers; post yourselves on polite literature.

"If you will begin at the start, there is no difficulty in observing all these rules, and that, with industry, is all that is required. There is one thing, however, that is very important, and that is, to keep all of your accounts carefully, and never let them run too long.

Charge reasonable fees, neither too low nor too high, and when you can do so have them secured. I have written a longer letter than I expected. Write me.

"Affectionately,

"J. D. GOODPASTURE."

CHAPTER VII.

As the years rolled by Judge Goodpasture found himself in a very different situation than previously, in regard to the education of his children. As appears from his letters to them from time to time, he always felt keenly his own lack of a thorough education, and one of his greatest ambitions was to see that they should escape the privations and hardships he had endured in consequence thereof. All of his children old enough to go to school up to this time, had been boys, and these he had sent away to preparatory schools, and then to college. But he was now in possession of a family of young girls as well as boys, with no good schools in reach of him, and it was thought unwise and imprudent to send them from home.

He had, besides, reached a period of life, when the conflicts and the exacting duties of a very large practice were growing more and more irksome. The profession of the law had never been to his taste. When a young man, it was the only road to political preferment, and gave at once a respectability and standing to those engaged in it that was offered by no other calling or profession. He disliked the eternal contention and wrangle necessarily incident to it. None of the incentives that had led him to begin the profession would now apply for its continuance. A poor, struggling boy in the beginning, he had long since made a competence for himself and family. Without reputation, and utterly unknown then, he had now gained all the standing in the profession that he ever expected to acquire.

Besides all this, he had long seen the advantages enjoyed by those who lived in better sections of the country, with railroad and other necessary adjuncts of modern life. Hence, he made up his mind to move. He first meditated moving to McMinnville, where he owned a very desirable little farm, and where there was a good female school, and then thought somewhat of going to Gallatin. Both of these, however, were finally abandoned for Nashville, and so, on Tuesday, October 21, 1879, we find him and the family, in the early emigrant style, moving in wagons through the country to that place. He had been there only a short while before and rented an excellent house on the fashionable Spruce street.

He and the family had quite a picnic of the trip, and when they reached Lebanon, the children went almost wild with delight. A circus had been there a few days before, and the gorgeous lithographic pictures of the wild beasts, excited their greatest admiration. Besides, they had never seen a town before, and were carried away by its gradeur. Those who have been raised in a city can hardly imagine the effect upon children or grown people either, for that matter, who see a town for the first time. Nothing they have heard or read seems to prepare them for it.

Jas. W. McHenry. They arrived at Nashville on Sunday afternoon, and their caravan attracted much attention. Luckily, their next door neighbor in the new home turned out to be Mrs. McHenry, an old friend, who had been born and reared in Overton County. She was the widow of James W. McHenry, a relative of the well known Cullom family, and one of the best lawyers who ever lived and practiced in Overton County. After the war, he moved to Nashville to secure a wider field for his talents, and was rapidly entering upon a paying practice when he died. He was in the prime of life and would undoubtedly have taken the highest position at the bar had he lived. He and Judge Goodpasture had been the best of friends, and when he moved to Nashville he insisted on the Judge going with him and forming a partnership for the practice of their profession. But the Judge's business at the time was thought to be too great to turn loose or abandon.

Mrs. McHenry was very kind to them, and her offers of assistance were greatly appreciated.

Builds a Home. Judge Goodpasture had been in Nashvile but a few days until he had purchased a place on which to build a home. In the very beginning he displayed that excellent judgment and foresight as regards the value and desirableness of city real estate that afterwards became so astonishing. He bought just outside the corporation, on the corner of Broad and Stonewall streets, a fifty foot lot, on which was located a very good two story brick house of four rooms and two basement rooms. The price paid was $2,500.00. This was only $50.00 per foot, without taking the worth of the house into consideration. In less than ten years he saw the value of the ground alone rise to $150.00 per foot.

He at once began to figure on building, and in the spring of 1880, he began the erection of a splendid residence, utilizing the house already on the lot, but building to it in such a way as to give it the appearance of a new house throughout. His addition, when completed, gave him a residence of fourteen rooms. He was his own architect, and could plan a house with undoubted ability. The drawing was the one thing that seemed to overcome him. But he worked at it most assiduously. Whatever he undertook, he did with his whole soul; and so in this case. If one drawing did not suit, he would make another. Finally his wife ran up on some of his remarkable plans and drawings, and inquired if he was laying out a new cemetery. That she should mistake his house for a cemetery lot and the windows for graves was too much for him, so he finally carried his plans to the carpenter firm of Wright & Co., and got Jacob O. Wright to make the picture for him. Wright did it to his entire satisfaction, but was indicted at the next term of the Criminal Court for following the the calling of an architect without a license.

Other Building Operations. The Judge also, a little later, purchased a lot on Cedar street on which to build a law office. At that time a large number of such offices were on Cedar street West of Cherry. The lot was just opposite the place of sitting of the Federal Court and was midway between the Supreme Court at the capitol, and the lower courts on the public square. How times change! In five years there was not a lawyer's office on Cedar street.

Judge Goodpasture had a passion for building.

and all his plans were in the direction of utility and practicality. He purchased not only the ground on which his office was built, but the entire corner of Cedar and Summer streets. The office building was a combination office and dwelling, the office, however, having no connection with the other parts of the house. He was very much pleased with it, and in one of his family letters says: "I will have my office done by the 10th of April; it will be the best office in Nashville." The plans of house and office were his own.

He also planned and built on a part of the same ground a very large, double tenement building. These were very handsome, and were rented before completed at $50.00 per month each. The office building, exclusive of the office of two rooms, was rented at $35.00 per month.

At this time his business in the Mountain Circuit was in a very unfinished condition, and he was constantly forced to leave home to attend the courts in the different counties in which he had practiced, and especially important to him were the courts of Clay, Overton and Fentress. These harassed him very much at times and almost, on a few occasions, destroyed the pleasure of even so agreeable a thing to him as building. Hence, we find him writing as follows on June 10, 1880: "I am inclined to think I made a mistake in building as much as I am doing; it gives me a great deal of trouble, besides, it is the most confining thing you ever saw. My dwelling is nearly done, and we are plastering the house adjoining my office."

His great energy, enlivened by a naturally active mind and a thoroughly confirmed habit of industry, would permit of no idle hours, notwithstanding the change from the country to the city, so that within the year, before he had learned anything much of the place or its modes of business (and they differ widely from the country, and especially from the country from which he came) we find him purchasing the ground and building a large dwelling for a home, a combination office and dwelling and a large tenement building. And during that same year, he was forced to attend all, or nearly all, the sittings of the courts in the various counties in which he had practiced. This had to be done in winter as well as in summer, and on horseback, the railroad at that time running no further than Lebanon, and sometimes the trips were made in desperately bad weather. In December, 1879, he wrote one of his sons: * * * "I hope you will come up and spend the Christmas at home. I only regret that I cannot be there. I am trying to wind up my business as fast as possible. I will not attend the Jamestown court any more, neither will I attend the Circuit Court at Livingston, but will be compelled for sometime to attend the Chancery Courts in Overton and Clay."

The Courts. With what feelings he must have attended the Jamestown court for the last time! He had been the first lawyer to appear in that court after the war; never missed a court there while he lived in the circuit, and was employed in so many cases at one time that the Clerk and Master said it would not have been possible to hold a court in his absence. When the writer was there in the summer of 1875, the Clerk and Master informed him that of the eighty new cases entered on his docket, he had been employed in fifty-five, and that these included all the causes of real importance. And it was this way from the beginning to the end—the confidence of the people of the county in his ability and integrity never wavered. and he had had control, practically, of one side or the other of every law suit of consequence in their courts for a period of nearly twenty-five years. Could he leave such a county for the last time with other than the deepest emotions? The court he attended there the year he moved was the last time he was ever in Fentress County.

He seems to have been mistaken in his statement in the letter above quoted, December, 1879, that he would not attend the Circuit Courts at Livingston, but would the Chancery of Overton and Clay, for we find in one of his letters, under date of June 10, 1880, an account of a trip to the Circuit Courts of Overton and Clay; of the trial of a very important murder case, and of his gratifying success therein. In criminal cases he preferred to defend, his sympathies being with the unfortunate. He liked the Chancery practice better, however, than either the law or criminal.

These courts, and a multitude of other unsettled business, not only harassed him in his building operations in his new home, but interfered with and prevented other things he had at heart as we may see from the following, quoted from same letter: "I would like exceedingly well to pay you a visit, but it does me nearly as much good to get a long letter from you. Then I am compelled to be gone from home so much; next Monday two weeks is Chancery Court at Celina, and first Monday in July at Livingston. I am compelled to attend both courts, so I can make you no promise as to the time of my visit to Clarksville, much as I would like to do so."

To the ordinary individual, it seems marvelous that a man of his age could or would ride on horseback, through a rough and mountainous circuit, to attend the various courts, look after closely and attentively innumerable unsettled notes and accounts covering several counties, keep up the taxes and rents on real estate owned by him situated in all sorts of inaccessible places, and yet find time to plunge into large real estate deals in Nashville, and plan and erect a number of large buildings. It only shows the nervous energy and active mind that characterized him through life. How he avoided serious mistakes in his multitude of schemes, planned and carried through, is the remarkable feature of it all.

Opens a Law Office.

When his Cedar street building was completed, he fitted and opened up a law office in it. He did not care much for practice, indeed, this was not the primary object in view. He desired some place of business of his own and wished to get his son, W. H. Goodpasture, who was then a law student at the Vanderbilt University, started off in the practice. This was characteristic of the man. Although still extremely active, and with many enterprises on hand, he had already begun to think much less of his own future than of those near and dear to him. Hence, the oft repeated expression in his letters of this time that "my chief ambition now is to see my children succeed well in life."

**Has
Pneumonia.**

In the spring of 1881, he made a trip to his old circuit to attend the courts, and on his return rode all day through a cold, early spring rain. He slept that night in a room without fire and with such large cracks that a damp, chilling draft passed over him. This gave him a most terrible cold, which went into a severe case of pneumonia immediately after his arrival home. A powerful chest and lungs, aided by a naturally strong constitution, pulled him through after a long and hard fight for life, but at one time he grew so dangerously ill that the absent members of the family were summoned.

He was attended during this sickness by Dr. T. A. Atchison, one of the ablest physicians who ever lived in Nashville, and a man who carried wit and good cheer wherever he went. The first call he made, he asked to see the patient's tongue. "Very foul, very foul; but Judge, you need not be at all frightened by this, as it is nothing uncommon for a lawyer to have a foul tongue."

Finally the patient became convalescent, and so Dr. Atchison said to him: "Judge, I am going to commence feeding you, and to begin with. I am going to have you given something so good that it will make your mouth water to think about it. I am going to ask Mrs. Goodpasture to fix you a nice dish of spring lamb and green peas." Now, if there was a single thing that could or could not be eaten, that he despised and abominated more than any and every other thing, it was sheep of any age or fixed in any way. He always maintained that no matter how well or hungry he might be, the very sight of mutton was enough to make him sick. The reader will, therefore, have to imagine his surprise and horror at the suggestion, and the doctor's at the effect it produced.

How little can we see into the future! In this conversation the doctor remarked that he would give fifty thousand dollars to be as young a man as his patient. The doctor is still alive and active, while his patient, for whose promise of life he was willing to pay so much, has gone to his eternal rest.

CHAPTER VIII.

Continues Building. With Judge Goodpasture's recovery came renewed activity, and we find him putting up a very large and handsome triple tenement on the corner of Summer and Cedar streets, himself planning the building and superintending its erection. These tenements he also rented at $50.00 per month each.

He had a remarkable tact for getting acquainted with every one of every station with whom he was thrown, and took great delight in making the humbler classes feel on good terms with themselves; was ever ready to praise their merits, sometimes extravagantly and not always with justice. But he did it through pure kindness of heart, and if gently accused of using a little "blarney," his reply would always be that it cost him nothing and made them feel good.

By this time he knew all the carpenters, builders, contractors, plumbers and everyone else engaged in the line of building. He would find out whence they originally came, who they knew and to whom they were of kin, and such information was never forgotten by him, especially if they or their ancestry ran back to the old Mountain District. He had a genuine sympathy for the hand of toil, and this class seemed to recognize and appreciate it. As an illustration, he had employed in the building of one of his houses, a mechanic named Carter, who was very poor. Some months afterwards,

Carter was taken sick, and sent word to Judge Goodpasture that he would like for him to come to see him. He obeyed the summons and called at the humble home, not once but several times. He found the family in need of the absolute necessaries of life and ministered to their wants. Carter died. The Judge's only acquaintance with this man was the brief employment in the building of a house. He had never seen him before that time and never afterwards until he called at the sick bedside. Why did poor Carter send for him in his extremity instead of to those he knew better? We do not know how it is, but the most ignorant can recognize a sympathetic soul. Even brutes can do this.

He was now living in his newly built home on Broad street, then the most popular and growing suburb of the city. The street cars at that time ran to his corner, and another line ran from there, with a good deal of irregularity and at long intervals, to the Vanderbilt. It then cost ten cents to ride from the city to the Vanderbilt and fifteen cents from Edgefield, or what is now East Nashville, and the cars went no further than to that point.

State Debt Problem. Tennessee was now greatly agitated over the settlement of her State debt. No question since the war had more thoroughly aroused the people. It was the first time in the history of the State, where all the great politicians and newspapers were to be found on one side of the question and the people on the other. Judge Goodpasture always manifested an interest in politics, and took sides on all public questions, not extreme as a rule nor strictly partisan, but firm in his convictions and open in expressing them. He was a strong "State credit" man, and ardently for the 50-4 compromise submitted to the vote of the people. One of the last political speeches ever made by him was on this question, in Fentress County, while attending the court there, about the time of moving. There was a large crowd in town, and he pleaded earnestly and effectively with the people. After the election was over, it turned out that Fentress was one of the few middle Tennessee counties to vote in favor of the compromise.

He was profoundly astonished at its defeat and greatly regretted it. He feared it meant repudiation of the entire debt. Never had there been more reason for astonishment. As said before, nearly every man of political prominence in the State, almost all the newspapers, and all the business, corporate and money powers in the large counties, towns and commercial centers favored it. Formerly, these elements had been all-powerful. In this contest, no one seems to have been opposed to the compromise except the people, and they voted it down overwhelmingly. Something in the same line, though not so successful, was seen applied to the nation, in the late Bryan campaign.

It seems certain, though he was never heard to say so in plain words, that he lived to see that, after all, the people in the main were right on this question and the politicians wrong. His oldest son, J. R. Goodpasture, a man very tenacious, and sometimes extreme in his views, but always vigorous in maintaining them, had been elected soon after leaving college to the Legislature, as a strong State credit advocate. We know that he has come to recognize the wisdom of the people, as have most of those who differed from them, and its compromise by the Legislature at 50-3 ended it as a political question. But it produced great acrimony and much ill-feeling while it lasted.

One of the results was the shooting of Senator L. T. Smith, and at Senator Smith's request, an investigation of the charges averred against him was ordered before a committe of the Senate. Judge Goodpasture had always been Senator Smith's warm personal friend. He had known him intimately for many years, both in a business and social way. In the meantime, W. H. Goodpasture had graduated in the law school at the Vanderbilt, and the firm had become that of J. D. & W. H. Goodpasture. They were employed by Senator Smith to represent him before the Senate committee. Charges against Senator Barrett and Speaker Morgan were at the same time investigated. A number of other attorneys were employed, both to prosecute and defend, among them Gen. Luke Wright, of Memphis. The investigation dragged through many weary weeks, the whole being published by order of the Legislature, making a book of seven hundred pages.

His Law Practice. About this time the firm enjoyed a peculiar run of practice. As said before, their office was located just opposite the Federal Court, which then sat in the Kirkman building, that is now occupied by the Conservatory of Music. Almost all the time of the court was taken up with small offences against the internal revenue laws. Now, if the "moonshiner" and "wildcatter" flourished at any one place beyond all others, it was in the Judge's old circuit. And he knew them all and by their given names, who their parents were, to whom they were related and to whom married. His ability to gather and remember family history, seems to have been natural and not acquired. They all flocked to him as one man in their petty troubles, and made the office their general rendezvous. He enjoyed it immensely—heard with patience the story of their troubles, and used his best endeavor to get them off as lightly as possible. From those able to pay, a small fee was collected, but none were refused because of their poverty.

At this time the firm also began to get a large but not a very paying practice in the Supreme Court. A Court of Referees had been established by the Legislature for the relief of the overcrowded docket of the Supreme Court. Many of the lawyers from the Mountain Circuit could not attend this court on account of conflicts with their own inferior courts, and of those who did, many could not be there to file exceptions to the findings of said court so as to secure a hearing before the Supreme Court. For somewhat similar reasons, many could not attend the sittings of the Supreme Court. Indeed, some of the attorneys up there, on account of the great inconvenience, expense and time required, never followed their causes beyond the lower courts. Judge W. W. Goodpasture, of Livingston, who enjoyed a large and lucrative practice, never, at any time, attended its sittings. Hence, the firm was employed by attorneys all over the Mountain Circuit, who could not themselves be present, to look after their several cases.

But the duties of the office were never able to divorce his mind from business. Even at the time when enjoying the largest practice of any man in his part of the State, he took time to give the maturest thought and most careful attention to matters of business. Hence, he watched the markets, attended the auction sales of real estate, looked at advertised property in all parts of the city and seemed to grasp relative values by intuition.

Real Estate Purchases. He began about this time the purchase of outlying vacant lots, and most of his early purchases were in the new suburb of West End. A remarkable thing is, that while he left in his estate a large amount of unimproved real estate, which after the depression could not, perhaps, have been sold at a profit, still, he never sold a piece of real estate at a loss in Nashville, and his dealings extended over many years. He was quick to make up his mind on a trade and never higgled over small matters. He seemed to know in a minute what he was willing to give, but after the trade was once consummated, he allowed himself to see only the good points in it. On one occasion he was walking along the street, and came upon two well known gentlemen and friends disputing over an extra lot on Belmont street, which they had gotten with others in a deal. Neither wanted the lot. Judge Goodpasture asked the price and exact location and on being told, said that he would take it if it would be an accommodation to them. Both said it would be a very great one, and the trade was made. It was only three or four years until the lot rose not less than three hundred per cent. in value, and was one of the best bargains he ever made.

At this time, by his love of enterprise, and the almost

universal example of those with whom he associated, he speculated to some extent in stocks in New York and grain in Chicago. But this he soon abandoned, on the ground that its rise or fall was largely in the power of the speculators, wholly outside of his control and afforded no room for the exercise of judgment.

Characteristic Anecdotes.

He never had any secrets, and if told one, the man who told it generally lived to regret it. Not that he intended telling it, or was indifferent on the subject, but they just came out in utter thoughtlessness, and the more important they were the more certain they were to unexpectedly appear. Drs. John and Alvis Ryan, sons of H. R. Ryan and nephews of Judge Goodpasture, were boarding with him and attending the dental and medical departments, respectively, of the University of Tennessee. They were at the office one noonday, and told him in great confidence and as a matter about which the utmost secrecy must be maintained, that the boys up at the dissecting rooms had just gotten in a Chinese subject, and that they had been especially charged by their demonstrator to mention the matter to no one. Any one who knows the peculiarities of this race of people and their superstitions, will readily appreciate the importance of the demonstrator's injunction. That night all sat down to supper. The table was filled by eight or ten Vanderbilt literary students, who were boarding at the house at the time. At one period of the meal, every one seemed to be out of anything to say and silence reigned from end to end of the long table. But it was soon broken by Judge Goodpasture, who remarked, "I understand they are cutting up a Chinaman out here at the medical school"—and then after a short pause—"but I believe, Ryan, you said to say nothing about it." Poor Ryan was utterly stupified and overcome by the announcement. The great secret had not only been divulged to a large crowd, but the very man who told it was named. He did not seem to think he had done anything very extraordinary, but afterwards remarked that "he would not have told it if he had thought at the time about Ryan objecting." It came out as purely and naturally as a clear spring from its source.

He had the happy faculty of getting a bit of amusement and entertainment from even the humblest callers on occasions. One long hot summer afternoon he was sitting in the office, when a very ordinary looking negro man entered, with the announcement that he was "a glass man," and was looking for a job. The Judge looked up at him in apparently the greatest astonishment. "A glass man, a glass man you say you are, my good friend, why, if you hadn't told me I would never have suspected your being so wonderfully constructed and of such remarkable looking glass." The darkey then explained that he only meant that he put in glass, and would like to do some work of the kind for him. The Judge said that he was exceedingly sorry that he had no work of the sort to be done, because he knew the applicant was a good man, but that if he did have any the applicant, of all other men in Nashville, would be the very one he would pick to do it. The negro looked at him in great seriousness and remarked, "You are the cleverest talkin' white man that ever I seed."

His sport with such characters was always good humored and was never allowed to become offensive. But he did not confine his attempts at wit to the ignorant and lowly, but to any friend he might meet, and sometimes they would prove quite a boomerange. Col. John H. Savage was a member of the Legislature, and the enterprising artist of the American had made and published in his paper a picture of the Colonel, sketched from life. Colonel Savage is a small man with an uncommonly large nose and small eyes. To this he added a peculiarity of dress, and wore an old cape overcoat for a great number of years, long after they had ceased to be fashionable. The artist had greatly exaggerated all these peculiar points but at the same time every one could at once recognize it, though the picture was an absolute scarecrow.

Judge Goodpasture met Colonel Savage the morning the picture appeared, coming down Cherry street, and remarked to his companion that he intended to get off a little wit on Savage. Said he, "Colonel, I see they have your picture in this morning's paper, and I'll tell you, I don't think I ever saw a better picture of a man in my life—it is a speaking likeness." "Yes," said the Colonel, "that's the art of these fellows—they can draw the picture of a snake and make it look like a man. Why, sir, these fellows could draw the picture of a jackass and still you would know it was J. D. Goodpasture."

Thus was his time occupied for the first five or six years after his removal to Nashville—winding up his multifarious business in the different counties in the Mountain Circuit, practicing law in a way, buying and selling real estate and building houses. He had been much missed in the section from which he had removed. The confidence of the bar and people in the soundness of his opinions seems to have been unlimited. They had grown to rely upon him, and to such an extent that long after removal his advice was much sought. As an instance, under date of October 17, 1883, one of the leading attorneys in that section writes him: "Herewith I send you an exact copy of a will. Would you be kind enough to give me your opinion of E. J.'s title. * * * Has she the complete power of disposing of it? I make this request to you from my own desire as well as at the instance of others."

He had gained this confidence by largely disregarding technicalities, and looking to the very right of every cause.

CHAPTER IX.

Judge Goodpasture had never been a man to travel or to be from home except for the necessary requirements of business. But the course of events now directed his thoughts in a channel, and to a section of the world, to which, in his busy life, he had never given more than a passing thought. In the summer of 1883, his son, W. H. Goodpasture, made a pleasure trip to the various countries of Europe. In the spring of 1884, he made an importation of Holstein-Friessian cattle on account of A. V. & W. H. Goodpasture. The business began to interest him, and he came near forming a company to import on a large scale, and did go so far as to send to his son in Holland an order for a number of head. In the summer of 1885, the same firm made a second importation. During this time he had studied over the importation question a good deal, and came to the conclusion that after all, cattle were not the things to import, but that jacks were: that mules did not depend upon fancy for their price; that they were a necessity to a large section of the country, and as staple as sugar and coffee, and that this would make jacks so. No jacks had been imported to Tennessee, since the introduction of the great freight steamers. Those previously imported were brought in sailing vessels, mak-

ing long and tedious journeys, that were trying in the
extreme to the stock.

When an idea or enterprise once took a firm hold of
him, he was all impatience until he carried it into effect.
So that during his son's absence in 1885, he was writing
letters to our minister and various consular representatives in Spain, and to jack men in the United States,
seeking information wherever obtainable. He con-
fessed that he could scarcely tell a jack from a hand-
saw, but did not allow this to dampen his ardor or
abate his enthusiasm. When, therefore, W. H. Goodpasture landed with his cattle in quarantine at Garfield,
New Jersey, he began to receive numerous letters on the
subject, all looking to an early trip to Spain, and expressing great confidence in the success of such an enterprise. The quarantine of cattle brought from foreign
countries is ninety days from date of sailing, which
makes it something like two and one half months in
which they are to be kept at the quarantine station, the
passage across consuming something like two weeks.

After the jack importation had been determined
upon, this delay of his son (whom he wished to accom-
pany him abroad) in quarantine, looked like a long time,
and he writes to know if an arrangement could not
be made for some one else to take charge of the cattle,
so that he could leave at once for Spain. Other letters
followed this still more strongly urging that the trip be
made at once. The difficulties in the way of this were
pointed out, and he finally agreed to wait until the
cattle should be released from quarantine and brought
home, but the trip to be made immediately thereafter.

From his various letters to Spain and elsewhere, he had received little or no information of value. Our minister and consuls in Spain knew nothing personally of jacks, and what information they received from others over there generally proved inaccurate and misleading. He had little better success in the replies to letters written in his own country. Few knew anything of the business. A gentleman, living in the far Northwest, who had once imported three or four, writes: "The information that I have obtained about Spanish jacks was gotten by the expenditure of much time, labor and money, and I do not care to make a gift of it to others."

In the meantime, he had taken in as a partner, Capt. R. H. Hill, an experienced jack man, a most excellent salesman and a good man. The connection was a fortunate one.

By the last of December, 1885, everything was ready for the start. His son had arranged while in quarantine to get free passes on the Monarch line, per S. S. Persian Monarch, running from New York to London, and they were to leave home so as to reach New York by the date of her sailing. They had been fortunate in stirring up such good company to go with them as Mr. W. B. Palmer and Mr. L. R. Campbell, both companions agreeable par excellence and especial friends. All were friends and intimates of Mr. R. F. Jackson. There was no better man to have along, and he wanted to go as badly as any one in the crowd, but could not make up his mind on the subject. He and the writer had gone abroad together in 1883, and Jackson had experienced something of this same trouble then. It looked at one time like his indecision might prevent the other two from going.

Leaves For New York. Judge Goodpasture and son were to go by way of Washington City, and there spend a couple of days, and had to be in New York for a few days, also, before sailing, to attend to necessary business. The boys were to go to New York direct, and, therefore, on December 19, 1885, the Judge and son left without them. They took John Terry, colored, along. John had been porter to the State Senate, and at the time of leaving he was private porter to the Governor. He did not resign, but secured a good man, Alfred Hart, to take his place, temporarily, during his absence observing the effete monarchies of the old world. He got Alfred from Bush's brick yard, who, it soon turned out, liked his new job a good deal better than that of carrying brick. He made himself so useful and polite that he has held the place ever since. John got to be a great man by his travels, but was never able again to become a public servant, to be the envy of the balance of his race.

They arrived in Washington City early one morning, and had no trouble in finding a good hotel for themselves but experienced great difficulty in getting quarters for John; for while Washington is more east than south, their people are still quite as particular in their treatment of the negro as they are in the Southern cities. They allow no mixing in public restaurants and hotels.

Congress was in session. The Judge went up to the capitol about the hour of meeting, 12 o'clock m., and met a number of the Tennessee Congressmen and

friends. Particularly agreeable was Judge Houk, of
Knoxville. Judge Goodpasture had practiced law before him, and had known him for a number of years.
All, however, were kind, and his two senators gave him
letters of introduction abroad, the letter of General Bate
being especially felicitous and complimentary. General
Bate was quite well acquainted with the American minister at Madrid, Hon. J. L. M. Curry, of Virginia, who,
as manager of the Peabody Fund, had been frequently
in Nashville, though the Judge had never met him.
He also called at the State Department to get passports.
Ex-Governor James D. Porter, of Tennessee, was then
assistant Secretary of State, under the Hon. Thos. F.
Bayard. Here was another old friend. Judge Goodpasture was one of the original supporters of Mr. Porter
in his candidacy for the governorship, and was a delegate to the State Convention that nominated him, and
on calling at the department was received with great
cordiality.

The Judge and party took the train that evening for
New York City. The coach was full, and all were
strangers to them. The only familiar looking object on
the train was a negro, with whom they soon got into
conversation. It proved to be Blanche K. Bruce, Register
of the Treasury, and formerly United States Senator
from Mississippi. He impressed them as being a big,
good looking mulatto of great vanity and not over-
much sense. He inquired of them where they expected
to stop in New York, saying that he always stopped at
the Hoffman House, which they would find to be a
very decent place, if they should try it. If men were
elected or appointed to office on account of superior in-

telligence or fitness. Bruce would never have gotten out of his native county. As it was, he had what was, in many respects. one of the most desirable offices in the gift of the President.

They stopped at the Continental Hotel and received the next morning the following gratifying line from Palmer: "I decided definitely this morning to go. Went down town and found Lem [Campbell] packing up, but Jack would not say much about going. Lem is cussing him for not deciding. He thought, perhaps, that I would drop out and that might break up the party, but now that I have assured him that I will go, and Lem is making preparations, Jack has to toe the mark or back out. and he is in his usual undecided condition. He is obliged to decide to-morrow, however. as we got a Herald last night and saw the steamer was to sail at eight a.m. Thursday. * * * Lem and I have decided to go without Jack if he does not come to a conclusion."

The steamer on which they were to sail had not yet arrived in port from her voyage from London to New York, though some days past due. The weather on the Atlantic had been severe and some uneasiness was felt for her. In the meantime, Palmer and Campbell had arrived for the trip. A day or two later the Persian Monarch came in. badly disabled, with twelve feet of water in her hold, notwithstanding the fact that her steam pump had been kept constantly going. Some of her crew had been lost. She had to lay up for repairs and the party had to look elsewhere for passage. This would, they found. keep them in New York some days longer, and this fact was telegraphed Jackson, at

Nashville, so that he could still go with them, if he would hurry up and come to a decision on the question.

They spent the time very agreeably in New York. They met several friends they had known in Nashville. Palmer, Campbell and the writer had been members of the Phi Delta Theta fraternity at college, and the alumni chapter of New York City invited the party to make headquarters at their rooms. These were centrally located, and they constantly availed themselves of the invitation, making many very agreeable acquaintances.

It was on the eve of the Christmas holidays, and the crowds in the neighborhood of the big down town stores were beyond anything they had ever seen. For blocks the streets were one solid mass of moving humanity, the foot passengers filling, not alone the pavements, but the streets as well. Judge Goodpasture remarked that Governor Hawkins was right when he said there were "a heap of people in New York." On Christmas day the streets were as completely deserted as a country village on Sunday. Every one seemed to be at home for the day.

They saw the big Christmas markets with all sorts of game, the Judge being greatly astonished at the enormous size of the sheep and turkeys. They went to Greenwood Cemetery, Brooklyn, and saw the monuments to Tweed and others. The Judge was afterwards at Vigo, Spain, where the great Boss was captured. All of them admired that wonderful piece of engineering, the Brooklyn Bridge. They went out Fifth Avenue, and saw the palatial homes of Stewart, Vanderbilt and others. Went to the top of the Equitable Building and viewed the city from that elevated point; ate their dinner on the highest floor of the Mills Building; visited the stock and produce exchange, Trinity Church and its old graves; read the Nashville papers in the reading room of the Fifth Avenue Hotel, and sometimes picked their teeth there; saw Jim Stokes' celebrated bar at the Hoffman House; went to the theaters and saw, among others, Miss Fay Templeton, a Southern girl; in fact, with plenty of time on their hands and nothing else to do, they tried to see everything worth seeing in the great metropolis.

Sam Bell Maxey. A very pleasant incident occurred during their stay. The Judge saw in the papers that Senator Sam Bell Maxey, of Texas, was stopping at the Fifth Avenue. He had known him intimately as a young man, the two being raised some twenty-five or thirty miles apart, but were thrown much in each other's society. They had not seen each other since before the war. The Judge called and was received by the Senator in his bed room. He got up, grasped the Judge's hand with great cordiality and said, "Why, Dillard, how are you?" "Well," said the Judge, "I can still call you Sam Bell, can't I?"

Senator Maxey gave him a speech he had recently delivered, and which he asked him to read, as he was a lawyer. He made a remark in this connection that was quite as true as it was complimentary to the South. He said that he had seldom written a speech, the habit being in his section, and all over the South, to speak without such preparation, and hence, he said, that in extempore and running debate, the speakers from the

North and East were far outclassed by those from the
South.

Only a few years after this, General Maxey died, and
Judge Goodpasture wrote up for the local press the following little sketch of him:

"Hon. Sam Bell Maxey, whose death is announced in
the press, was well known to a section of Tennessee
when a young man. The press dispatch states that he
was born in Todd County, Kentucky. I do not know
how this is, but his youth and young manhood were
spent at Albany, Ky., a small village and county seat,
five miles across the Kentucky line from Overton
County, Tennessee, now Pickett County. His father,
Rice Maxey, was clerk of some of the courts at Albany.
At that time, in Kentucky, the same man was allowed
to be clerk of more than one court.

"I was not acquainted with the subject of this sketch
until after his graduation from West Point. On his
return from the war with Mexico, where he served with
credit, he was made a deputy under his father, and both
practiced law at Livingston, Tenn., where I was then
living. His mother was a Bell, a well known and distinguished family in that part of the State, a connection
of which he was always proud, and a name which he
always used. He was a dressy man, very much so for
that day and section, and was looked upon by the people
as something of an aristocrat. But he was always polite,
affable, courtly and dignified, and among those with
whom he was acquainted and with whom he associated,
he was well liked and popular. His older brother,
(there were only two of the boys) was also a graduate of
West Point, and also went out at the first call of his

8

country to seek glory on the bloody fields of Mexico. But, like many others who went out from that section, he never returned. I am not certain whether he was killed or died from the exposures incident to army life. He was said to have been a man of great talent and most promising future.

"I have most excellent reasons for remembering General Maxey perfectly. As young men, we not only practiced at the same bar, but were rivals for the hand of the same fair one, and finally when I won and went to get my license, he, as deputy clerk, issued it to me, and generously refused the fee which the law allowed him for the service.

"Sam Bell's father, Hon. Rice Maxey, was a pious and popular man—a Baptist—well educated, well to do, and a leading man in his section. He was very proud of his boys and his solicitude for their success was intense and continuous. The last time I saw General Maxey was in the winter of 1886. I happened to be in New York, and learned that he was stopping at the Fifth Avenue Hotel. I had not seen him since the war, but on my approach he instantly recognized me and put me fully at ease by calling me by my given name. Fully thirty years had elapsed since we had met, and he showed the politician's talent for recollecting faces.

"General Maxey has numerous relatives in Tennessee. Varney Andrews, a large farmer and prominent citizen of Clay County, married a sister of Rice Maxey, the General's father. Mr. Andrews lived all his life in Clay and left a considerable family. A brother of Rice Maxey lived just across the Clay County line in Kentucky, but his children all moved into Tennessee and raised families, who still live there. One of the children of this brother was John L. Maxey, who became a very prominent man, and was for a long time Chairman of the County Court of Clay County. He is still living. Another son lives in Celina, where he keeps the village hotel. There are many others scattered about over that section of the State, and. so far as I know them. they are all good people.

"General Maxey was married in Overton County. Tennessee, to a Miss Denton. a relative of the Hon. H. Denton. of Cookeville. Tenn. There was no issue as a result of this union. and when I met General Maxey in New York he was accompanied by a young man whom he had adopted and raised. and whom he had named after himself, Sam Bell Maxey.

"Albany. the former home of the Maxeys, is a small village and county seat. But among the few young men practicing at her bar when Sam Bell was a young man. and who also practiced in all the courts of Overton County, a number afterwards became famous. As young men together, there was Sam Bell Maxey. afterwards United States Senator from Texas; Thomas Bramlett. afterwards Governor of Kentucky. and a distinguished lawyer of Louisville, where he settled after the expiration of his gubernatorial term. And there was Preston Leslie, who became a well known Circuit Judge. Governor of Kentucky. Territorial Governor by appointment of Cleveland. and who. I think. has lately settled in the West. He is the uncle of Hon. Benton McMillin. Not as a practicing lawyer, but as a young man with the others, was William Bramlett. He married in Overton County, a daughter of Rev. John

L. Dillard, went to Texas, studied law, became distinguished, and for a long time occupied a position on
the bench.   He was a younger brother of the Governor,
and was educated in Overton County.   A remarkable
thing is, that all these men who became so distinguished,
were members of the Baptist Church."

CHAPTER X.

The party were greatly rejoiced one morning to see Jack make his appearance. He had at last made up his mind to go, and had gotten to New York in plenty of time, thinking the steamer would sail a day earlier than it did. They went around and bought tickets for the Alaska, an ocean greyhound, and one of the fleetest steamers developed up to that time. For some years she held the record for quickest passage. Their money matters were arranged, the party were all in good health and fine spirits, and were at last ready to embark upon the boundless deep. It was to be the first trip of all the party except two, and they had the liveliest anticipations of the voyage and the trip—what it would look like to get out of sight of land, who would be seasick and who would escape. All agreed that Jackson would be the first to succumb, as he had generally managed to be the unluckiest in every party of which he had been a member.

The voyage to Liverpool was without any especial features. They embarked at 11 o'clock, a.m., December 29, 1885, having spent, altogether, eight days in New York City.

The cuisine of the steamer was first-class, and the attendance excellent. They enjoyed, for the first time, melons for breakfast in mid winter, and many other much appreciated delicacies. Sure enough Jack was sea-sick right away. Campbell followed hard in his wake, as did Palmer also. Judge Goodpasture did not exactly get sea-sick, but the rolling and pitching of the vessel, with the rattling of chains, the splash of the big waves, rolling over the deck, and the constant cracking and screeching of timbers, produced the most fanciful and sometimes surprising dreams. They were, besides, quite as unpleasant as they were unreal. He had always been a great smoker, and had carried with him his old hickory pipe with cane stem and his favorite brand, Knights of Labor, smoking tobacco. But smoke did not taste right to him. While he did not get sea-sick, he came closer to it than was really comfortable.

About the second night out, the weather became rather rough, and the big waves began to sweep the deck. The water would strike the front part of the vessel and come rolling down the deck in a torrent, and with a good deal of noise. From the cabins, this noise of moving water was hard to locate. The Judge was awakened from a light slumber and heard it for the first time. He occupied a lower berth. Instantly, he was all attention. He first put his head out and listened. Then he called to his companion in the upper berth and desired to know if he could hear that water. Of course he could. "Well," said the Judge, "I would give a good deal to know just exactly where that water is."

The passage, being in midwinter, was rough and windy throughout. A very fast vessel rocks and pitches much worse than a slow one, and does not change her course for any sort of weather. Those who wish to gain two or three days in time of passage, pay very dearly for it, the slow boats being a great deal the more comfortable. On this trip for some days in succession, passengers could only walk from their state rooms to the dining saloon by holding to a rope, stretched along the passage way for the purpose; could not go out on deck for a bit of fresh air, as the huge waves were continually sweeping it; and would often be thrown from their seats to the floor in the smoking room. Many very comical and a few painful scenes of this sort were enacted. At the dining table, all of the dishes including one's own plate, had to be kept in bars, and liquids like soup, coffee, etc., had to be held in the hand, if not, it would soon be found in one's lap instead of on the table. The very greatest mistake made by travelers in general is to cross on a very fast ocean steamer.

Foreign Newspapers. But, finally, there was sighted the much looked for land on the other side, and the boat was soon discharging her mail at Queenstown. Some enterprising boys rowed over from the town with papers for sale. Every one of course was eager and hungry for the news, and there was a great scramble to get them at double and even treble the ordinary price. The boys quickly sold out and as quickly left the boat. They sold the passengers as well as the papers. Not a paper was under a week old. It was really no great loss, however, as Irish and English papers have the least possible news in them, and generally nothing to interest an American. There are no real newspapers published outside of America. The make up of a London daily is one of the most amazing things to the American met with abroad. The great papers like the Times, Standard and others, give full reports of the trials in the Bow street police courts, including the age, residence and occupation of the accused, the name of officer making the arrest, and where and under what circumstances made, all of the material evidence in the case, the remarks of the magistrate and of the attorneys as well. Then there is the big editorial page, with articles on the driest of dry subjects, and written in the ponderous Johnsonian style. Then a contributor's page, filled with articles by our old friends, "constant reader" and "vox populi." Then a page of what passes for news—a few cables from Reutgers on the continent, all short and unsatisfactory, a few more from the English colonies, maybe something from South America, and an occasional line from the United States. Of course any news of the English Court is recorded. Then the balance is advertisements. No Sunday papers, no illustrations, no big issues, no enterprise, no interest. An ordinary American paper has more news in one issue, than any paper in Europe has in a week, and a New York daily will have more telegraphic matter in a single number than a big London paper will contain in a month.

As the party steamed up the smooth and placid waters of the Mercy toward Liverpool, sea-sickness having taken wings, they all busied themselves writing home to friends, so that they might devote their entire time to sight seeing, on landing. All were in fine fettle except Jack. He had one day felt so sea-sick that he thought himself obliged to have fresh air. So he ventured out on deck. The waves had been rolling over it, and it was consequently wet and slippery. Jack was standing near an overhanging life-boat. He is quite a tall, slender man with very elongated limbs. Suddenly, the ship gave a big roll, Jack's head went down and his feet and legs went up, and went sufficiently high to strike the bottom of the life-boat with a good deal of force. This greatly impeded his locomotion, intensified by the fact that he had left home with a pair of new shoes.

The Stop in Liverpool.

But they were soon at the docks of Liverpool, and were taken in charge by the custom officers, who examined their baggage, (luggage is the word used over there) for fire-arms and spirits. They went direct to the North-western Hotel, a most excellent hostelry, made so, largely, by its enormous American custom. Campbell registered them, and put John down as Hon. John Terry, the result of which was, that he got altogether the best room of any man in the party.

There are very few elevators in Europe, but the American travel through Liverpool is so great that this hotel has been forced to build one. In England, they are called lifts. When the party had gone up to their proper floor, and were passing through the long hall-ways, they saw on every corner "To the Lift." "By the way, gentlemen," said the Judge, "had you discovered in what a peculiar way these people over here spell left?" And when told of his error, he said it sounded more like left than it did like elevator anyway.

John got into some trouble here. That afternoon, when he had been gone for a short time to get his supper at a restaurant, he returned to the hotel in a good deal of excitement, saying that so many people crowded around him, he was afraid to proceed. So one of the crowd had to go with him for the first meal or two. He was a rather remarkable looking negro, six feet one inch, well dressed, with a broad brimmed soft hat, (a kind unknown in England) erect in his walk, a splendid physique, intensely vain in his way, but polite and obedient at all times to his employer. He was extremely superstitious and believed strongly in dreams. These rendered him very unhappy whenever he chanced to eat too much supper. He had crossed on the steerage of the boat, and the vessel had produced the same disturbing sort of dreams that they had with Judge Goodpasture. One of these was so vivid that, early one morning, he sent for the Judge and son, and begged them, if the boat should go down, to send for him, so that they might all go down together. And they promised him faithfully that they would do so.

But John soon got used to the attention he attracted. In fact, he grew to like it. Judge Goodpasture succeeded in convincing him that it was all on account of his good looks and splendid appearance. This was easily done after he had occupied his gorgeous room at the Great Northwestern, and because, later, in Paris, where the party had registered at Gallignanni's, and where Campbell had again put it Hon. John Terry, his was the only name that appeared in the list of recent prominent American arrivals. So that, what had, at the beginning, been a cause of fear, became a source of great pleasure and gratification.

They visited a good many places in Liverpool that interested them, but while it is a large city of more than a half million of people, it is still purely commercial, and has not much to interest or detain the traveler. Nothing there or elsewhere, though, so much interested Judge Goodpasture, as their ordinary dray horse. They are enormous in size. The North and West have an idea of it, because of the very large importations of the breed brought to those sections, but the ordinary Southerner can have no appreciation of their huge appearance without seeing them. The Judge stopped one man and asked him the weight of his horse. "Oh, something over a ton," said he. A pair of these great horses were seen pulling an extraordinary load along the quay, and some one asked the driver if he did not have a very heavy load. "Ten tons," was the reply. One can scarcely believe that a single pair of horses would haul a load of twenty thousand pounds, but the streets of the city are of stone, fairly level, and the hauls of comparatively short distances.

The party went to see the cotton exchange, which fixes prices all over the world; visited the great docks and saw the loading and unloading of vessels for and from ports of every country on the globe; and took in the sights of the town generally. At night, they went to see the Christmas pantomime at the Princess Theater. These holiday pantomimes are unknown in America, but are enormously popular here, performances being crowded to the limit for weeks at a time. It was very beautiful, very novel as well as very interesting and entertaining.

After their return to the hotel that night, Judge Goodpasture went to see how John was getting along in his fine room. He had retired, but before doing so, had bathed as thoroughly as possible, put on his cleanest linen and tied his head up in his wash towel. He was determined to preserve untarnished the immaculate whiteness of his sheets and pillow slips. The Judge inquired of him if he thought he could be comfortable in there. John said he thought he could. He had a brass bedstead, burnished until it shone in the greatest splendor. John said, "Judge, do you see this here bedstid? Well, sir, that's gold, they ain't no brass that could look like that."

Foreign Rail-Road Trains. Early the next day they took the train for London, occupying a third class coach of the Midland Railroad. These coaches were very comfortable, equal to second class in many parts of the continent, and there being six of them, they were allowed a compartment to themselves. The coaches over there, and all over Europe, are divided into compartments, and entrance is made from the side and not from the end. Instead of one smoker, as in America, there are usually quite a number in each train, and unless the cars are very much crowded, small parties can always be given a compartment to themselves. These are conveniences, but they are the only ones. They have no means of going from one compartment or coach to another, no lavatory, no drinking water, and no retiring rooms. To the American, these are not only conveniences, but they are looked upon as necessities. The engines and coaches are very small and light, and if one occupies a rear coach in a long train, his hair will fairly stand on end as he rounds the curves, for the English, as far as our observation goes, make faster time than do our American trains. The American, we believe, are said to have the record for fastest time for a single run, but we know of no American road that makes the regular schedule as fast as the "Wild Irishman" or the "Flying Welshman." They have better bridges, better arrangements for entering and leaving towns and stations, and absolutely no obstructions on the track.

The trip through the country was immensely entertaining to the whole party, but to the Judge, more than any of the others. He always enjoyed the country more than the cities. Of the former, he never grew tired. In the latter, he chaffed and fretted until the time of departure. He was particularly struck by their manner of stacking and preserving straw. It was done with great precision and beauty and was heavily covered with thatched straw. The Judge gave his enthusiastic endorsement to the plan.

London. They arrived in due time at London, and found the ground covered with a light fall of snow. They were to stop at a most excellent boarding house in the very heart of the city and the center of amusements, kept by Mrs. Dysart at No. 12 Arundel street, Strand, a place where one of the party had stopped on more than one occasion previously. They took a closed, four wheeled cab from the station. These London cabs are rather smaller than the American, and all five of them were to go in it. John was to ride in front with the driver. They entered the cab, Campbell occupying a seat in front. When they had barely seated themselves, Campbell declared, with great emphasis, that with five people in there, it was unendurably close, and that he was bound to have air. He discovered that the windows could not be let down, and this made him want air worse than ever. Finally, John mounted the high perch of the driver just as the horses started, sat abruptly down to the rear of the seat, and crashed through the glass directly over Campbell's head, the glass pouring down upon him in a perfect deluge. The Judge remarked: "Don't be alarmed, Mr. Campbell, he is only trying to accommodate you with a little fresh air." They had plenty of fresh air after that, and paid two or three dollars for it at the end of the journey. They had plenty of air, too, a week later, in driving back to the station, when a boy threw a snow-ball through the glass window.

They were very much on the go in London for the next few days, visiting numerous places of great historic interest, the House of Parliament, the statue of Prince Albert, without doubt the handsomest in Europe, at least to the ordinary visitor; through the Bank of England; riding on the top of omnibuses and watching the panorama of fleeting houses and crowds on High Holborn, Fleet street and Rotten Row; seeing Regent Park and London Bridge; going through St. Paul's, one of the best known churches in the world; and a great many other places no tourist can miss, but which have been described until a repetition would be a bore.

It was very remarkable the way Judge Goodpasture, at his age, and having grown rather fleshy, was able to get around over the city with his crowd of lusty young fellows. He was on the go from morning until late at night.

All wanted to go to the Drury Lane Theater to see the great pantomime—Aladdin and his Wonderful Lamp. It had been written up and illustrated in the American periodical literature, Harper's Weekly having given an especially good representation of it. They wanted to see the "Dream of Fair Women," and the historic representation of Nell Gwynn, who had played in this theater over two hundred years before. All the reserved seats and boxes had been sold for weeks beforehand. But the first floor or pit (with our theaters in Nashville it is the highest priced part of the house) is never reserved, but is open to a scramble for all those who have been unable to get reserved seats. Only ordinary benches, however, are provided for occupants of this part of the house. They went early—at least an hour before the opening, and took their stand with a crowd who had gathered directly in front of the ticket office. The price of seats was only two shillings (about fifty cents). The crowd increased rapidly and continuously, and before long they were jammed in together as closely as sardines in a box. The entrance door and ticket office were opened simultaneously, and there was an awful rush and scramble that baffles all description. There did not appear to be any women in the crowd, and if any, they were very few. and must have been of the most daring.

In the push and rush and scramble, men were carried clear off their feet and onto the backs of the surging crowd. Judge Goodpasture had all the buttons torn off his overcoat. Some big burly fellow, in trying to get over the crowd, got his foot in Jackson's overcoat pocket. and tore it down to the hem. Jack would have been mad had he not been so rejoiced at getting through with whole bones. The party were carried on through the door by the surging crowd. but once inside, relief was instant, and they secured good seats. All were in a crushed and perspiring condition.

The theater and pit are enormous in size, and the latter was filled to the last seat in an incredibly short time. Those occupying boxes and seats in the dress circle came in leisurely, and much later, in full dress, looking superbly handsome and very gay and happy; and the Judge's party thought it not strange that there should be envy and discontent at classes, there seemed such a distance from their place to those above them. And then they looked so entirely satisfied and comfortable, with an abundance of room, elegantly upholstered, cushioned seats, a maid to take charge of their cloaks and wraps, separated from the crowd in railed off boxes, in which they received short calls, and chatted gaily with the young society men of the town. The Judge's party sat below on common, hard, old field school benches, crowded and nudged by those sitting next them, mixed up with the mob, and only thankful that they were allowed to live and look up with envy at their betters. Oh well, they could stand it, for they would soon be back at Nashville, where they could strut the streets "as big a man as old Grant."

A pretty tough experience, but they all felt fully repaid (unless it was Jack), after seeing the performance. It surpassed their wildest dreams of spectacular display.

While in the city, they called and presented their letters to ex-Governor Waller, who was then the Consul-General to London. He was an intellectual, short, stout looking man, and treated them very kindly. He afterwards made a telling speech in the national Democratic Convention at Chicago, in 1896, which some of them heard.

CHAPTER XI.

 They left grim old London town for Paris by way of Dover and Calais. The boat in which they crossed the English Channel was quite a small one, and soon began to bob up and down to the great discomfort of the passengers. It was after midnight, and as the sail is a short one, no private rooms were provided, but all the men had to pile up on cots in one large saloon. A double row of cots, upper and lower, as in a sleeping car, extended entirely around the saloon. These cots were provided with ominous looking tin vessels, for it seems that people will get seasick crossing the Channel who can defy the ocean. John got pretty sick crossing the Atlantic but would never acknowledge it, seeming to feel that it would, in some way, be to his discredit. As he had been in a different part of the vessel from the others in coming over, he could conceal it from them to a great extent. But not so in this little boat. All lay down. Jack was soon heaving, and in a little while so were the other boys, and so were numerous other passengers on all sides. The boys looked around to see how John was resting. He had run his curtain around so as to conceal himself as much as possible, and was very slyly drinking out of a dark colored bottle, in appearance very suggestive of whiskey. He afterwards acknowledged that there was so much sickness around him that he was "bleeged to take something to settle his stomach."

9

When they landed at Calais, and had their baggage examined by the custom officers, they took a light breakfast at a very good restaurant (that is kept open all night for the benefit of travelers) although it was not yet light. Here they boarded a train for Paris. It was the first time in life that Judge Goodpasture had been in any place where English was not the current language, and it seemed to come on him all of a sudden that here was, indeed, a people who did not comprehend a word that he said. About eight o'clock that morning, when they had stopped at a station for a moment, a very polite, farmer looking old gentleman, took the train and came into their coach. The Judge turned on him saying: "You low down, dirty villian, get out of here at once or I will kick you out." "Oui, oui, monsieur," said the old Frenchman, bowing and smiling as he took his seat. The boys roared with laughter. They afterwards found this to be a dangerous sort of pastime.

They were now passing through the province of Normandy, and as the train sped along, they looked out on the most beautiful agricultural country in all the world. Normandy may not be its prettiest province, but sunny France, as a whole, stands unrivalled in beauty and fertility.

Paris. When they arrived in Paris, their baggage was again examined, as the city has a municipal custom duty, and on a multitude of articles not taxed by the State. Among these are food products of all kinds. They arrived about 11 o'clock a.m., and after depositing their baggage at the hotel (they stopped at the Grand Hotel de Suez, across the Seine and near the Latin Quarter), went out in town. As all of them were hungry, they stopped in at a restaurant to get breakfast. People on the continent breakfast at 11 or 12 and dine at 6 or 7 o'clock. They were handed a bill of fare, and the only thing any of them could make out was beefsteak. Therefore, each ordered beefsteak. As they were very hungry, all agreed that they ought to have a little more variety, so one of the boys picked out something on the bill of fare, after examining it with great care, and pointed it out to the waiter. His order was understood. Then each of them in turn took it and very solemnly pointed out to the astonished waiter the same thing. They speculated a good deal while it was being prepared, as to what it would turn out to be. Some thought it might be horse meat, as the Parisians are said to greatly enjoy that delicacy. Judge Goodpasture said it made no sort of difference to him what it was, just so it was not sheep. They were already devouring their steak, and about the time they had finished it, in came the waiter with six several orders of green string beans, cooked without bacon or grease. The Judge declared he always did like beans, and that these gave him a splendid opportunity to finish off a good meal. He asked for vinegar. John had never seen any olive oil before, and as it was in a vinegar bottle, and very much the same in appearance, he very naturally mistook it for vinegar, and passed it over. The Judge poured it bountifully over his beans without discovering his mistake. The first bite was of so unexpected, nasty, slimy taste, that he came as nearly as possible having a case of sea-sickness on shore.

Of course they went to see the great art gallery at the

Louvre, the tomb of Napoleon at the Hotel Des Invalides, House of Deputies, rode through the Champs
Elysee, saw the Arche de Triomph, the Column Vendome, the Grand Opera (the most expensive amusement
building in the world), and watched the ever changing
kaleidoscope of the gay boulevards. In the evening.
they generally found something to entertain them. A
part of the crowd went to see the divine Sarah (Bernhardt) at the Theatre Francais, while others enjoyed
the music at the Eden Theater. If amusement is the
thing sought, every taste can be satisfied in Paris. Still,
there are things that cannot be found even there.
Jack's foot was still troubling him greatly, the effect of
having tried to kick the bottom out of a life-boat on the
steamer, coming over, and he went to all the drug stores
he could find in the city for a certain kind of liniment.
without success, having finally, much against his will,
to take a French article, the efficacy of which he was
in great doubt.

Leave for Madrid. They were to take an early train for
Madrid via Bordeaux, and the hotel
gave them an early breakfast. They
were asked what they would have to drink. All said
coffee except John, who said he would take brandy;
and he gave a pretty lucid explanation of it—that he
could get plenty of coffee at home but "sich drinks as
this here French brandy was a scace article to meet up
with."

They had a very pleasant time for a part of the way,
going to Madrid. They passed through Bordeaux during the night, and next day found themselves speeding
along the beautiful fields of Southern France. Every-

thing was green, and the air was balmy and delightful. They crossed the Spanish frontier early in the afternoon of the second day, and reached the foot of the Pyrenees before night. Here wild strawberries and roses were in bloom, though it was in the month of January. They had not gone more than half way up the mountain before a very heavy snow began falling, and it was growing steadily colder. There was no way of heating the car except by the introduction of a long hollow iron, filled with hot water. This was only good for the feet and seemed to have no effect on the car. It became most disagreeably cold. To make matters worse, a piece had been broken out of one of the windows of their compartment, through which the cold wind came whistling. They had started from Paris with a good lunch, and got along well for the first day, but on this day, they had had little, if anything to eat, the mountain stations being illy provided. They finally secured three sandwiches and a pickled bird.

Madrid. The snow continued to pour down, and it was greatly feared that they would become snow bound in this cold mountainous country, and they shuddered at the thought of it. They did not sleep any that night, and arrived early the next morning at Madrid, stopping at the Hotel de Londres, in the center of the town.

They found themselves in the midst of the most distinctive people in appearance they had yet seen. The male portion of the inhabitants were walking leisurely about, with long Spanish blankets wrapped around their bodies, moving with all the dignity of old Roman Senators, and wearing broad brimmed sombrero hats.

Beggars were going up and down the streets playing wretched tunes on still more wretched guitars.

Here they saw for the first time, though the sight became very familiar later, in other cities of Spain, female asses being driven about for the sale of their milk. When a purchase is made, the herd is stopped, one is milked and the amount ordered is turned over to the purchaser absolutely fresh and warm. It is greatly esteemed over there by invalids. At the hotel, they tasted for the first time goat butter. It is mean, sticky and very inferior. Spain has no dairy breed of cattle, and uses the least possible amount of milk, none to drink and only a small quantity for coffee, as most people drink it with only sugar and brandy.

They were not a little astonished at some things noticed at dinner. People in European hotels dine at what is known as table d' hote—that is, all sit down at one long table, and the meal is served in regular courses. There is no ordering from a bill of fare as in America. If one should not like what is brought in a course, he must wait until that is over before he can get the one to follow. In Spain, there are usually eight or nine courses, and the hotel fares are better than in other countries of the continent. It takes an hour and often more, to dine. In the center of the table were placed cigarettes, in packages of five hundred. Wine and brandy being free, some of the party supposed cigarettes were also, and helped themselves. After the meal, the whole package was sent to John's room. John thought that perhaps his good looks had once more gained him special favors, but upon inquiry it was found that they had been charged about four dollars for them. They compromised by paying thirty cents for what they had taken, and returned the package.

At the table, the party were divided, and on opposite sides. Campbell remarked: "I say, Good, this fellow sitting beside me is looking at you mighty hard." "Yes," replied the party addressed, "and he looks like a pirate." Campbell agreed at once that he was a villain, when suddenly the man turned and said in good English, "Where are you from?"

Meet the American Minister. They called on the American minister, Mr. Curry, and were treated with great cordiality and kindness. Americans do not get to Madrid very often, and he seemed really rejoiced to meet some genuine Americans and Southerners. At his urgent solicitation, they called several times before leaving the city. On one occasion, he had just dressed to go to a diplomatic meeting, wearing the conventional dress suit—a dress that is prescribed by Congress, at least the law prescribes that all American representatives abroad shall dress in the garb of American citizens, except those who have held commissions in the United States army, and these are entitled to wear the uniform of their rank. Mr. Curry's military services had been on the other side, and so he could only dress as a civilian. This, he said, often proved embarrassing. All the other diplomatic representatives dressed in the full uniform of a ranking officer, with sword and other trappings. Under these circumstances, when he would meet with the representatives from other countries, he was in danger of being taken for an interpreter or a servant. The waiters at all the leading hotels and cafes in Europe wear full dress suits. The Charge d' Affaires was Mr. Stroble, a native of one of the Carolinas, a graduate of Yale and an exceedingly nice gentleman, whose endeavors to make their stay pleasant were greatly appreciated. He spent several evenings with them and carried a part of the crowd to Toledo to see the town and the Escurial Palace.

Among others to whom he introduced them was a young American dentist, who was getting into a fine practice. Americans are the best dentists in the world, and are scattered about all over the continent. They are better paid than are the natives, and receive a more desirable class of patrons. No science has made such rapid advancements in theory, practice and instruments, and most of it has been done in America. Few of these late discoveries have yet reached the native European practitioner.

They were very much gratified, afterwards, when Mr. Cleveland, in his second term, made Mr. Stroble minister to one of the South American countries.

Art Gallery. We cannot leave Madrid without a word or two on the National Art Gallery, though to describe such places is generally tiresome. This collection was made by Philip, when the best specimens of the old masters were very cheap, and an appreciation of high art at its lowest ebb, and his purchases have been held, until now they are priceless. It is not a large gallery but there is scarcely a painting in the collection that is not the genuine work of a famous name. It is by far the completest collection in the world of the works of the famous Spanish artists, Ribiera and Murillo, and the largest collection known to the writer of the Flemish painter, Reubens, besides containing excellent canvases, too numerous to mention, by Rembrandt, Raphael, De Vinci, Paul Veronese, Tintoretto and others. It is by no means the largest gallery in Europe, but it is without doubt one of the most valuable and select. This was a great surprise.

Judge Goodpasture thought Madrid the handsomest city he had ever seen, and his stay there was enjoyed more than in any other. The Judge and some of the others went out one evening with their interpreter about two hours by sun to buy a pipe, but all the shops were closed for the day—not because of some celebration but by custom. They waited until next day and had to search two hours before they could find one. The Spanish do not smoke pipes, but a great many use cigarettes and a few, very bad cigars. Neither do they chew. Chewing tobacco cannot ordinarily be bought in the country.

Madrid has the finest drive of any city in Europe, a hill with winding roads, from the top of which an unsurpassed view is had of the entire country as far as the eye can reach. All fashionable life drives up there of an afternoon, and as many as two thousand carriages can be seen in line of a pleasant day. Their horses are prettier and more stylish than in any other of the great cities of Europe or America. Nearly all of them are Arabian barbs, and are usually stallions. They are bought in Andalusia, and are smaller than the light horses of France and England. So much importance, in a social way, is attached to the possession of a pair of horses and carriage, by the people of the capital, that it is said, they will live in a garret and subsist on beans and bread alone, in order to drive in the afternoon.

Everyone with whom the Judge consulted here advised him to go to Andalusia for the best jacks. Accordingly, he and his son and John, parted from the boys, who were going from Madrid to Toledo, and took the train for the ancient city of Cordova. A good part of the way lay through the most sterile, driest and dreariest country to be found anywhere. Mile after mile was passed over without seeing a shrub or living thing, here and there seeing large towns without a single inhabitant, a mournful suggestion of Spain's former greatness. She once supported a population of more than sixty millions of people; now she has less than seventeen millions. All this arid desert through which they passed once bloomed like the rose, and supported a large and prosperous population. But it has ceased to rain in those parts, and there is no water for irrigation.

Go To Cordova. On arriving at Cordova they stopped at the Hotel Orientale, recommended by Baedeker, and a most excellent place. They secured an interpreter early the next morning, one Baccariza by name, who had little information and less sense, was vain and sensitive to a degree, but whithal, a kind-hearted and good man. He had some experience, too, that was thought would make him valuable. He had been the interpreter and guide to General Grant and party when in this part of Spain, and had assisted Leonard Brothers, of Missouri, in purchases when they made an importation of jacks a few years before. Baccariza said that he knew nothing about how or where to find the stock, but that he could talk, and that he knew a gypsy who was a stock commissioner and the best about the town. We never got to know the name of this commissioner further than Louie. Gypsies are thick in Spain, and instead of being altogether nomadic as with us, a large number of them live in towns, and are well to do citizens.

CHAPTER XII.

Judge Goodpasture engaged Louie, and began to scour the country for jacks. They found nothing, practically, except gray ones, some of these, however, were excellent animals. Even with their limited experience, they knew that the black were the ones for their market. They could hear vague rumors of black jacks in Catalonia in the North, and on the island of Majorca, but it seemed almost impossible to get information on which to rely in Spain, and especially through a fool interpreter. But after they found that only gray ones could be had around Cordova, W. H. Goodpasture took the train for Valencia, a city on the Mediterranean almost opposite Majorca, about half way to Barcelona. When he went to the station, he was greatly surprised to find Palmer, Jackson and Campbell on the train. They had been to Seville and the Alhambra, and were now on their way to Paris by way of Valencia. They stopped off for a day at the latter place.

The trip was destined to be a fruitless one. The American consul could not speak English, and Mr. Goodpasture had no interpreter and was unable to secure one in the town. He had recourse to the English consulate where he was well treated, but none in the office knew anything of jacks. He heard it said that the biggest and best mules came from Majorca, but even here, the preponderance of opinion was, that Andalusia, and especially Cordova, was the best place to buy good jacks. So he returned to Cordova, and buying was at once begun.

Traveling to see jacks in the country was done largely by rail, but sometimes it was necessary to take carriages to points remote from the railroad. Jack buying and mixing with the peasants is a very pleasant occupation, and would have been especially so if they had been able to find what was wanted.

One day they drove so far out into the country that they had to spend the night in a small village. There was no hotel there, and they stopped at what is known as a posada, that is, a place where teams are accommodated. The woman who ran the place agreed to furnish them sleeping apartments, but could not feed them. She consented though, to cook their food if they would buy it. This was entirely agreeable, and they had the good woman to make the purchases for them, giving her carte blanche as to what and how much she should buy. The result was everything desired, and they had a good dinner—soup, omelette (for which Spain is famous), cooked with young, tender asparagus tips, chicken cooked on a spit which revolved in front of the fire, the woman from time to time pouring basting over it; sausage, fruits, cheese and black coffee. The bread was, of course, cold, and was placed on the table in spikes about three feet long and three or four inches in diameter.

Judge Goodpasture sat in the corner of the fireplace and smoked, while the cooking was in progress. These fireplaces are very deep and eight or ten feet wide, the

fire occupying a small place in the center. No large
wood is to be had, either here or in France, but their
fires are altogether of brush, obtained from trimming
the hedges and trees. The Judge was very anxious to
talk to the busy females, but nothing is more unsatisfactory than a social conversation through an interpreter.
He did find out, however, from the servant girl, whom
he pronounced the best looking woman he had seen in
Spain, the amount she received per month for her services. He also found out that she had no sort of desire
to go to America. They ate dinner with their fingers
and pocket knives.

After their return to Cordova, W. H. Goodpasture took
the train to Jativa, in the province of Jaen, near the Alhambra, to see what was to be had there, but not enough
could be found to justify shipping the distance. On his
return, he went to Malaga, where he investigated the
question with the aid of an interpreter named Lobo.
Lobo was said to be flighty and of weak mind, and had
taken up the calling of guide, courier and interpreter,
not having sense enough for anything else. While there
were innumerable small pack jacks found in the Malaga
district, there were none large enough to import. All,
there, at Valencia and Jativa were gray. These various
trips are mentioned to show how they were ignorantly
groping about and striving to find something they knew
to exist but were utterly without information as to where
it existed. Six or seven hours ride from Valencia by
boat, less than a single night, would have carried them
into the home of the biggest black jacks in Europe. It
seems strange that specific information could not be obtained about them, but the Judge and son were unable to

talk the language, did not know of whom to inquire, their interpreter had no sense, and their commissioner was interested in selling in his own section, his employment depending upon it.

They completed their purchases in Cordova and the country surrounding it, getting two black jacks and a black jennet out of an importation of twenty-two head. They paid considerably more than the regular price there, the gypsy commissioner doubtless getting a good share of the excess. But if there is any way to help this, they never discovered it, even with the added experience of later importations—in fact, they were worse robbed on the second importation than in the first, or, possibly, in any succeeding ones.

Judge's Friend. An old fellow sold them a rather common jack at an uncommonly high price, considering quality. They soon discovered that they had paid too much, but said nothing. It put the old Spaniard in great good humor with the world in general, and when they had paid him, he had more money in his pocket than he had ever had before in his life. He took a great fancy to Judge Goodpasture, although neither could say a word to the other, and would follow him around wherever he went. If they went out to the suburbs to see something, a distance too short to take a carriage, he would get his old gray horse for the Judge to ride, while he himself and the rest would walk. If they took the train to some far off village, he would go too, paying his own railroad fare, and carrying his food with him for the trip. The Judge was partly responsible for this. He would pat the old fellow on the back, and have the interpreter tell him he was the greatest and one of the very cleverest men he had ever had the pleasure of meeting in Europe. After these speeches, he would invariably offer the Judge a cigar. This grew to be quite comical, for the same thing, with variations, was gone over day after day, whenever the Judge wanted to see a little fun, or smoke a bad cigar.

Dr. Plumlee. After completing their purchases, the jacks were collected in a stable at Cordova and put in charge of John. They had arranged to ship from Malaga to London, and thence to New York. The boat was not to leave for some time, and they preferred to keep the stock in Cordova until the time of sailing. One day, when they had been to the stable looking at the stock, and were returning to the hotel, they saw coming, what looked like one of the most enormous men ever seen, walking leisurely in their direction. The Spanish are quite a small people and do not wear overcoats. But they were surprised to see that this man wore a great heavy one that came to his heels. This greatly increased their interest and astonishment. Upon getting a little closer, the Judge turned, the very picture of amazement, and said, "Upon my word, I do believe it is Plumlee." And so it turned out to be, Dr. B. S. Plumlee, an old friend from the good county of Clay, who had taken the fever and had himself come for jacks. Now, Plumlee is a thoroughly good fellow, uncommonly handsome and smart, and an interesting talker as well. A splendid suit of new Paris clothes added to the importance of his appearance. The Judge ceased to be a great man after his advent, except in the eyes of his Fidus Achilles, and everything was "Senor Doctoree."

Nothing would do Plumlee but that they should go back and show him their stock. He looked through the lot with great care, one at a time. As intimated, the Doctor is a rarely shrewd man. So he praised them all to the extent the occasion seemed to require, but apparently was not taken with any in particular. Finally, he suggested to the Judge that as he wanted to go to Poitou, France, and purchase, he would not buy in Spain, but still, if the Judge would sell him two or three of his at a fair profit, which he said he was willing to pay, he thought he might trade with him. The Judge told him he did not desire to make any money off of him, as he was on the ground; but Plumlee said that would be all right, and the Judge agreed to price the stock to him. At his request, the Judge priced each of the jacks and a part of the jennets. Plumlee walked down the line and said: "I will take this one." All right said the Judge. "And this one," said Plumlee. "Plumlee, you have got to stop right there," said the Judge, with emphasis. He had picked out the best two year old jack in the lot and his only black jennet, and she in foal. "You may have the two selected, but I would not go home," declared the Judge, "with all the best jacks yours for a thousand dollars. You will have to buy the balance like we did, here in the country."

Judge Goodpasture, on leaving Cordova, thus writes a friend, describing it:

Description of Cordova. "Cordova, as Campbell would say, is a funny city. It has about sixty thousand inhabitants, and is about three thousand years old. With the exception of a few modern ones, there is not a street in the city that is

10

straight for one hundred yards, and are from eight to fifteen feet wide, all paved with rock. There are many places of great interest. The bridge across the Guadalquivir is a stone structure in first rate repair, and was built by the Romans more than two thousand years ago. There stand in the river three stone water mills, each quite as old as the bridge.

"The Mosque at this place is the greatest wonder of them all. It is one of the largest churches in the world, being about 600 feet by 450, and is supported inside by 1050 large columns, made of marble, porphyry and all the finest stones of the East. Many of these were brought from the ancient city of Jerusalem. It was built in 712. The main chapel has two organs, each 75 feet high, and are of comparatively recent date, being placed there 150 years ago.

"The country around Cordova is the richest I have ever seen. It will bring from fifty to seventy-five bushels of corn to the acre, and everything else in proportion. I was out on a large farm near the city yesterday. We were in a pasture field of a thousand acres. Upon it were grazing some goats ,some donkeys, and about five hundred head of cattle. These cattle were all of solid colors, either jet black or dark red, the most of them very large, with enormous horns, many of them five feet from tip to tip. In the herd was a big black bull that would weigh about 2,500 pounds, with horns more than two feet long. He started toward us, and was followed by probably a dozen others. Our interpreter and ourselves made for some small trees on the bank of the river. In our flight we came upon the herdsman, who assured us that there was no danger unless the whole herd should come.   We did not disturb the cattle any more.

"The goats were of a dark red color, and very **large,** with two wattles under the neck about four inches long, and udders almost as large as those of cows.   They drive herds of these into the city and sell their milk. Many are slaughtered as kids.   They raise every kind of stock here that is to be found in Tennessee.

"The peasants live hard; they eat little meat, but subsist on cheap bread, wine and fruits, with more or less beans.   One can see a man that has lived in a hovel, on cheap bread and beans come out and strut the streets in a flashy cloak with red velvet lining and a fancy turban on his head.   A stranger would think he was one of the nobility.   I suppose no people in the world are fonder of dress than the Spaniards, or dress better. They are a very handsome people, both men and women, and polite to excess.   If one meets an acquaintance a dozen time a day, he always shakes hands.

"In Cordova, the ladies, except the poorer classes, seldom walk out on the streets.   They can be seen, however, through the windows in passing.   The young folks, I am told, make love at the windows.   One frequently sees a nicely dressed young fellow, standing outside at the window, talking to some beautiful young woman inside.   These windows are made safe with fixed iron bars like a jail.   The young ladies are all beautiful.

"All kinds of fruits and vegetables are plentiful here: oranges, large and fine, six cents a dozen; figs, and grapes of every kind, cheap; wine by the barrel, eight cents a gallon, in quart bottles eighteen cents.   Coffee is not much used at the table, being drunk principally at the cafes. Everyone uses wine at every meal, a quart bottle being placed at each plate. I do not think they use to excess any other drink. I have not seen a drunk man in Spain."

Judge Goodpasture never displayed much talent in the matter of finding his way in a city, and was especially troubled in Cordova, with its multitude of narrow, crooked streets, running in all directions. He never went out there alone without getting lost. He could not inquire of anyone, and would walk until he suddenly and very unexpectedly, found himself outside the walls of the city, on the Alameda, near the railroad station. Luckily, the station and hotel were on the same street, and in this way he could find his way back. Strangely enough, every time he was lost he finally, after much tiresome walking and worry, suddenly came out at the same place, and each time would surprise him worse than the preceding one. It made no sort of difference in what direction he tried to go, he would finally arrive at that place all the same.

Malaga. They shipped their stock by rail to Malaga, and arrived there a little before night. Malaga is built quite similarly to Cordova, the streets just as narrow and crooked, making it quite as easy to get lost. John, the interpreter and the writer, went to the stable to feed and attend to the stock, the Judge being quite tired, remaining at the hotel. But after a bit he concluded he would follow, and left the hotel alone. He was soon lost. There is a very pretty little park in the city, not over one hundred yards square. The Judge ran into this park four or five times, until it looked like he could not get away from it. He was by this time very tired indeed, and had ceased trying to find the stable, and was endeavoring to get back to the hotel. In the meantime, he had forgotten its name, if he had ever noticed it enough to learn it. Finally, after being about broken down, he saw in front of a large building a gentleman who looked like an Englishman, and so he proved to be. The Judge told him his trouble; that he was lost and did not know the name of his hotel, or where it was. "Well," said the gentleman, "this is the place right here, where you ate your supper." He had walked rapidly for an hour and a half and was intensely relieved.

Finding one's way in a strange city is as much a natural talent as any gift that can be suggested. Some people find their way seemingly by intuition, without any sort of trouble, while others will lose all sense of direction, and go the wrong way quite as readily as the right. But any sort of man, with any degree of talent, would be excusable for getting lost in Cordova or Malaga.

They had a very queer and very persistent visitor just before sailing for London. A farmer living near Cordova had three jacks which he was very anxious to sell at a big price. They had left there without seeing them. In his anxiety to sell, the owner put them on the cars and shipped them to Malaga. When he arrived, he did not have the money to pay the freight, which he expected to pay out of the proceeds of his sale. He was in a fix. The Judge had bought his full complement, and could buy no more. The poor fellow insisted, and continued to insist, until they sailed away and left him in his trouble.

CHAPTER XIII.

We cannot leave Spain without a word as to the Andalusian women. Andalusia was, for a long time, occupied by, and in complete possession of, the Moors. Their splendid mosque at Cordova, the beautiful palace of the Alhambra, the grand castles at Jativa. Malaga and elsewhere, all proclaim them to have been a great people, and it is now generally admitted that, at that time, they were in advance of the Spanish. These Southern provinces, the fairest and most fertile of the country, were conquered by Ferdinand and Isabella and confiscated and occupied by their subjects, the larger part of the Moors leaving the country. But many remained, and in time became mixed with, and absorbed by, the Spanish population. This has given to the women of the latter, the most glorious eyes that ever spake love to mortal. Heavy eyebrows, a small downy mustache, intensely black hair, a rather small but perfect figure, small feet and hands, excellent taste in dress, the head covered with lace mantillas, out of which those magnificent eyes shine luminously—this is the lovely senorita of song and story. She is not the most sensible of women, nor the best educated, nor yet the least frivolous, but from a purely aesthetic point, she is the most attractive of all her sex.

Judge Goodpasture thought her mustache her chief

attraction, at least he made Baccariza think so. When
he saw a woman, old or young, good or bad looking,
who had been particularly blessed with this hirsute
adornment, he would call the interpreter's attention to
it, and to how very becoming it was. So Baccariza
brought his wife all the way up to the hotel one day,
that the Judge might see what a fine mustache she had.
She looked like one of Shakespeare's witches, but as in
duty bound, the Judge was duly enthusiastic. Still, the
fact remains, that the Andalusian woman surpasses all
her sisters in the one matter of beauty, though all, or
nearly all, are of the same general type, and do not
present that great variety that is found in America.

Judge Goodpasture wrote as follows of the voyage
he had now undertaken:

Malaga to London.

"On the 10th day of February, my
son Willie, John Terry, colored, and
myself, embarked on the good ship
Cadiz, at Malaga, Spain, bound for London.

"Malaga is located on the Mediterranean coast, about
one hundred and fifty miles from Gibraltar. It contains
a population of 126,000 people; is a city of great commercial importance, its principal trade being in fruits
and wines, a large proportion of which are shipped to
the United States. My purpose, however, is to describe
the voyage and not the country.

"We steamed out at six o'clock p.m. The bay looked
beautiful. The hills of Malaga were adorned by the
still standing castles and fortifications of the Moors, and
the declining sun seemed to be in unison with the fading
glories of the country.

"Our captain was a very inquisitive as well as communicative man. He knew everything known by his passengers for the last twenty years, and if each succeeding passenger did not learn it all, it was his own fault, for he was sure to hear it.

"Our voyage for the first one hundred miles was devoid of interest, being in the night. However, about daylight, I was awakened by our captain, to see some historic battle fields on the coast, but have forgotten their names. There is a history about nearly everything and place in Spain. A little after daylight, we found ourselves in sight of Tangier, Africa. Our ship did not land, but we saw the city from the bay—churches and towers and public buildings, and the view as we passed out, was that of a handsome but curious city. Leaving the African coast, we were soon between the two pillars of Hercules and into the Straits of Gibraltar. Here we were in view of three of the greatest fortifications in the world. The best known is, perhaps, Gilbraltar, and then comes the Moorish fortification, which is said to be the strongest defensive point, naturally, of any military post in existence. A little below these two is the Ceuta fortress of Spain. If the three should act in concert, the combined fleets of the world could not enter the Mediterranean. It would be a hard thing to accomplish even as against Gibraltar, the English having kept this point up to the highest standard of modern warfare. She has two one hundred ton guns that shoot through eighteen inches of solid steel, and through six or seven inches at the distance of ten miles.

"Soon after passing out of the Straits, and having lost sight of 'Gib,' as the place is familiarly called, we entered the bay of Trafalgar, where Lord Nelson gained his great victory over the combined fleets of France and Spain. Our captain pointed out the position of the French and Spanish, as well as that of the English, and showed us where Lord Nelson was killed.

"He related many amusing incidents of the battle, one of which is truly worth relating. He said: 'In one of the English ships, a passing cannon ball struck a sailor and cut off one of his legs. In his agony, he called on a fellow soldier, an Irishman, to carry him to the cockpit. The sailor shouldered the wounded man and started, but before he had passed below, another ball took off the wounded man's head. The Irishman, in the noise and confusion of battle, had not noticed this, but as he went below, he met one of the officers who asked him where he was carrying that man. 'To the cockpit,' was the ready response. 'Yes,' said the officer, 'but there is no use of that, his head is shot off.' 'Is that so,' said the Irishman, looking back over his shoulders, 'he told me it was his leg.'"

"After leaving Trafalgar, we passed the city of Tarifa. Here we could not land, as cholera was raging in the place. Our next stopping point was the ancient city of Cadiz. We were here for a day and night, and had the opportunity of taking a general view of the city, which we found to be clean and beautiful, with few indications of its great antiquity. It was founded by Hercules about eleven hundred years before Christ, and now has a population of 65,000 souls, though at one time it was much larger.

"We proceeded from Cadiz to Lisbon. Portugal, the capital of the country, and a large town of about 280,000 inhabitants. In the bay lay five English iron-clad warships, constituting what is known as the Channel Fleet, each ship manned by about eight hundred men. One of these ships brought the remains of Peabody to America, and another was in the bombardment of Alexandria, and has in her side a dent, six or eight inches deep, and as large as a half bushel, made by a cannon ball in that engagement. The Duke of Edinburg had just been appointed to the command of the fleet, and the King of Portugal dined with him on the day of our arrival. They had quite a big time of it. We remained here five days, saw the church in which Columbus was married, still in good preservation. Lisbon is a city of hills. Here our ship took on two hundred bales of cork.

"From Lisbon we proceeded to Vigo, Spain, a dirty little town with a fishy smell, on one of the finest bays in the world. Here we took on 460 boxes of eggs for London. There is a company of Americans at work in the bay here, mostly from Philadelphia, with the best divers to be had, attempting to recover the gold and silver in the galleys that were sunk about 160 years ago. They have found one of the ships and recovered some logwood, and are expecting to get the gold. They are to give a certain per cent of all the money recovered to the Spanish government, if they do not forget to tell the government that they have found any.

"We had so often been told of the dangers of the Bay of Biscay that we left Vigo in some dread, but we crossed it in safety. The good captain—to quiet our nerves, I suppose, told us about, and showed us while crossing the place, where, a few years ago, a number of English warships were caught in a storm and one of

them upset and went down with 500 men on board,
everyone of whom perished. In passing down the English Channel, it was a matter of great interest to us, and
to John in particular, to look at some half dozen or more
wrecks. Of some, the smoke stacks were visible, and of
others, only the masts. These wrecks were suggestive."

They landed safely at London, and carried their stock
to Mills' stable, four or five miles from the place of landing, and two or three from where they expected to
embark. While unloading at the docks, a slick artist
relieved Judge Goodpasture of a fine gold watch, which
distressed him very much, it having been a gift from his
wife. Nothing was afterward heard of it.

Judge Goodpasture thus describes the section in which
they had stopped in one of his letters: "We are here
in the black bottom of London, in fact, nearly all of
London is black bottom. It is certainly the most god-
forsaken, rough city in the world. There is, however,
including the House of Parliament, the banks, etc., a
portion of the city about as large as Nashville, that is
grand beyond description; the balance of the city is as
bad as you can imagine it. We stayed four days in the
neighborhood of Moody and Sankey's Tabernacle. I
reckon a more abandoned place you never saw: poor
beyond description, and wicked beyond belief."

They remained in London one week, giving their
stock a good rest, as they had been fourteen days in
reaching London, having sailed about 1,700 miles, and
on March 3rd embarked for New York on the steamship
Assyrian Monarch. It was raining when they sailed,
but no wind, and a smooth sea. On Sunday night,
March 7th, they had religious services on board. This

is required on all English boats, weather permitting. The duty is imposed on the captain, but he is allowed to call on any minister who happens to be on board, and is willing to conduct the services.

Storm at Sea. Judge Goodpasture thus writes home describing his first sight of a genuine storm at sea: "About five o'clock on the morning of March 8th, I was awakened from my slumber by a terrible noise and rolling of the ship. The most of the passengers were thrown from their beds. I put on my clothes as best I could, and looking out found that a fierce storm was raging. The captain was on the bridge at the time, and was unable to get down for four hours. He held on by main strength, and a part of the time had himself lashed to the bridge, fearing that he would be washed overboard. He was drenched with spray. The wind blew at the rate of sixty miles an hour for eleven hours, and at times even harder. The sails were not only blown to pieces, but entirely away, by the terrific force of the gale. I looked out through a port hole at the raging waters. No man can describe a storm at sea. It is unlike anything else. The wind seemed to lift the waters up, and it looked more like a dreadful snow storm, the spray being blown in all directions, than anything of which I can think. The waves looked like great mountains, partly obscured by fog or snow, and the ship careened thirty degress. The officers and sailors throughout the entire storm were cool—the first officer in particular, who indulged in many most amusing anecdotes, and tales of past experiences in sailing over nearly all the waters of the known world. In order that we might know when the time of real danger arrived, he told this—that he once had a very timid minister on board during an unusually nasty spell of weather. To quiet his nerves, he called attention to the profanity of the sailors, who were having to work on a wet, slippery deck, and in a cold drenching spray. and told him that as long as their profanity continued. he need have no fear—it would cease at once in case of danger. Now, the weather grew worse, and at last reached the proportions of a gale. Many of the passengers were frightened, and with the minister at their head, assembled in the dining room for prayers. The minister opened the meeting. While he was in the midst of an eloquent appeal, some of the sailors passed along the deck violently cursing everything in sight. 'Thank God,' said he, 'the sailors still swear.'

"After the storm was over, we found that some of our machinery was broken, and our ship was standing still. It took four hours to repair it."

These storms are very wearying and bruising to stock, but seldom result fatally. The jacks and jennets were put in stalls, their heads facing the center and not the sides of the vessel. Heavy strips were nailed to the floor, about two feet apart, so as to give them a footing. Before leaving Spain, they had made a number of swings to hold the weak and injured on their feet. On this trip they never allowed the stock to lay down, because they had been told they would grow so stiff that it would be impossible for them to stand afterward. This was a great mistake. If allowed to lay for a reasonable length of time, there is no such effect, but they are greatly rested by it.

They shipped this time and subsequently, except their

last shipment, between decks. This will do in winter or early spring when bad weather may reasonably be expected, but a more serious mistake could hardly be made in summer. They once suffered a loss of over five thousand dollars' worth of jacks in a few days' time that was directly attributable to shipping in this place. If they had been shipped on top of the deck, unquestionably all would have been saved. It was, however, a very natural mistake. All the insurance companies charged higher rates on top, as in case of a severe storm all might be washed overboard. But the danger of a severe storm in summer is very small—we have never seen one at that season that would have been at all hazardous.

During the prevalence of a storm, like the one above described by Judge Goodpasture, the stock must be watched very closely to avoid accident. The stalls are built up in front of the jacks, with strong oak plank or other stout wood, reaching a little above the chest. The feed troughs are fastened to the upper planks. The jack is tied to the posts on either side, which holds him in position and prevents his interfering with his neighbor. On this trip, they had several thrown entirely over the front part of the stall and out into the passage way. When this happens, the immediate presence of the attendant is necessary to release the animal's head.

This was a hard time on John, but he was faithful and attentive. More or less sea-sick through it all, losing a great deal of sleep, constant watching and working, the depressing effects of bad dreams and fears for the safety of the vessel, made the voyage a pretty tough experience for him.

New York and Home. They at last reached New York, having been fourteen days in sailing from Malaga to London and sixteen days from the latter to New York. This, with delays at different places, together with six days by rail from New York to Nashville, was a very long and trying trip on both man and beast. They made the journey without further accident than the loss of one animal, the fine black jennet owned by Dr. Plumlee. They had agreed to bring his two or three head along with theirs. They regretted this loss very much, because she belonged to their friend, and was, besides, a very superior animal.

Judge Goodpasture came home on a passenger train from New York, and prepared to receive the stock by the time of their arrival. He had a very interesting interview published in the American, and had awakened a good deal of interest in the public. Dr. Plumlee had gotten home some time previously, having declined to buy in Poitou on account of the very high price.

The stock arrived in Nashville the latter part of March, but rather late for the market, which only really covers the period from January to April inclusive. After their long journey, it was impossible to get them in first-class condition in time for the spring demand. Still, several of them were sold at profitable figures, and the others were carried over for the following year. One of the very best of the lot was a jack named Alfonso, purchased from the royal breeding stables at Cordova. He was a large steel gray jack, 15¼ hands high, and the best of the variety they ever saw, before or since. As said before, the Andalusian was not the popular jack for this country.

CHAPTER XIV.

Second Importation. Judge Goodpasture busied himself for the next few months watching the jack market, attending to his various real estate deals and making a trip to Sparta and the Mountain District.

He was not satisfied with his first importation of jacks. He became more than ever convinced that black jacks could be found in Europe, and the sales he had made of the gray, made it certain that an importation of black ones would bring great profit and credit as well. A second importation was, therefore, determined upon, and arrangements were made to go for them during the summer, so as to have them in good fix for the winter and spring trade.

All was ready, and he and his son left Nashville on the 7th of July, 1886. Their faithful groom, John Terry, was left behind because of the expense. It was not then known how much travel would have to be done to find the kind of jacks desired, but the Judge left with the determination to keep looking until they were found.

He seems to have been a bit sad in leaving on this trip. He thus writes his wife from New York, under date of July 9, 1886:

Trip to New York. "The day we left home was one of the saddest of my life. We got to Louisville at 2 p.m., and staid there until 7. I was feeling gloomy, and in the evening late, I went down to the bank of the river, to nearly the same spot where I sat upon a rock thirty-six years ago and watched some fishermen. I found a log at this place and sitting down on it remained there for an hour. I thought of nearly everything I had done for the last thirty-six years, and where I would be at the end of thirty-six years more. But few people at that time would know I ever lived, perchance some might pass through a grave yard and point to the mossy headstone and say "I knew that man when I was a boy." Such is life.

"We left Louisville at 7 p.m. It was not long until I heard the conductor call out Frankfort. I looked out in the dark at Kentucky's capital. I never saw it before. I went back and tried to sleep, but I could not. After a little I heard the conductor cry out Lexington. I looked out again to see if I could recognize the place. I was here exactly thirty years ago. Everything in an instant came to my mind as vividly as if it had been but yesterday. I had just helped nominate Buchanan for President, and was going home full of political enthusiasm. What a change since then!" He closes this unusually sad letter by saying: "Remember your imperfect husband in your prayers."

This was a feeling very rare to Judge Goodpasture on these trips. He had the happy faculty of dismissing from his mind all thoughts of business left behind, and entering with enthusiasm into the undertaking on hand. He was an ideal traveling companion. In the best of humor at all times, rarely growing tired, never fretted, always ready to agree on what to do or where to go— a thing oftentimes hard for travelers to do; always well, and an adaptability to places and conditions equaled by few men. He was soon acquainted with those with

whom he was thrown, and had a way of making everyone like him.

Sails for London. They sailed for London per S. S.
Lydian Monarch, July 10. The voy-
age was not an altogether pleasant one.
For the first five or six days they were in a dense fog.
This almost precluded sleep on account of the incessant
blowing of the fog horn, and besides, it was uncom-
fortably dangerous. Indeed, the steamer did run into
the Alice Frances, of Boston, off the coast of Newfoundland, about two o'clock at night but with no more serious consequences than a very bad scare and an uncom-
fortable feeling for the balance of the night. They
never knew what became of the other boat.

The steamship fare was rather bad, and was made
much worse on account of a somewhat peculiar circumstance. Having about 550 large bullocks on board, it
was necessary to take the most northerly passage in order
to keep in a cool atmosphere. While the steamer lay
in New York, innumerable flies had congregated on her,
attracted by the great number of cattle on board. By
the time they reached the coast of Newfoundland, the
wind was blowing the blasts of December or January.
This did not agree with the flies, and they were dropping
about everywhere and in everything.

They stopped only a short time in London, and ran
down to the famous seacoast watering place, Brighton,
and took the train from there to New Haven—thence
by boat to Dieppe, and from there by rail to Paris.

Brighton to Paris. Judge Goodpasture writes as follows
of this part of the trip: "After a day
and night in London, we left at 11 a.m, for Brighton,

arriving there at 2 p.m. We saw most of the city. It has 128,400 population, and at least one thousand hotels and first-class boarding houses. It is on the English Channel and is a great summer resort for the aristocracy; is handsome in the extreme, and was the summer home of George III. We visited his palace and private theater. They look as new as if just built last year, being kept in perfect repair. They are located in the heart of the city ,and are surrounded by a large and handsome park. This property has all been bought by the city and is kept as a place of amusement.

"We reached Paris this morning at 11 o'clock, had our breakfast, gave out our washing and then nearly walked ourselves to death looking at the city. We got in our wash by dinner time (6.30 p.m.), all right. Willie and Mr. Bernard have gone out to-night, but I am going to bed as soon as I finish this letter. I slept none last night. We crossed the Channel and no one could sleep. There were more sea-sick people than I ever saw before all put together. Taking it all together, we have had a pretty rough voyage. People are wearing over-coats here—it is quite cool and wet."

Paris to Barcelona. From Paris they took the train for Barcelona, Spain, intending to go through without stopping; but when they arrived at Nimes, one of the extreme southern towns of France, they found that they had missed con-nection, and would have to lay over about three hours. They arrived just before daylight, and concluded to pass away the time in looking at the town. They went first to the city market, always a place of especial in-terest to Judge Goodpasture. He enjoyed seeing the kinds of people and the odd and interesting characters found there, as well as the variety of things for sale. These southern markets are extremely rich in variety of fruits. Nimes is an old Roman town with many curious and well preserved specimens of the works of the ancients.

They had breakfast at a coffee stand near the depot. It consisted of a very good cup of coffee, and the deligtful bread to be found in every part of France, which, on account of its shape, the Judge called ram's horn. He pronounced it one of the best breakfasts he had eaten in Europe, so it is to be supposed he was hungry.

They went to the station a little early to take the train, but did not have to wait as long as they had expected. They hurriedly got aboard in a compartment with plenty of room, the Judge lighted his hickory pipe and settled back to enjoy the beauty of the scenery of this old country that has been in a high state of cultivation since before the days of Christ.

When they had gone about one hundred miles, a guard came along to examine tickets, and informed them, by many signs and much jabbering, that they were in the wrong train. As a matter of fact, they had taken a train going straight back to Paris. There was nothing to do but to get off at the first station and take the next train for Nimes, which they did. When they got back, the station agent, who divined the trouble they had gotten into, took the Judge by the hand and led him over to one of the several railroad tracks and put his hand on it, pointing out at same time the direction they were to take. He then took out the Judge's watch and showed him the exact time it would leave. They had

to wait for some time, and without especially desiring it,
they were given another opportunity of sight seeing in
the ancient city of Nimes.

Their instructions had been so exact and so impossible to misunderstand, that they boarded the right train
next time and had no further trouble until they arrived
at Cerbere, the last station in France, and near the
Spanish frontier, where they arrived at eleven o'clock
at night. As they had eaten nothing since morning,
they had supper before retiring, and a very bad one it
was.

They left at five o'clock the next morning, entering
a long tunnel immediately on leaving the station.
When they emerged, they were in Portbon, Spain,
which, like Cerbere, is a custom station, and where the
baggage was examined. Here a very beautiful young
Spanish woman entered their compartment and rode
with them to Barcelona. She afforded them much entertainment. When they grew tired of looking at the
magnificent mountain scenery on the outside, they had
scenery quite as attractive with which to regale their
eyes on the inside; and when they discovered to a cer-
tainty that she did not understand English, they enjoyed
discussing her conduct and appearance. It afforded
diversion for the balance of the trip, but more than once
she looked rather suspicious as to the subject matter
of their conversation.

On arrival at Barcelona, after a journey of forty-two
hours, in addition to stops, they went to the Hotel Central. It is not recommended by Baedeker, but so far as
their experience went, it was the most satisfactory hotel
in all respects at which they ever stopped, either on this

or subsequent trips, in Spain or elsewhere. The charges were quite moderate. only eight pesetas, or a dollar and sixty cents per day. which included breakfast and dinner, the only meals served in continental hotels. An excellent restaurant was attached to it, at which they obtained delicious bread and coffee on first rising, the hotel breakfast being served from 11 to 12 m.

Discovers an Interpreter. They at once began a search for an interpreter, but without success. As they had little Spanish money, they concluded to try and find their bank correspondent and draw some. Their bank here was Vidal Quadras Hermanos. After finding the address in the directory, at the hotel, they secured a city map and from it succeeded in finding the place, but no bank was in sight. They looked in vain in every direction, although at the address given. In their perplexity, they showed the address to a plain looking citizen standing idly near. He looked carefully at the address and then at them, and to their amazement said: "Do you speak English?" They replied that they used to indulge in that greatest of luxuries, but had not had the pleasure for some days past outside of conversations with each other. He then showed them the bank, which turned out to be on the third floor of the building, directly in front of them, but with no sign to indicate its location. They asked their new found English speaking friend to wait for them, which he consented to do. After transacting their business in the bank, they rejoined him—found that he was a Frenchman who had been to New Orleans and there learned English, but had lived for the last fifteen years in Barcelonia. He was a coal agent, and had never acted as an interpreter and did not know one single thing about jacks, but he said he could talk, and knew a man that could tell them all about jack stock. They engaged him, and thus, chanced the first employment of John Rives, who became the most famous interpreter in all Spain, and whose services were often engaged by cable from the United States in order to be the first to obtain them. No man has ever assisted in the purchase of more jacks for export to America.

They went at once to the stables of the man who knew all about jack stock; found that he had gone to his home at Sabadell and that they could see him the next day (Sunday), as it was to be a great feast day there, and if they waited until the following day they might miss him, he being a man whose business carried him all over northern Spain. His name was Jose San Marti, and he was the biggest mule dealer in Spain, importing large numbers from France. He looked to be about sixty, very erect, with piercing eyes, very handsome, and extremely intellectual in appearance. They were kindly received by him at his home, and he agreed to go with them on the following Wednesday and show them jacks for the consideration of four dollars for each head purchased, and all his expenses. They agreed to his terms. His intellectual appearance was not deceiving. He was sharp and shrewd, and the compensation paid him was a mere bagatelle to what he made out of them. They never discovered this until divulged by the interpreter subsequently, and it would probably never have come to light had not he and the interpreter fallen out with each other over a division of the swag.

CHAPTER XV.

After agreeing to the terms of the commissioner, Judge Goodpasture had nothing further to do in the town, and devoted himself to an observance of the festivities of the occasion. It was a glorious Sunday, their first, on this trip in Spain. The sun shone down just enough to give beauty to the shady parks and evergreen forests. A gentle Mediterranean breeze fanned the cheeks, and made the growing crops in the fields around to waive and ripple as the bosom of a lake. The thermometer was not higher than at an American mountain resort, and the atmosphere looked perfectly clear, until one turned toward the tall blue peak of the Montserrat.

A great day it was to the people of the little city of Sabadell—the annual feast of the town, mixed up, as everything else is, with the church. The streets were gaily decorated with evergreens, flags, flowers, saucy looking peasant girls, and high bred dames. The proud seignor, with his broad sombrero, stalked the streets in all his imagined grandeur. The great organ in the old cathedral was pealing forth its grand notes, accompanied by a choir of trained voices and a band of fifty or sixty instruments. The multitude had assembled at the church, and were going through the exercises there in the forenoon so as to be in time for the afternoon exercises at the Plaza de Toros, and the evening entertainments at the numerous ball rooms.

A bull fight was to take place at 4.30 in the afternoon. and to insure themselves good seats they went down at three.

The Plaza de Toros here, built upon the plan of the Coliseum of Rome, is an immense circular building with seats and boxes extending entirely around, and in the inside a ring for the combatants. From the top of the building that day, floated an immense Spanish flag. and around it a thousand lesser ones.

The crowd had already begun to assemble, except in the reserved boxes at the top, and was composed of both sexes and all degrees of humanity. The justly famous small boy was there, selling bottled soda water, fans. programmes, etc. Buying one of the latter they found that they were likely to see an uncommonly interesting battle. The famous Munchao, of Madrid, was to fight that day—so was Alaban, of Valencia; Rocher, of Seville; Lopez, of Madrid, and half a dozen others, more or less known to the ring and to fame.

The crowd soon assembled, and the private boxes, especially, shone resplendent with brilliantly jeweled senoritas, and the most sparkling and brilliant of all the jewels were their jet black eyes, made brighter still by immediate expectation and suppressed excitement.

At precisely 4.30 o'clock, the president, who was the mayor of the town, entered his private box, the band began to play, the men to yell and the women to wave their handkerchiefs and fans. The president gracefully bowed his acknowledgments. Fans seem to be quite as necessary there as they were to the Roman ladies at the gladatorial combats in ancient times.

Everything then being ready. the trumpet sounded. and the whole bull fighting company marched into the ring, glittering in their gorgeous costumes.   How graceful and majestic they looked, these bull fighters, as they passed by in their close fitting suits. trimmed in gold and beads.   As soon as they had passed in front of the president, he threw the key of the toril (the cell of the bull) to a man dressed in black, wearing an enormous black plume in his hat. and mounted upon a spirited Arabian barb horse, that reared and plunged to the great delight of the crowd.   These horses are trained to thus act. and it gives a fine exhibition of graceful horsemanship.   When thrown down, he endeavored to catch the key in his hat. but was prevented by the plunging of his horse.

A curious part of the calvacade was four immense Norman horses harnessed together. wearing plumes on their heads, and used for the purpose of dragging the slain from the field of battle.   The different performers now took their places in the ring, and the door of the toril was thrown open.   The public curiosity to see the first rush out of the bull was intense, as none knew whether he would behave well or ill, and they judge there of his character by the manner in which he behaves upon first entering the ring.

The bull, an immense red one, fresh from the Jarama mountains, then rushed into the ring.   He had long sharp horns like the native breeds in Texas and Mexico. an exceedingly thick neck, raised far above the level of his back, and a defiant look.   Every movement showed great power and activity.   No one who has not seen these bulls, raised in their natural state, high up in the

mountains, can imagine their ferocity. An enraged lion
would not appear more dangerous. They are very expensive, costing the management four or five hundred
dollars each.

On entering, the first object that presented itself being a man, known in ring parlance as a matadore, he
charged him. The man saved himself by dextrously
jumping the wall around the ring. These bull fighters
are all athletes, and can run and jump like those in an
American circus. Other matadores approached waving
their red flags, and the bull charged them but without
result. Soon he espied the mounted picadores. These
are men on horseback, and armed with long poles, in
the ends of which are fixed sharp spears. They wear the
broad brimmed Thessalian hat; their legs are encased in
iron and leather, which give a heavy look, and the right
one, which is usually presented to the bull, is the better
protected.

The bull charged the first one he came to, and the
picadore, holding the lance in the right hand, turned
his horse to the left and received the onslaught of the
bull on the point of his weapon. This did not stop him,
but possibly only added renewed fury, for he buried
his horn completely in the hip of the horse, raising him
from the ground, and pitching horse and rider in a mass
upon the arena. A cloud of dust rose from the imperfectly sprinkled ring, the matadores rushed up waving
their red flags to attract away the bull, while others
hastily pulled the poor picadore from under the horse
and carried him from the ring. "Bravo, bravo toro,"
shouted the multitude, and women and men lost a sense
of existence in the excitement of the moment. The bull

was now charging anything in reach. and the horse that he had just brought to the ground was raised to his feet. a picadore placed upon his back and he was ridden forward again. the blood shooting out in a spurt at every step.   "Isn't this thing terrible?" said Judge Goodpasture. and he began to light his pipe, his universal recourse in case of any unpleasantness.

Again the bull attacked and received a fearful gash in the neck from the picadore, but planting his horns full in the horse, he raised him high off the ground, pitching the picadore over the ring wall and letting the horse fall a dead beast. a vanquished foe, in the ring.   He attacked the next he could reach, and again with his terrific force piled man and beast on the ground.   The rider was assisted from the ring, the horse raised and another rider placed upon his back.   The poor horses were all blindfolded, and when this one was raised and ridden forth to the awful encounter, his entrails were seen to be hanging down almost to the ground.

A large Newfoundland dog, led, we suppose, by bad company down to the ring, and by curiosity into it, making no war upon any one. and intending none, greatly to his surprise. suddenly found himself pitched ten feet into the air.   It was his death warrant.

Other horses were attacked and their riders unhorsed, and soon the scene of battle was indeed a gory one. Dead horses lay about the ring, others had wounds through which the blood gushed or their entrails protruded. and the bull still fought game and looked more defiant than ever.   Here the trumpet sounded, and the first act of the bloody drama was over.

The next act. that of the chulos, is short and interesting. The picadores leave the ring. The sole object of the chulos, as they are termed, is to enrage the bull to the highest pitch. They entered the ring bearing shafts with arrows in the end, and marched directly toward the bull, pointing the shafts at him. These arrows have barbs to prevent their coming out when once stuck. One of the chulos advanced and just as the bull bounded forward and stopped to toss him, he stuck the arrow into his neck and dextrously jumped to one side. These arrows were provided with crackers, which, by means of a detonating powder, explode the moment they are affixed to the neck. The agony of the infuriated animal on this occasion made him bound and jump high in the air, greatly to the delight of the audience. To the bull, it was an ever present, unseen, unattackable foe, and his fury soon knew no bounds.

The trumpets again sounded, the arena was cleared for the third act, and the great espada, the star of the company, the executioner, stood before his combatant. On entering the ring, he addressed the president, threw his cap to the ground, dropped to his knees and swore to do his duty. In his right hand, he held a long straight Toledo blade, and with his left, he waved a red flag. He thus enticed the bull, who charged him, and he quickly jumped aside. He did this again and again, when at last he got him in the desired position. When the bull then jumped forwad to gore him, the sword was buried to the hilt just between the shoulders and near the left one. The sword remained in his body but the bull fought on. Finally the espada succeeded in drawing it out, and buried it again in nearly the same place. The bull coughed once or twice, fell to his knees and then to the ground and immediately expired, the blade having pierced the heart.

How furiously the people cheered then! Hats, cigars, fans, handkerchiefs, and all the property which Wemmick terms portable, was showered into the ring. The bull fighter, the great man of the day, gracefully bowed to the crowd. The four big Norman horses then entered, and commenced the operation of dragging the dead from the field, leaving in their wake one broad track of blood.

Thus ended the first fight, and, as those that followed were but repetitions in the main of the first, we shall not attempt to describe them.

After three bulls had been killed, the fourth and last proved to be one of unusual ferocity and power. He had killed all the horses entered. The mob cried for more; the management refused. The musicians started to leave the place and a row occurred in which walking canes and fists played an important part. At length the mob began to tear up the seats and to throw them into the ring. Quiet and order was restored by a squad of gendarmes armed with drawn Winchester rifles. These gendarmes or civil guards rank higher and have greater powers, than police; will shoot when necessity seems to require it, and will preserve good order at any price. There could be no law or order in Spain without them. France has the same system.

Such were their first observations at a bull ring, which, let critics say what they may, is *the* sight of Spain. Its brutality is undeniable, and its place ought to be with a less civilized people. It was introduced by the Moors, and has withstood the influence of the pious

Isabella, the Catholic, and survived the bulls of the Pope, and may be counted a permanent and fixed sport of the country. One visit is enough to satisfy even the most curious American, whose humanity has been educated more than his cruelty.

The Judge went to one of the numerous balls that night. It was in an immense pavilion, and decorated regardless of all expense and trouble. There were a large number of private boxes, hung with costly curtains and laces, for those who wished to see, but did not care to mix with the multitude or to dance. The crowd was crushing, the dancing attractive; many lovely costumes; the women of course beautiful; plenty of light, good music, and doubtless much love making. It lasted until 4 a.m., when the crowd dispersed, for many had to go to Monday morning's confession at 6.

The Judge, of course, left for the hotel early, and on retiring, tried long and hard to banish from his mind the cruel barbarity of the afternoon's sport.

CHAPTER XVI.

Barcelona. The Judge returned to Barcelona early the next morning, and had nothing to do for two or three days but look about the city. Barcelona is the only really modern town in Spain, broad streets, well built business blocks and handsome residences. It is very ancient, but has undergone a renaissance, and now partakes more of the French than the Spanish in appearance. It had a population at this time of something more than 350,000 souls. A magnificent alameda runs from the bay clear through the city, dividing it into two parts. This and the quay were greatly appreciated by him, because he could always find his way back to the hotel when he came upon either of these two points. He mentions this fact more than once in his letters, and congratulated himself on escaping his Cordova and Malaga experiences.

Some of the streets are models, not only very broad, but lined with three or four rows of sycamore shade trees, and are kept perfectly clean by sprinkling and sweeping.

There is a permanent circus here which gives performances every night, including that of Sunday, general admission being fifteen cents. He attended this one night and enjoyed it. The jokes of the clown were in pantomime to him, but his imagination supplied the deficiency.

He and his son had given out their wash during the morning, and when they returned to their rooms in the evening, one of the hotel clerks, who spoke a little English, came up very gravely, bearing one of their shirts. "What is the matter," said the Judge, "we want it washed." "Yes, yes," said the boy, "but look, it is broken," and pointed to a small rent in the garment. "All right," said the Judge, "go ahead, and have it washed and bring us back the pieces." To this he agreed and retired.

Buying Jacks. They found no jacks in the immediate vicinity of Barcelona, but on going out into the country from twenty to one hundred miles they found the very thing for which they had been so long looking. At Grannollers, they bought a magnificent five year old, 15½ hand jack called Jumbo, which was afterwards sold for $2,000.00, and they secured him at a figure they were never afterwards able to duplicate. They also purchased fine specimens at Vich, at Agua Fria, Gerona and elsewhere. Although this is the home of the Catalonian jack, they rarely found more than three or four at any one place, and were unable to buy, as a rule, more than one or two of sufficient merit to import, from a single owner. They would sometimes find these jacks on the railroad but often they had to take a conveyance and drive some miles into the country. Purchases cannot well be made without two men to assist—an interpreter to talk and a commissioner to find the stock.

They made Barcelona headquarters, at which point they received their mail, and radiated through the surrounding country. The finest jack purchased on this trip was one known there as "The King of Jacks," bought near Vich, and the finest specimen of his race they had seen up to that time. He was a model in form and color, about fifteen hands one inch high. They would have preferred him larger. He had won several prizes in their local shows, and had never been beaten. In this lot were also Paulito, Peacock and Monarch, that became famous afterwards in different states of America.

Majorca. When they had bought about eighteen, the interpreter, Rives, and W. H. Goodpasture, made a flying trip to Majorca, an island in the middle of the Mediterranean, not so much to purchase as to see what was to be had there, as no American importer had ever visited it; and they had long heard vague rumors of their fine mules and jacks. The trip was made by boat from Barcelona, leaving about ten o'clock in the morning and arriving early the next morning in Palma, the capital of the island. On arrival, they stopped at the Fonda La Balear, the leading hotel of the place, which proved to be most excellent and cheap, and located in the center of the city.

Here they met Mazantini, the most successful bull fighter in all Spain. He is an Italian, and differs from other espadas, in that he drives the sword into the head, just behind the frotal bone and penetrates the brain. He had fought in Palma the day before. Everyone looked on him with the greatest admiration—he was the beau ideal of the populace wherever he appeared. This adulation seems to have had some effect, as he modestly told Mr. Goodpasture, after an introduction, that he was the greatest espada who ever entered a bull ring. He makes from fifty to seventy-five thousand dollars each summer season. There are no bull fights in winter.

They employed as commissioner to show them the stock of the island, one Francisco Fortesa, who was afterwards employed by a number of Americans in importing. They drove all over the island, measured and priced jacks, and looked at a most lovely country. The people depend largely on irrigation, but a richer or more fertile spot can scarcely be found in Spain. The export of nuts, principally almonds, is enormous. This delightful nut, hulled and parched with a little salt, is to be found generally on the hotel tables of Europe, while pickled olives are never absent.

There is not very much on the island to attract visitors who are not drawn there by business. The surface of the country, the towns and the people, are nearly identical with those in Catalonia. A great deal of corn is raised but purely as a second crop, wheat or something of that sort being grown on the ground first. The valleys are very pretty, being planted in regular rows of trees such as the almond, orange or olive; and the ground being covered with beans (a very large variety, used for feeding stock entirely), corn or alfalfa, presents a very luxuriant appearance.

The women here, as in Catalonia, are by no means so beautiful as are those around Cordova and Malaga. Those found at the stores, markets and on the streets, wear short sleeves and low necked dresses. This is generally quite becoming. The hair among the peasant women is plaited, hangs down their backs and is universally black, but among the higher classes, it is arranged into a knot on the top of the head, similarly to the styles prevelant in France, and a very handsome way of wearing the hair it is, particularly if there be a heavy suit of it. Like the women of Venice and Andalusia, they wear a good deal of lace on their heads. This fashion ought to be introduced into the United States; no bonnet or hat is half so becoming. They wear the most outrageous shoes, the heel being very high and located near the middle of the foot, and the toe very sharp and narrow. All colors of shoes are worn except black, which are not considered fashionable. The foot of the Spanish woman is her pride, and its smallness is much remarked upon by strangers.

The Judge remained at Grannollers, where it had been arranged to collect the stock. He must have been a bit lonely, as he was unable to speak to a soul in the town. Most of the jacks had been collected, and he spent much of his time in looking at them and seeing them fed. They were a grand lot, far beyond what they had expected to get—all jet black, large, well formed and none older than five years. The Judge repeated over and over again that the collection seemed to him like a dream—that he could scarcely believe it real.

They were quite convenient to him, too. He writes to his wife that they occupy the first floor of his hotel, and that he slept over them every night. That sometimes he would hear them all braying at one time, making good strong music. Those who have heard one jack bray can imagine the effect of eighteen. He likewise never tired of going to the market, and spent much of his time very pleasantly in this way.

To Marseilles. From Grannollers the jacks were shipped to Marseilles, France, from which point they were to be embarked for New York. At Portbon, they stopped to feed, and here each jack was examined carefully by a veterinary surgeon before they were allowed to be shipped out of the country. While here it was discovered that they had failed to make a declaration before the United States consul, at Barcelona, and obtain a permit to ship from him. In this declaration, the age, sex, size and color of animal must be given and where purchased, also price paid, and it must be made before the consul nearest the place of purchase. So the Judge and Rives continued the journey with the stock while W. H. Goodpasture went back to Barcelona for the required papers. On their way to Marseilles, a stop of several hours was made at Cette, France. This is the most important city for the manufacture of wine in France. They buy up the cheaper grades in France and Spain, and by processes known to themselves alone, so treat it as to make it closely imitate different grades and different kinds of wine. It is then labeled the genuine article, and is shipped to wholesale dealers all over the world. Huge casks, fifteen to twenty feet in diameter are to be found here.

The Judge arrived safely at Marseilles, where the stock was unloaded and carried to stables. He had to remain there for some eight or ten days, waiting for the sailing of the vessel on which he had engaged to ship. Having so long to stay, with little to do and an interpreter to show him around and do his talking, he was enabled to see much of a very beautiful city. Rives was brought along, he being, as before mentioned, a Frenchman, and, of course, quite as much at home as in Spain.

Marseilles is the first seaport of France, located on the Gulf of Lyons, and enjoys a large trade in the Levant and Algiers. The latter is by far the most successful of any of the numerous attempts of France at colonization. and her trade is monopolized by this city.

While there. a steamer came in with a large number of African donkeys from Algiers, these diminutive animals being used in the parks for the children to ride, and to draw small market carts on the streets. Judge Goodpasture was greatly taken with them, and the importer offered him the pick of the lot for fifteen dollars. He selected a very beautiful three year old jennet for his young son, Dillard, Jr., who exhibited her the following fall in the State Fair at Nashville. She was shown in the ring of jennets three years old and over, and as a matter of sport, the judges tied one of the prize ribbons on her bridle and awarded her a prize of one dollar (which the Judge paid) to the intense delight of the boy. After keeping her about a year, she was exchanged for a saddle pony, on which he took a real prize at the next fair. and which he afterwards sold for three hundred dollars.

Judge Goodpasture's great facility for getting acquainted has been mentioned before in these pages. It was never better illustrated than on an occasion in this city. He was one day at the jack stable, and observed a man with a pair of Poitou mules. He proceeded to measure them, and was asked by the owner in French if he wished to buy. He replied that he could not speak French, and the owner said that he could speak a little English. whereupon, the Judge at once entered into a conversation with him. and found that he had been. during the war, a cook on one of Amon L. Davis' boats. Davis was an old Tennessean. thoroughly well known to the Judge, and he and the Frenchman were soon the best of friends.

Marseilles is a lovely city, much on the style of Paris, with splendid streets, beautifully shaded, and lined with many magnificent hotels and cafes. Indeed, the latter are scarcely surpassed in any other city of the world. The quays are the most bustling, busy and interesting part of the town, being constantly thronged with crowds of turbaned orientals, as well as Greeks, Italians, English and French, who are engaged in the business of the place. The city trades all over the world, but especially in the East, and the variety of races found on the streets, drawn there by business, is a genuine study.

Opposite the mouth of the harbor, is the curious old Chateau d'If, in which Mirabeau was imprisoned, as well as the Count of Monte Cristo, made so famous in the novel of that name by Dumas. The Judge was greatly interested in it, on account of this novel, having seen James O'Neil play a dramitization of it in a theater at New Orleans.

One of the finest drives and promenades in the world is the Prado here, leading from the city, out several miles, to the bathing beach. It is shaded by eight rows of spreading sycamore trees, all numbered and so trimmed as to be uniform to a remarkable degree. The Judge was out there several times, and greatly enjoyed watching the gayeties of the bathers, but could never be induced to take a plunge. He had never learned to swim.

With visits to the botanical and zoological gardens, among the finest in Europe, the quays, fortifications, cathedrals, drives, parks, etc., the time went swiftly by.

and they soon found themselves and stock loaded on the ship and steaming out of the bay.

Cette. The first stop was made at Cette, France, where several thousand empty wine casks were taken aboard and piled up on the upper deck, until the ship had something of the appearance of a Mississippi steamboat overloaded with cotton. While here the captain gave a dining to his father and friends. Rives was still with them, but left at this point to take the train for Barcelona. One leaving Cette, Judge Goodpasture bade good bye forever to this part of France, with many pleasant recollections of his visit.

Almeria. The next stop was at Denia, Spain, where the ship took on board ten thousand bushels of onions and other freight for New York. Then they went to Valencia, where the cargo of wine casks was discharged, and fruits and raisins taken on. Then they stopped two days at Almeria, Spain. It was Sunday and intensely hot. They could see long lines of pack donkeys, bearing heavy burdens down to the ship landing, driven by the toughest class of people seen in Spain—very dark in color, dressed somewhat differently from those of any other part of the country, and looking more than half savage. From appearance, they must have had more of the Moorish blood than is found in other sections of Andalusia. The town is very rugged, high, steep hills, rising at intervals. Caverns have been dug out of the sides of these hills, in which a considerable population resides. These abodes may be cool, but they present an awful appearance of dirt and squalor.

They next stopped for over a day at Malaga, but no further description of this town is necessary.

Heavy Losses. The jacks had been located between decks in the vessel, and having a large cargo, but little room was given them. They were able to get a fairly abundant supply of air, while the vessel was in motion, and the ventilators properly adjusted, but when lying in port, it was unendurably hot and stifling. In consequence of this intense heat and lack of fresh air, three jacks were lost at Almeria and one at Malaga, the four being easily worth five thousand dollars. Among the number was "The King of Jacks" before mentioned, whose superior they had never seen, and which they thought would be the greatest ever imported to America with the possible exception of old Mammoth. He was worth anywhere from $2,000.00 to $2,500.00.

A rather amusing circumstance happened at Malaga. The steamer was anchored out a half mile from the shore. When the dead jack was reported to the crew, they simply hoisted him and threw him overboard into the sea. That was late in the evening. Early next morning, it was found that he had floated ashore and was beating up against the docks of Malaga with the incoming tide. The boat was informed by the authorities that they would not be allowed to discharge such undesirable cargo on them, and the captain was forced to send in a boat and crew, who hitched up to the jack, and with great labor, rowed him out some miles into the sea. The Judge was feeling sufficiently badly about his losses but was much amused at the circumstance,

Sails for Home. At last they left the Mediterranean and her detestable ports and stops, and as soon as they were fairly out at sea, the jacks immediately revived. They had employed a good man to attend to them. He could speak no English, but was an adept in signs, and they got along with him fairly well. It was a long voyage but an uneventful one. The captain was a tyranical commander but at the same time a jolly man, who enjoyed good wine and good eating. He especially delighted in very old Rochefort cheese, and the older they were and the more skippers they had, the better he liked them. This shocked the Judge, and the captain having observed this, appeared to eat them with more relish than ever. One day, when eating a particularly lively piece of this cheese, as he carried a bit to his mouth, a skipper jumped into one of his eyes, and made it sting and water for some time. The Judge enjoyed this hugely, and expressed the wish that the whole army of them would follow the good example.

At the end of a tedious trip, they landed in Brooklyn. They had never before landed there. As soon as possible they got through the custom house. It is a queer thing that our custom system should be allowed to remain so complicated that one cannot get through his own property, but is forced to employ a commissioner who follows the business, and whose charges are usually exhorbitant. At that time, live stock imported for breeding purposes, and of a new and valuable breed, were allowed to enter free of duty. After being passed through the custom house, they had to be examined by the official live stock examiner. This took a good part of the day.

Brooklyn. With much trouble and intense worry, they succeeded in getting a stable in Brooklyn, until they could make arrangements to ship their stock. The following morning, when they went down to the stable, the proprietor, who had never seen a jack before, informed them that he had no idea that they were such horrible animals, that he had slept none that night on account of their noise, and that his neighbors suffered almost as much; that they must move them that very morning, and that he would help them do so. One can form some idea of their noise, when it is known that Perry & Lester, who erected a jack stable in West Nashville, near the stock yards, were enjoined by the neighbors from keeping them there, on the ground that they were a public nuisance.

They shipped by way of the Lake Erie and Western Railroad, and got home without accident and without special incidents. Captain Hill had erected in their absence commodious jack stables near Cockrill Springs, and he and Mr. Hayes were on hand to receive them. On this trip Judge Goodpasture came through with the jacks. They were six days coming from New York, and he and his son fed, watered and attended to the stock in transit. They shipped in Arms Palace cars and no stops were made, food and water being carried in the car. This was a very severe trip for a man of his age— little sleep, irregular meals and constant exposure to the night air and drafts. But he was never a man to pay attention to any amount of labor or exposure—he had an idea that neither hurt him, and appeared to give no thought to the subject. In fact, up to this time, he had scarcely felt the effect of his years, and believed himself to be able to successfully withstand anything.

CHAPTER XVII.

The jacks were gotten into good shape for the winter and spring trade, an excellent catalogue was printed and distributed and the stock advertised in the principal agricultural papers. The firm had great success in the sales of this importation, together with the gray ones brought over on the previous trip. The last importation were sold at what would now appear high prices, ranging from $800.00 to $2,000.00.

The Judge spent the winter attending to his home affairs and assisting in the care and sale of the jacks. He also argued some important cases in the Supreme Court during the winter. One cause especially interested him—that of Gore vs. Stafford. It had been twice tried in both the Circuit and Chancery Courts, and once by the Courts of Referees, altogether five times, and Stafford had lost at each trial. It was an important case, involving the title to an island. After losing before the Referees, Stafford employed Judge Goodpasture's firm to assist his local attorneys before the Supreme Court. The record was much the largest before the court at that term, containing something like two thousand pages. Stafford gained it, Judge Caldwell who delivered the opinion of the court, being the same judge who had delivered the opinion in the Court of Referees, thus reversing himself and five previous judgments. a most uncommon legal triumph.

By the middle of March, 1887, all of the jacks of both importations were sold but three: one of these being a jack imported by him individually named Paulito and which he afterwards sold for $1,200.00; Alfonso, the best jack of the first importation, and a three year old colt. They made good seasons that year, and holding them over proved a profitable investment.

Third Importation. Having been so successful in the sales of this importation, another was at once resolved upon, and on May 1, 1887, the Judge and his son, and once more "Hon." John Terry, left Nashville for the third importation, and sailed per steamship Chateau Margaux, May 4.

John was not put in the steerage this trip but in the second cabin, where he had plenty of wine at his meals, which he had grown to appreciate very much. His only trouble seemed to be that of having to occupy a cabin with two white men, one of whom was continuously sea-sick. This unsettled John's stomach again, but as the sea-sick man divided his bottle of brandy, he was, in a measure, compensated for other and disagreeable features.

All who have ever been at sea will remember how the water seems to rise like a high rolling hill in the distance. This hill was a matter of much speculation to John, who said he had, all his life, heard old men say that water would seek its level.

The passenger list was small but composed of a queer conglomeration of nationalities, a very few of whom could talk with each other. Among the number was a Frenchman from Hayti, together with his negro wife and two mulatto children, an old Greek, who was unable to talk to anyone on board, two Arabs from Jerusalem, a German Jew and family, three or four Spaniards, several Frenchmen and three Americans. Altogether, there were nine distinct nationalities on board.

The Greek passenger died during the voyage and was buried at sea. The captain conducted the funeral service, delivering a short but serious and appropriate address. It was very affecting to all the passengers, but to one of the Arabs it was almost overwhelming. They were Moslems, and had a horror of being buried by a Christian dog. This Arab was named Jusef, and could speak a few words of English. The Judge soon got acquainted with him. Jusef said he was well fixed at Jerusalem—that he had a wife and two donkeys, and that he made them work for him a plenty.

Bordeaux. They landed in Bordeaux, France, May 17, 1887, after a very smooth, pleasant and uneventful voyage. They at once telegraphed to Barcelona for Rives, and were two days hearing from him. He replied that he was engaged by another importing firm. They then searched for another, and finally found a man, a stevedore, named Paul Carles, who could speak English but had never acted as an interpreter, nor heard of breeding jacks. He and the Judge had an amusing interview. Carles agreed to go with them for ten francs per day and expenses. They desired to start at once. Suddenly Carles turned to the Judge and said: "Sir, do you know my terms?" The Judge replied that he thought it ten fracs per day and expenses. "No sir," said he, "it is, that I require twenty-four hours notice." "Then," said the Judge, "I now give notice that in twenty-four hours we will leave Bordeaux." This was satisfactory, and at the end of that time they left to attend several fairs to be held in southern France.

French Fairs. They visited a number of these, the one at Arles being the best, but found no jacks good enough to import, though they found any number of other kinds of live stock of the best quality. These fairs are not such in our sense of the word, but are more in the nature of huge annual markets, which the whole surrounding country attend, bringing whatever they may have for sale. It is the best of all places to see the varying types of peasants. It is made a general holiday as well as market, several dances being in progress throughout the day, traveling shows and slight of hand performances doing a thriving business, and every one making a big day of it.

On such a day, the leading hotel of the town, at breakfast time (12 m.), is a place worthy of study. The long dining table is continuously crowded. The women rush in with armfuls of bread, three feet long, like they sometimes carry stovewood in this country. A part of this is distributed on the table and the balance stood up in one corner of the room. Two or three barrels of wine stand near with faucets in them, at which two women are kept busy filling bottles for the use of the guests. Many of those who have finished the meal linger at the table to drink one or two more tumblers of wine and smoke a cigarette. By the time they have eaten a hearty breakfast and drunk a quart of wine, each feels in a good humor with the others and as they all talk at the same time, a very babel of noise rises with the volumes of smoke. It is a sight never seen in America.

Leaves for the Pyrenees.

After visiting these fairs and running down a number of false rumors about the location of fine jacks. it was recognized that there was nothing to be had in this part of France. and they left for the mountains, passing through Toulouse and Carcassonne. They reached the end of the railroad, and the foot of the Pyrenees, at a village called Quillan. Here, in looking over a breeder's directory for France. they found that one Ribo. gill. of Porte, in the Cerdan. was a breeder of stallion jacks. They telegraphed him. France being on a war basis. the telegraph lines are not confined to the railroads. but run into the mountains and every part of the republic.

Courtois & Co.

Upon investigation. it was discovered they would have to drive over the mountains in a carriage; that it would take not less than three days, and that there was no bank at Porte from which they could draw money. As they were running short of funds, W. H. Goodpasture was sent back to Carcassonne to draw some. though it was not at all certain that he could get it there. It turned out to be a holiday, and the banks were all closed. Next day. he found that the banks there did not deal in such exchange, it being a rather small place, so he returned to Quillan.

The following day he went to Toulouse, where his letter of credit had a regular correspondent, Messrs. Courtois & Co.. and carried with him his passport as an identification. Toulouse being an interior city and having had little business in this line, they declined to pay a draft on the credit, unless authorized to do so by Brown. Shipley & Co.. of London. on whom the credit was drawn, it having been issued by Brown Bros. & Co., of New York. This placed Mr. Goodpasture in a predicament. He was expected to return to Quillan on the seven o'clock train that evening. The interpreter had been left there with Judge Goodpasture. However, he concluded to wait, much against his will, and gave the bank the money to cable, paying for the answer at the same time, a queer custom that is enforced in France where the message requires an answer; and also gave them a telegram to send Judge Goodpasture, explaining the matter, and luckily taking a receipt for the same. The latter was never sent, and when his son failed to arrive at the expected time, it threw the Judge's party into the greatest consternation. The amount to be drawn was some four thousand dollars, and the Judge jumped to the conclusion that some one had seen him draw the money, had followed, robbed and possibly murdered him. A sleepless night was spent, and when the morning train came in without his son, the uncertainty of the previous evening appeared certain and hope was abandoned. The Judge telegraphed to Bordeaux, Toulouse and Carcassonne, and began making preparations to start out on the sad search by the next train. He had very little money, but the inn keeper at Quillan told him that he need not pay his board bill.

Fortunately, before the train left, he received this telegram in answer to one he had sent: "Drew money this morning, gone—Courtois." This relieved him at once. His son arrived with the money that evening, and was greatly astonished to find that the bank had failed to send his telegram at the time of the cable. He had not been well treated by the bank in other respects. Altogether, the mistreatment was so gross and its consequences so serious, that they thought the firm deserved a lesson that would stay with them as long as they remained in business. They, therefore, wrote them a letter just as strong as they could find language to make it. The matter was fully reported and referred to Brown, Shipley & Co., who, after making a thorough examination into it, and hearing the statement of the bank, promptly removed them as one of their correspondents and substituted a rival bank. No other action was ever taken in the matter.

Drive Over Mountains. It was a long, dreary drive over the mountain from Quillan, a part of the way being over an unfinished road, where it was necessary to walk a good part of the time. Ancient castles crowned the tops of the high mountain peaks, giving a very romantic appearance, and occasionally a wild goat could be seen scrambling along the rocky cliffs. Ice cold water poured down the sides of the mountain, the streams being fed by the melting snow.

They entered a small valley, in which was located a little village, inhabited by the most provincial people they had ever met. The Judge said that undoubtedly no white man had ever put his foot in the place before. Only Americans were white men to the Judge, just as all the outside world were barbarians to the Greeks. By ransacking the town, buying ham at one place, eggs at another and potatoes at a third, they were enabled to have a very good dinner.

While the meal was being prepared, the Judge looked around the village. A horrid old woman, evidently the virago of the place, said something to him, but as

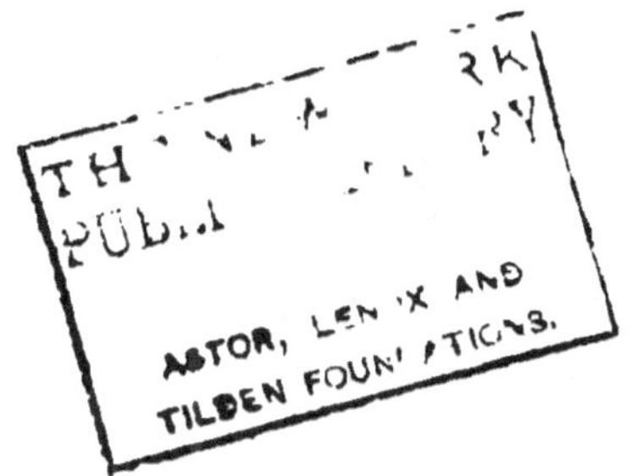

GREAT EASTERN.

he did not understand it. he paid no attention to her. She repeated it louder with a like result. Then she was good and mad, came up to him, and with a loud voice and many gesticulations, gave him several pieces of her mind. The Judge retreated to the place where the dinner was to be served, and where the interpreter had remained. The old woman followed with a number of younger people close in her wake. "Oh," she said, "you can talk and you can hear. but you think yourself too fine a gentleman to speak to me." And thereafter the Judge kept close in until they left.

Before entering the valley of the Cerdan, they spent the night with one J. B. Merlat, at the village of Fourmigueres, an innkeeper and stock commissioner, whom they employed. He proved in all respects the most reliable and competent of any ever engaged.

Great Eastern. They found an abundance of good jacks here. It is on the frontier of France with Bourg-Madame on the French and Puycerda on the Spanish side. Sixteen head were purchased and, both collectively and individually, they were the best lot ever imported to America. Among the number was Great Eastern, a jack that has stood unrivaled for size, general form and excellence. either in Europe or America. He was five years old, sixteen and one-half hands high, short, black hair, long body, unequalled head and ear, large, clean bone, and beauty to a remarkable degree. In fact. he filled the ideal of a perfect jack. He had taken the first prize of a thousand pesetas at the International Jack Show. at Puycerda. and his reputation had extended all over that part of Europe.

While on the subject, it will. perhaps. be in order to

state, that at the request of the executive committee of the American Breeders' Association of Jacks and Jennets, his picture was inserted in the first volume of the Jack Stock Stud Book, as a perfect specimen of the Catalonian breed. After getting him home, the Judge was offered four thousand dollars for him on a guarantee of his complete recovery (he was then suffering from the results of the trip) which he declined. He was certain the jack would recover in his own hands, but feared to risk him with another. There were a number of other very fine animals in the importation, among them a sixteen hand jack that took third prize in the ring at Puycerda being shown against Great Eastern.

John Distinguishes Himself. John succeeded in distinguishing himself on this trip. One day, they were examining a most beautiful specimen of rather small jack. Just as W. H. Goodpasture stepped in front of him for a closer inspection, the jack suddenly jerked loose from his owner and grabbed Mr. Goodpasture by the overcoat, tearing it almost off him, and very nearly jerking him down. Releasing himself, he and the balance of the party, the Judge leading the van, made their escape over a stone fence. This examination was sufficient, and they at once left. As they drove off, the last they saw of the owner, he was after the jack with a pitchfork.

It seems the old farmer had experienced trouble in abundance with him before, and was growing very tired of it. He sold him for a song to a young, strong and risky farmer hard by, who thought the jack had not been properly handled. But after having him a few days and being nearly killed, he grew quite as sick of him as had his previous owner. Hence, he telegraphed Judge Goodpasture to make him an offer for him. The Judge then called John in and told him all about the jack, and asked him if he thought he could conquer him, otherwise he would not want him at any price. John said he certainly could. The Judge telegraphed an offer of three hundred franc—a little less than sixty dollars— if the owner would deliver him at Bourg-Madame and have him shod all around. This was accepted, and one evening in came the jack, led by two men. He had on a big heavy bridle with a rope in either ring. Each man walked at his side and held one of the ropes, making it impossible for the jack to jump at either because he would be held by the other. In addition, he had a rounding steel band with double rows of teeth, fitted over his nose to hold him back.

He was brought up in front of the hotel and John went out to get him. Now, John is six feet one, has unusually long, muscular fingers, with no surplus flesh whatever, and is a most powerful man. While the two men held him, he went out and secured a firm hold on the jack's lower jaw, his fingers meeting inside the mouth. Then, to the amazement of the Frenchmen, he asked that the bridle be taken off. They had to be told to do so a second time. As soon as this was done, the jack began to rear and plunge and try to strike John with his fore feet, but as he did so, John, by a quick wrench, threw him to the ground. The jack bounced up like a rubber ball, at once renewed the fight and was again thrown. By this time, John was gripping his mouth so tightly that blood was spurting from numerous places in his lips. The Judge called out to

John to kill or conquer him. To shorten the story, it is only necessary to add, that John so thoroughly subdued him that he followed him without bridle or halter into the stable. The Judge presented him with a new suit of clothes, and as long as he remained there, he was the biggest man in Bourg-Madame. The jack was never afterwards any trouble to them, but thoroughly docile and obedient. He was sold to a Texan for $750.00, but when spring came, his old viciousness reappeared, and having no one who could re-conquer him, he was turned out with the horses on the ranch, to run at large.

The March Across The Mountains. They finished buying June 17, and started for Tarascon, the nearest railway station, at four o'clock on the morning of the 18th. The distance from Bourg-Madame to the railroad is forty-two miles, over the Pyrenees. The jacks had to be led, and a man was employed for each. Their excellent commissioner, Monsieur Merlat, engaged these, and saw to their getting off early, so as to go the day's journey before the sun became too hot. They were given a dollar per day, and fed and housed themselves on the trip.

It looked like a little army as they passed out of the town that bright June morning, all the jacks braying and the men singing and shouting rough badinage to each other. The Judge insisted on leading a jack himself. They went in single file. It was a jolly procession and attracted great attention. They would sometimes pass by women working in the fields. This was always a great time for the men to get off their jokes. And sometimes these were rough beyond anything permitted in this country. It was all taken, however, in good part, and the women would usually parry them quite successfully.

The first day they went fifteen miles to Porte, at the foot of the steepest part of the road up the Pyrenees. From this village they could look up and see the snow covering the entire mountain top. Here the men chipped in and bought bread, wine and dried beef from which they made a hearty breakfast. They slept in the hay that night.

The Judge and son went to the Delmonico's of the place, a house composed of a stable underneath, and a small place of entertainment above. One of the daughters of the house was a plain but extremely good natured woman of about forty years of age. She was very solicitous of pleasing and making them comfortable. The Judge seemed to think of no way of compensating her for such kind attention except by letting it out through the interpreter that she was the best looking woman he had seen in France, and a few other like compliments. This gratified her immensely, and she redoubled her efforts to entertain them—slew a kid, killed her fattest chicken and feasted them to all the good things on the place.

In going over the mountains next day, they stopped for a few moment's rest, as they did quite often in going up very long and steep climbs. Here the Judge's jack stepped over the guttering of the road bed onto a slightly elevated bank, not more than eight inches high, to graze. When ready to start, the jack refused to come down. The Judge pulled and persuaded, but for some time in vain. Finally, the jack reared as though going to jump a high fence and gave a fearful leap, landing in the middle of the road and almost jumping over the top of the Judge's head, who was the very picture of amazement and surprise.

After three days of tedious travel, they arrived at Tarascon, where they proposed to rest for a couple of days, with all the jacks except Great Eastern, he having become somewhat lame. They had instructed his leader to take no risks of injuring him if he was a week in coming or even more. Here one of their largest and fattest jacks died from having been traveled too hard in crossing the mountain. Great Eastern not arriving, they made arrangements to have him cared for, and decided not to ship him in this importation but to send back for him after his perfect recovery.

They shipped to Bordeaux via Toulouse, and sailed from there with fourteen head, landing safely in Nashville with the entire number.

The Voyage To New York. They had a lot of good company and a jolly time on board coming home. Capt. C. C. H. Burton and Frank Lester were on board with a most excellent importation —one among the best ever brought over; also Mr. A. B. Murray and Mr. Rutherford, with an importation large in numbers, rather undersized but containing some very handsome animals. All these people were well known to them and were appreciated companions.

On these French boats, breakfast is not served until eleven o'clock and frequently later, and as they were generally up early and expected to be busy with the stock, this feature of the trip did not look very pleasing. Fortunately, in going down the Geronne, Bordeaux being eighty miles up the river from the Bay of Biscay, they stopped to take on some freight at a small town called Paullac, famous for its claret wines. Here two of the party went ashore on a boat, the steamer being anchored in mid stream, and bought two hundred and fifty eggs, a fine ham, onions, lemons and a freshly cooked hog's head for the benefit of the Judge, who esteemed it a dish of especial delicacy. On board, they soon made a bargain with the chief cook to furnish them with bread and hot coffee, and to cook the ham and eggs. These they had for a seven o'clock breakfast every morning during the voyage, and no man was ever heard to complain of the lack of variety.

One of the passengers was a Frenchman who had lived for a time in the State of Missouri and could speak English. He was very talkative, very irascible, and an utter stranger to the meaning of a joke. He was above sixty years of age and felt privileged. His little weaknesses and eccentricities soon became apparent. His name was Crossa. After getting fairly settled down and started, the Judge one morning said: "Mr. Cross-eye, this is a very fine morning." The old fellow looked at him rather hard but answered that it was. The next day at breakfast, the Judge said, "Mr. Cork-eye, how long do you expect to remain in America?" Mr. Crossa looked at him harder than ever and was silent for a time, but finally made some sort of reply. But on the third day the climax was reached. The Judge asked: "Will you kindly pass me the bread, Mr. Cock-eye?" Then the old fellow jumped up from the table in the greatest rage, and it was with some difficulty that he was restrained.

All was quiet after this until one day Mr. Crossa

spoke of having once lived in America; that he was in "Mizzuri" for about eight years. And the Judge, with great gravity, told him that if he had lived in misery for that length of time, no one could well blame him for going back to France. This came near precipitating the whole trouble over again.

Crossa was very fond of wine, as are all Frenchmen, and stated that he would rather do without bread at his meals than wine. So at dinner that day, Frank Lester started the matter by giving the balance of the crowd the wink and pouring out a full tumbler of wine; all the others followed suit, drank it and refilled, and before the old fellow could well get started on his meal, all the wine was gone. He ordered the waiter to go for more. The waiter disappeared and returned with the information that all had been served that was given out for the meal. And the old Frenchman said he would as soon dine with a set of hogs as with such a lot of Americans.

They arrived home the last of July. In transit from New York, the jacks grew so tired and sleepy from incessant travel and constant standing on their feet, that they began to fall and had to be stopped and rested at Cincinnati, from which point the Judge came home on a passenger train. All were gotten to Nashville in good condition and placed in the old sales stable of Hill & Goodpasture. The partnership with Mr. Hill ended with the second importation.

CHAPTER XVIII.

After resting for only a few days, W. H. Goodpasture, carrying John with him, returned for Great Eastern. On arrival in the Cerdan, he offered a reward of one thousand pesetas to any one who would find him a jack of equal merit. No one ever claimed the reward. Mr. Goodpasture purchased seven more jacks and a French coach horse, and in September, arrived safely home with them all, including Great Eastern.

A very quick trip had been made in order, if possible, to get back in time to show Great Eastern in the State Fair. The jack arrived in Nashville only two days before the meeting and was too much affected by the trip to be exhibited. But he was shown in the stables to large and admiring throngs of stock men.

A most excellent cut of him from a sketch by the artist A. C. Webb, was soon afterward made for illustration in the stock papers of the country. This was stated by a member of the Farmers' Home Journal Company, of Louisville, to be the first illustration of a jack ever to appear in a paper, which is, without doubt, true. There were few people who believed it to be a correct representation of the animal. The cut was made by the Methodist Publishing House, who sold a copy of it to a local printer, who intended to use it as a cut in his jack bills. A lawsuit resulted, the court holding that the picture, unless copyrighted, belonged to the public.

This stock was also sold easily and at good prices, except Great Eastern, who was farmed to a breeder for the season, where he contracted lung fever and died. The winter and spring was passed in caring for and selling this stock.

New Partnerships. The following summer, the firm formed a partnership for an importation with Lyles and Parmer. former importers, and W. O. Parmer and W. H. Goodpasture went for the stock.

A Visit To Mexico. Judge Goodpasture concluded to rest that summer, and he and wife took a pleasure trip to Mexico. They left about the middle of June. 1888, and made their first stop at St. Louis, examining all the important points of interest. Among the things seen particularly entertaining to the Judge, was the cyclorama of the battle of Missionary Ridge, where he recognized the pictures of Governor Porter. General Cheatham and others.

It was during the memorable Cleveland and Thurman campaign. Now, like the old Roman. he himself was accustomed to carry a red bandanna. Mrs. Goodpasture, having shipped her shawl in her trunk, he loaned her his bandanna to protect her head from the drafts on the train from St. Louis to Kansas City. Every one on the train recognized the sign, and some were heard to remark that there sits a good Democrat.

They stopped a day and night in Kansas City, long enough to see all there was to be seen. The town is too new to have much to attract visitors, unless it be streets graded down a hundred feet below the houses and which cannot be reached by their occupants. They next visited Las Vegas. where they spent a night. and the next day went to the Hot Springs. Here they made the entire ascent of the mountain. which grew a little tiresome to the Judge, but they were rewarded by a fine view. They were especially pleased with Las Vegas and the springs, and enjoyed their stay there very much.

They stopped for two days at El Passo, where they were delighted to meet Mr. A. G. Hodge and wife, with whom they stopped. These were old friends who had boarded at the Judge's for two or three years. and had been great favorites with the family. Their stay was most agreeable, and every attention was shown them. Here they first learned of the Mexican flood, and that the trains had been stopped for some time on account of it. They left on the second train that went out over the road, and had to stop altogether at night. and often in day time they would have to wait until an employee walked in front of the train to see if the track was in condition to be passed over.

At Leone, where the flood seems to have been the worst. they were forced to stop an entire day. This is a large town, and they found the people sleeping in the parks in the greatest destitution, the town being submerged in water. A large number of people were searching the rivers for the dead.

They arrived at Mexico City in the night. On the way down, they had become acquainted with two sisters of charity. On alighting at the depot, no carriages were to be had, all being engaged. They were relieved from this unpleasant predicament by the sisters, who kindly offered them seats in their carriage and had them driven to the hotel Iturbide, at which they stopped.

Here they met Major Foster, a Tennessean, who showed them many courtesies. They also met Mr. Bowling and wife of Bowling Green, Kentucky, a place not more than sixty miles from their own home.

They at once devoted themselves assiduously to seeing the sights of the town, examining the great aqueducts built by Cortez, seeing the place where Maximilian was shot, the private burying grounds of the city, and the monument of Juarez. This monument the Judge thought one of the finest and handsomest he had ever seen. They went to Guadalupe and saw a natural soda fountain boiling up from the ground, the shrine of "My Lady of Guadalupe" and the cathedral. Near here, they saw the tomb of Santa Anna, a very plain and unassuming one, and such as would indicate that his countrymen were not very proud of his memory. They brought home some flowers from his grave. Before returning to the city they ate a regular Mexican dinner.

Through an introduction by Major Foster, they were allowed to visit the military school, where they were treated with much consideration and shown everything. When they entered a class room, the professor and all the students would stand until they left. They went to Chepultepec, from which point they could see the smoke rising from the volcano Popocatapetl. They were much struck by the street railway system, the lines having first, second and third class cars, and a baggage car for freight. The conductors use horns instead of bells for stopping them.

They visited the American legation and were well received, being invited to the Fourth of July ball, which they did not find convenient to attend. They were

much impressed with many of the Mexican public buildings, and especially by the Senate building on the
square. They attended a Sunday entertainment given
on behalf of the flood sufferers. It was given in the
building erected by the government at the New Orleans
Exposition. The music was magnificent, and a great
many of the best people were there in very handsome
costumes. They also saw what is a beautiful sight in all
countries and is appreciated by all classes, a grand military review.

They spent a week in the Mexican capital, and during
the entire time the weather was cool and delightful. It
rained nearly every day, but only in showers and interfered little with sight seeing. They returned to the
United States via El Paso. Along the road they bought
baskets of delicious strawberries, and were informed
that they were to be had every day in the year, but would
not bear shipment.

Nothing in the country seemed to so much impress
the Judge as the plowing in the fields by the natives.
He had been a famous plower himself in his boyhood
days, and always prided himself on his ability to run a
straight furrow; but these Mexicans could surpass anyone at it he had ever seen; not one, but all, seemed to
do so.

At El Paso they changed their return route and went
to Los Angeles where they stopped for two days, seeing
the noted ostrich farm, visiting the town's watering
place, and watching the surf bathing. The Judge was
much impressed by the many improvements noted, and
the general air of prosperity. Among other things, they
have built one of the finest drives in the country. From

here they went to San Francisco, where they remained eight days, stopping at the Palace Hotel, at that time the largest in the United States. They went to the ship building yards, and saw the warship, Alabama, launched. They ran out and spent a day at Oakland, a beautiful suburban town, one afternoon at San Rafael and an evening at the Golden Gate. In the city, they visited Sutro Heights, which they thought the prettiest place yet visited. These lovely gardens and grounds are really private and filled with fine residences but the public are kindly allowed to enter and admire them.

Of course they went to Chinatown—no visit to San Francisco is complete without it. Their visit was much facilitated by a letter of introduction from a Chinese merchant which gave them an entrance into places not open to the public. They examined the Joss House, and at night, the Judge visited the Chinese theater.

Leaving San Francisco, they next stopped for a couple of days at Salt Lake City, where they were in time to see the celebration of the landing of the pioneer fathers in the Utah Valley. There were speeches by Cannon and others, and one of the widows of Brigham Young occupied a seat on the platform. They visited the celebrated Beehive, one of Brigham Young's numerous mansions, his grave, the tithing house and the great temple, not yet complete, but a most magnificent building. They had been at work on it for more than twenty years. They were at Garfield Beach and saw the multitudes bathing in the lake.

They next visited Colorado Springs, Golden Gate Park and Manitou Springs. Near here Senator Palmer has his summer home. They were at Denver for a day, spending the time driving over the city. It is a handsome and well built town, but contains nothing of especial interest.

There were few things to disappoint them on the tour, the general trip being a most agreeable surprise. But a few were so to the Judge, and among these was the noble red man of the West. Instead of finding the man of splendid carriage and fine physique which he expected, he pronounced them the lowest order of human beings he had ever seen. All were dirty and filthy, all looked half starved and all seemed to be beggars. And if it were possible to be so, the women looked worse than the men, illshapen, undeveloped and almost naked.

The Garden of the Gods was also disappointing. They had passed through the grand canons and other scenery that was so much superior, that the place looked tame and insipid. Taken as a whole, however, he pronounced it the greatest and pleasantest trip he had ever made.

During the absence of W. H. Goodpasture in the early summer, Judge Goodpasture had purchased a lot just to the rear of the fair grounds, on which he erected an excellent stable and feed store, and in which he exercised his talent for practical economy, purchasing the lumber in person and superintending the erection of the buildings. On his return from Mexico, a part of the importation was put in the new stables. Among the number in the last lot brought over, was a half sister to Great Eastern; a fine three year old, which was afterwards sold for a thousand dollars, a good price for a jennet, and especially so for an untried one

Leave for Importation of Horses. The French coach horse that had been imported had attracted a great deal of favorable attention and a half interest in him was sold for $750.00, the horse having cost in France $300.00 in round numbers. This led the Judge to think there might be money in well selected coach horses. As Messrs. Lyles and Parmer, partners, could attend to the jacks in his absence, he determined upon the importation of a small number of English Cleveland bays, and he and W. II. Goodpasture left for England the latter part of August, 1888.

On arriving at New York, they had the opportunity of attending the grand ovation tendered Senator Thurman, then the Democratic nominee for Vice President, at Madison Square Garden. There were full twenty thousand lusty Democrats present, packing the great building and all seemed to be yelling and waiving red bandannas. The old Roman was so feeble as to be able to speak only a few words, inaudible to most of the crowd but was followed by Governor Flower, whose voice rang clear and strong to the limits of the vast crowd. Several other Democrats of national reputation spoke. It was the biggest political gathering the Judge had ever seen.

Glasgow. From New York they sailed on the Anchor Line steamer, Furnessia, for Glasgow, Scotland, and landed on September 18, in Glasgow. They at once began an investigation into the horse business, visiting the stables of David Riddle, one of the best known of all the Scotch breeders, being the owner of the Prince of Wales, perhaps the greatest Clyde sire at that time in Scotland. After examining what

Mr. Riddle had in the city, they, in company with his son, visited several breeding establishments in the country, but purchased nothing. returning to the city.

The Glasgow exposition was still in progress. which they went to see. It was quite elaborate and contained many interesting things.

On the streets of the city. they were much entertained at seeing the costumes of the Highlanders and were astonished that such a dress could survive so long. They took the train, after a stay of two days, for London. going by way of Edinburg. York and other cities, and in passing through the former could see some of the fine monuments-and castles. This train was the fastest on which they had ever ridden. The distance from Glasgow to London is four hundred and fifty miles. This they made in nine hours. including stops. The schedule during the hunting season is eight hours.

London and Its Attractions. On arriving in London, they went to their former stopping place with Mrs. Dysart. They had not yet discovered where to go to find the horses desired. and determined to stay some days in London informing themselves.

The city had many very attractive things to be seen just at this time. Among others which they attended was an evening performance at the Irish Exhibition. There was a perfect little Irish village. with a herd of Kerry cows, the smallest cattle in existence, and the villagers showed how they carried on their dairying. the linen industry and many other things. There was a historically correct representation of Blarney and Drogheda castles. A company of Irish cavalry gave a fine exhibition of riding and field sports. Dividing themselves into two companies, they put on wooden helmets with long plumes in them, and armed themselves with stout sticks. At a given signal, each charged the other and tried to knock out the plumes from the helmets, and it looked like they would knock each others heads off in the undertaking. Later, as infantry, they stormed and took Drogheda castle, one of the most realistic fights imaginable.

They also went to the French exhibition one evening. In addition to a splendid display of the products of France and her colonies, there was given a fine exhibition of the French soldier in the field, camp life, etc., and of their campaigns in Africa and Egypt. Besides the large company of French soldiers, mounted on excellent horses, there was a large company of Arabs, commanded by a native Sheik. They rode pure bred Arabian horses, which was in itself a most entertaining sight. These gave an exhibition of life on the plains and desert, their modes of worship and government, their games, and, finally, in a marauding expedition, captured and carried off a caravan crossing the desert.

Like all visitors to London, they made it a point to visit Madame Taussaud's. It is the best display of wax figures in Europe. They entered a long hall filled with life like counterfeits of all the notable people about whom there was a public curiosity, and leisurely examined them in passing down. Suddenly Judge Goodpasture stopped and pointed some distance down the hall to the solitary figure of a man standing with his back to them. The Judge said that, looking at the man's back and from his position, it looked exactly like Andrew Johnson. They strolled on down, and when they reached the figure, sure enough it was Johnson, and so perfect that the Judge felt like shaking hands with him. If there were any other Americans to be seen they are not now recalled.

In making inquiries in the city, they discovered a breeders' directory for the kingdom, and found the exact information desired, the names of the breeders of various kinds of horses and their addresses. In this directory, they were astonished to find that England had a jack breeder, Mr. C. L. Sutherland, and that he lived only a few miles out of the city in the county of Kent. Not discovering how to reach him by rail, they took a carriage and drove through what is considered one of the prettiest parts of England. They arrived about eleven o'clock in the morning, and found Mr. Sutherland still in bed, but he got up and treated them with great hospitality. He had the Maltese and Catalonian breeds of jacks, an excellent specimen of the latter, but asked a price for him altogether beyond reason. He had formerly owned a fine Poitou, but had sold him at auction in France for more than a thousand dollars. He had them to dismiss their carriage and remain to dine with him. After dinner, they walked over to the home of Mr. Darwin, the scientist, where his widow still lived. The lawn, in front of a fine old English country mansion, is covered with large oaks, and around it is a circular path made by Mr. Darwin in walking the lawn in his long periods of meditation. He seemed to have been a sort of Socrates in this respect, and it has made a profound impression on his neighbors.

They returned to London by rail, and that evening attended a performance at the Crystal Palace. a place where every visitor does or ought to go.   Here the lighting was beyond anything they had ever imagined.   The place is several miles out from the city, and in going on the train the Judge unfortunately got a cinder in one of his eyes that gave him great trouble and a poor opportunity to enjoy the brilliant scene.   The lights on the grounds were of every color and seemed to be numberless.   A great castle was made of these, an immense birdge, a music stand, and the walks, lined on both sides with thousands of lights. wound their way through the shrubs and flowers.   There was splendid music and the performance wound up with a grand ballet.   They left immediately after, and happened to get into a car occupied by a large number of those who had taken part in the dance.   They were surprised to see how beautiful and fairy like they were on the stage, and how ignorant and common place they appeared off it.

Next day they went out about forty miles to see Mr. Palmer's herd of prize winning short horns. and horses. Mr. Palmer is very wealthy and lives in the city, but they were well received by his manager and shown everything on the place.   They arrived after dinner, but as hungry as two wolves.   However. they were invited to lunch, and were set down to a leg of cold mutton, and cider, equal, it appeared to them. to the best champagne. They had never seen any in America like it.   How the Judge did bemoan the fates that day, that denied him the privilege of eating mutton, particularly as he sat by and saw his son eat it ravenously and actually appear to enjoy the performance.

Purchases. The following day they left for York, the very heart of the Cleveland Bay breeding district. They examined a large number of Yorkshire Bays as well as Clevelands, the former having an infusion of the thoroughbred blood, but they determined to adhere to their original intention and buy only the pure breed. They purchased a number of fine young horses around North Allerton, an excellent one at Stamford Bridge, and the best horse of the importation from Mr. Baker, of Ingmanthorpe Grange, called Ingmanthorpe Boy, No. 846. These horses were registered in the English Cleveland Bay stud book.

They ran up to Manchester and had a look at that large manufacturing city, and that night saw a performance at the theater by Mr. and Mrs. Kendall, who afterwards created such a furore in America. They then went out to the fair at Altringham, where they had been invited by Mr. John Kirby, from whom they had made a purchase, and who was to be one of the judges in the light harness ring. Here they purchased a three year old Clyde-shire horse, of great size and beauty, of Mr. John Brown, a tenant on the lower farm of Lord Egerton. They had not intended the purchase of any large horses, but when they thought of the sensation he would create, could not resist the temptation. They also secured an Exmoor pony that was afterwards sold to A. V. Goodpasture, and from which he has raised quite a herd. Before leaving Yorkshire, they visited the well known Booth farm of short horns.

They had the stock collected at Liverpool. While waiting for the sailing of the boat, they attended a performance at the Princess theater by Miss Mary Anderson, in "A Winter's Tale." This was one of her last appearances. She came to the United States soon afterwards for a tour but was taken sick and returned to England where she soon afterwards married and retired from the stage.

They shipped on the steamer Oranmore for Baltimore, where they landed without accident or loss of stock. After resting a few days they shipped to Nashville, Judge Goodpasture accompanying the stock on the train and aiding in their care. They arrived home the latter part of October, 1888.

CHAPTER XIX.

The following winter was pleasantly spent attending to the stock and making sales. The Judge had built a nice double office near the stable, where they had big fires, entertained numerous visitors and attended to a very voluminous correspondence, extending all over the United States and Southern Europe. Inquiries for jacks came in from every section of the country from Vermont to California, and scarcely a day passed, except Sunday, when they did not have visitors to see the stock.

In the early spring, they closed out the jack partnership with Lyles and Parmer, and prepared to make the largest importation of jacks ever yet made to America. Preparations were completed, and on May 4, 1889, the Judge and son sailed on the French steamer Bourgoyne for Havre. It was the year of the Paris International Exposition, and Judge Goodpasture had been appointed a commissioner to it.

There was a full complement of passengers on board —quite a crowd of Mexicans, all nice men, a number of negroes from Hayti and several South Americans. A negro woman of the party had a maid with her, who gave the most assiduous attention to her mistress, who was sea-sick most of the time. One woman of unknown nationality, who sat just opposite to them at the dining table, had such a heavy beard that she shaved every morning.

They did not stop at Havre, but went directly to Paris, stopping this time at the St. James Hotel on the rue St. Honore. On account of the great crowds coming to the exposition, they found hotel rates about double what they had previously been.

One of the first places visited was the exposition, the greatest ever held up to that time, and, in many departments, unexcelled since. They were particularly pleased with the beautiful architecture of the buildings, and greatly admired the Eifel tower. It is admitedly one of the greatest pieces of engineering of the time. It was gratifying to note that the elevators were put in by an American firm. The villages of the different nationalities were very curious. Those who filled the African looked as familiar to the Judge as the occupants of a Southern cotton field. At night, they visited a Spanish circus performing in the city. It was unlike anything seen before, and was one of the most enjoyable entertainments ever witnessed in Europe.

From Paris they took the train direct for Bordeaux. On arrival, they found that other importers had gotten the interpreter Carles, and they had to search for another. They succeeded in getting an English speaking clerk out of the office of Th. Columbier & Co., ship brokers, a young fellow of abundant education but little else to recommend him.

Some Good Luck. They hardly knew where to go. Catalonia and the Cerdan were both overrun with importers, and they did not desire to meet the competition. Leaving the baggage at Bordeaux, they concluded to investigate an unexplored part of the French Pyrenees, and took a train to a point near Tarbes. On the train a gentleman informed them that if they would get off at Lannemezan he was sure they could find what was wanted. They got off but found no jacks, and were advised to go to a certain town about twenty miles from the railroad. They went and were again disappointed. They returned to Lannemezan, intending to take the train for Bordeaux and then for Barcelona. But their innkeeper insisted on their at least going to Trie before leaving, where he was certain there were a few good jacks. They went but with little hope. Here, to their surprise, they entered a section never before visited by an American importer, and, after a little investigation, found a large number of fine jacks. Most of them were of the Catalonian breed, though they bought a sixteen hand Majorca and two Poitous. For the first time they bought jennets as well as jacks. The price of these was very low and the quality good. They left home prepared to purchase the largest importation ever brought over, but their plans were yet enlarged by the opportunities presented.

Go to Poitou. After buying all desired in that section, they returned to Bordeaux and drew four thousand dollars by telegraph from their Nashville bank, which was in addition to the amount of their letter of credit. They then went to Poitou, principally to the provinces of La Vendee and Deux-Sevres, and were a good deal around the towns of Poiters and Niort. They were greatly astonished at the appearance of this race of jacks, none of which had ever been introduced into America. Prices were likewise astonishing. They sold here for about as much as do the Spanish in

America, but their mules showed such great superiority over those of all other breeds, that they determined to import some at any cost. Their previous desire to get some of these jacks was greatly intensified by a visit to the chateau and great farm of the Count of Exea. He had two rarely good specimens of the Poitou jack, and about one hundred and fifty Poitou mules, one and two years old. The Count, who lived right among the Spanish breeds, told them that the progressive mule breeder in this day of low prices and close competition, could afford to keep and feed no other than the Poitou and make anything. The mules would sell in the open market for almost a third more than the others.

They found the French breeders greatly in advance of their own, that they had long maintained a stud book (limited to the Poitou breed) and published a monthly, with a large circulation, in the interest of mules and jacks. Besides, an excellent book had been gotten out on the subject.

Judge Goodpasture made a large purchase of Poitous, both jacks and jennets, principally of M. Roy Phillippe and M. Sago, the latter being an officer of the stud book organization, and the gentleman who had reared the two great jacks they had seen at the Count of Exea's. They purchased, in order to advertise the breed and to give a proper appreciation of it, the finest and highest priced jack found in all Poitou. He was a two year old, 15½ hands high, and a body and bone that dwarfed the ordinary jack stock. The bones of all Poitous are enormous in size, and the hair so long that they look like wild animals.

After the completion of these purchases, they returned to the Pyrenees for those bought there, and collected them at Lannemezan, the nearest railroad station. The stock occupied several cars, and by a special dispensation, they were allowed to go on the train with the jacks. They arrived at Bordeaux a little after daylight. The city lies on both sides of the Geronne—about 35,000 on one side and 250,000 people on the other. When they alighted from the train, the Judge could not tell on which side of the river they had stopped, and asked the interpreter, Mr. Duthil. "On zees side, saire," was the reply. "All right," said the Judge, "I was afraid we were on the other."

Toulouse. As they came through Toulouse they were delayed for several hours, which they put in doing the town, though they had been there more than once before. The Judge took an interest in going to the market where horse flesh is sold and examining the steaks, cuts and roasts. He said it looked rather good—a great deal better than mutton, and he thought it more civilized to eat it. His animosity was kept constantly alive on the mutton question, because it is found on the tables of France and Spain oftener than any other meat except chicken. From the market they went to the place where the horses are slaughtered. Here such an infirmary of old cripples and broken down hacks were collected as no man ever saw outside of a horse eating country. All sorts of unfortunate horses were there, a good many mules and a few small jacks. The Judge thought they ought to be made to kill better stock or stop the trade. There is no attempt at imposition in the sale of this meat: it is sold strictly as horse meat. While passing through the city, a good many chickens were seen running at large on one of the back streets. The Judge remarked to Duthil that in his country they would be stolen, and asked why it happened that this did not occur here. "Because, sir," was the reply, "in France it is against the law to steal." But the Judge paid him in his own coin at Havre.

Ship Home. On arriving with the stock at Bordeaux, W. H. Goodpasture went to Poitou and collected those there, and brought them to Bordeaux. They now had fifty-two head. They were unable to ship from this port again, and arranged for the Persian Monarch to call for them at Havre on her voyage from London to New York. They shipped by rail from Bordeaux to Havre. They were gratified to find that Messrs. Kniffin and White, of Danville, Ill., had purchased a few jacks in Majorca and had arranged to ship on the same boat. They had run short of funds, and the Judge proposed to loan them some, although he had never met them before. Duthil took him to one side and advised him not to do it. He said: "You do not know these men and how do you know you will not lose your money?" "Because," replied the Judge, "these are not Frenchmen, but Americans." And Toulouse was revenged.

In the hotel at which the Judge stopped, he saw a large advertisement of the furniture dealer, M. Bonpasteur. The English translation of this name is Goodpasture. He had previously seen a Bonpasteur street in Calais. These were the only times he had ever seen or heard of the name, outside of his own kindred in America.

When the boat arrived at Havre, they led the jacks down to the steamer, and arranged with the proprietor of the stable the stock had just occupied to haul down the extra halters, blankets and buckets. But they never came; he thought it more profitable to steal them than be paid for their hauling.

On the voyage they had much bad luck. They lost by death many of the Poitous, including the great two year old. He had such a fine coat of hair, long and silky, that the captain had him skinned in order to make a robe of his hide. The next best of the lot was a yearling which also died. The losses, altogether, amounted to several thousand dollars. They had few mishaps with the Catalonians, losing an excellent one, however, at Salamanca, New York. Notwithstanding all this, they landed in Nashville with the largest and most expensive importation ever brought over. It represented a greater investment than any importation before or since that time, and reached high water mark in the business. When gotten home and stabled, they, with the horses and other jacks on hand, gave them a stable of above fifty thousand dollars worth of breeding stock for sale, assuming proportions never before approached by anyone in the jack business.

This was the last importation made by Judge Goodpasture personally, though W. H. Goodpasture, in August, 1890, made an importation for the firm of twenty-one head, ten jacks and eleven jennets. The McKinley tariff bill having been passed during his absence, he had to pay a duty on landing them. This duty was a severe one, amounting to thirty dollars per capita and twenty per cent ad valorem.

The firm, in the meantime, had made the largest sale to Missuori parties ever made in a single transaction, amounting to over eleven thousand dollars. The business carried the Judge much over the country—to Kentucky, Missouri and elsewhere. He made no trips further West than Kansas City, though he sent several jacks by other parties to Texas, consisting mainly of the less valuable animals.

Results of the Business. The results of Judge Goodpasture's embarkation in the importation of live stock was far-reaching in its effect. Indeed, it may be truly said, that no man in the South has ever accomplished more. At the time he entered the business, less was known of the different breeds of jacks and jennets than of any other character of live stock. This may be said to be true, even in those sections in which they were best known, while in many parts of the country, there was absolute ignorance on the subject.

Judge Goodpasture was himself wholly unacquainted with the different breeds when he began the importation business. It is a matter of the utmost importance that the jack breeding sections be made familiar with all the different races, because there is a vast difference between them, not only in appearance and color, but also in their value as adapted to our country. At the time the Judge entered the business, but two classes of imported jacks were commonly known to breeders, comprehended in the broad terms Spanish and Maltese, although in Spain there are three distinct breeds, differing as widely in appearance and characteristics as do any of the varieties of horses or cattle. There was much reason for this

popular ignorance. Although the mule and jack are
among our most ancient domestic animals, the latter
antedating possibly the horse, and certainly our Christian civilization, and notwithstanding the fact that the
jack is the highest priced domestic animal known to
man, still the field was absolutely barren as to literature. There is no good reason known for this, but its
effect was inevitable. Even the agricultural press paid
little attention to him.

15

CHAPTER XX.

The first importation made by Judge Goodpasture came from the Southern provinces of Spain, and were of the breed known as the Andalusian. In Tennessee, breeders had experimented some with them, those first introduced having reached us through either Virginia or Kentucky. The king of Spain, in 1787, presented to General Washington a jack and jennet of this breed, the former being called the Royal Gift. About the same time, he was presented with a Maltese jack by the Marquis Lafayette. The Maltese jack was crossed on the Andalusian jennet, the result of which was a very famous jack called Compound, that proved to be much more popular as a breeder than the Royal Gift, which was said to have been selected from the royal stud, and was near sixteen hands high, but ill shapen and ungainly.

Not many years after this, the great orator and statesman, Henry Clay, imported a few Andalusians into Kentucky. No two men of the day could have added greater popularity to a breed, and being of a distinctively gray color, the cross in our native stock was accepted with little or no protest until the later importations of the distinctively black breeds.

The Andalusian is one of the most distinctive of the many races of jacks. As before said, they are found only in the Southern part of Spain, embracing the whole of the kingdom of Andalusia, and are evidently of an ancient race, for we read of them, and the profits arising from their use in propagating mules, during the Roman occupation and before the time of Christ. Columella, who, in the reign of the emporer Claudius, published a treatise, which has been handed down to us, on the husbandry and economy of the Romans, gives very particular directions for breeding jacks and mules. He was a native of Cadiz, Spain, owned large estates there, and tells us that the best mules were raised in that part of the country. But at this time, the best of the breed is found in and around the city of Cordova.

As a race, they are distinctively gray in color, sometimes, indeed, practically white, in rare instances black and occasionally blue. The larger ones, such as would be selected by an importer, range from fourteen and a half to fifteen hands, though the country literally teems with small pack animals twelve or thirteen hands high. They have a most excellent leg, the bone is large and firm, and freer than are the other breeds from what is commonly known as jack sores, viz., a running sore that appears on the inside of the knee and hock, and which sometimes gives a great deal of trouble. They have a fairly good head and ear and are really a meritorious jack. While many have been imported, they are not now popular on account of their color. Judge Goodpasture frankly admitted the objection, and abandoned them after a single importation. Even that one was made because of a lack of information.

We have heard at least one importer complain of their not breeding regularly; this has not been our observation of them. So far as we have seen, they are as much to be depended upon in this respect as any others. The cross of the breed is now scattered all over the country, as in addition to those brought over before the war, they have been imported in the last few years by Mr. Lyles, of Kentucky, Goodpasture and Hill, of Tennessee, Messrs. Leonard, of Missouri, and in 1889 quite a large importation by a firm in Arkansas.

The Catalonian. After Henry Clay's importation of Andalusians, his son went to Spain in the consular or diplomatic service, and while there, sent to his father's Kentucky home an excellent specimen of the black breed, supposedly the Catalonian. So much pleased was Mr. Clay with this jack that a year or two later he imported a number of others. A picture of one of these ornaments one of the rooms in the old homestead at Ashland. Mr. A. C. Franklin made a small importation to Tennessee many years ago, purchased, it is understood, around Barcelona. These were, undoubtedly, Catalonians, and some of them became famous breeders.

Judge Goodpasture, in making a second importation, determined to find the black breed. He found them in the North of Spain, principally in the province of Catalonia, but, later, he discovered the same breed in the Pyrenees of France. No jacks had been imported as far South as Tennessee for many years until he revived the business. He brought over from Catalonia the largest and most select importations that had ever been made, and for the first time made prominent the characteristics of the different Spanish races.

The Catalonian is a very popular jack, and justly so. For the propagation of mules of a certain quality they are unsurpassed. They have many valuable qualities,

and among these is that of color. Sunburned blacks are
sometimes seen, but the great majority have a very
glossy, jet black coat of short hair that is greatly sought
after. Besides, they are a jack of good size, varying
from fourteen and a half to fifteen hands, in some instances reaching sixteen hands or higher. While they
have not a large bone, it is a very flat, clean one. They
have great style and beauty, and are of superb action,
and many have been used in the best jennet herds of the
country.

The area from which they come covers some hundreds
of miles, extending from the Mediterranean coast in the
North of Spain to the French side of the Pyrenees, taking in what is known as the Cerdan, which lies partly in
France and partly in Spain. Although they are found
in both countries, they are still bred only in the mountains of the Pyrenees. They are scattered all over the
South of France bordering these mountains, about Toulouse, Tarbes, Pau and elsewhere. These were, never-
theless, imported from their mountain fastnesses as colts
to take their places in the stud when sufficiently old.
Many of the best Catalonian jacks introduced into this
country have been purchased in France. Judge Goodpasture made two entire importations from there and one
from the Cerdan.

For style and action they are possibly unequaled, certainly not surpassed, by any other race. This is noted
too with great force in the case of jennets. Our native
jennet stock are proverbially dull and lazy; they move
about in the most composed manner, with an entire
lack of appreciation of modern ideas of "get up and go."
Such a thing as playing in pasture or paddock is far

beneath their sense of dignity and decorum. Age fastens upon their feelings and spirits long before they reach the responsibilities of being matrons. But the imported will play and run about their lot like colts, and some of them can trot equal to a horse. The Judge was, on one occasion, while buying, driving on a government road in France. His team was a spirited pair of Tarbes horses, with a great deal of the oriental Arabian blood coursing through their veins. The driver was no less spirited; a defeated soldier of France in their late clash with Germany, he still had enough of the fire of enthusiasm left to try to pass everything on the road. The Judge saw ahead of him, driving at a smart gait, a man in a two wheeled vehicle, drawn by a fine looking jennet, and ordered the driver to overtake what promised to be a valuable acquisition to his purchases. This was what the driver wanted to do any way, so he cracked his whip and started off at a merry clip, but the man with the jennet refused for sometime to be overtaken, and the Judge had to drive for a full half mile, at the limit of his speed, before coming alongside of him. It is needless to say that he purchased the jennet, and she was afterwards sold at a long price in the United States.

One rarely sees a drop-eared animal in the breed, and when he does, it generally has some physical cause, such as a hurt in shipping, disease or something of the kind. The race are most excellent breeders, as they have proven in all the jack producing states, their mules being handsome, quick, active and good sellers, and it is said that they mature very early. Judge Goodpasture imported a very large number of the breed, and they are now scattered all over the West and South. and the good effect upon the breeding interests can scarcely be over-estimated.

The Majorca. Another of the popular breeds imported by Judge Goodpasture was the Majorca. Attention was called to the great size and black color of these jacks in a letter to the Nashville American by the firm, written from Spain, sometime before any of them had been imported to America. They are found, principally, on the larger of the Balearic islands, known as Majorca, and, so far as is known, the Judge's firm was the first American importers to visit the island.

Majorca lies in the Mediterranean, about fifteen hours sail by steamer from Barcelona. The breed of jacks found here is one of the purest in Spain. As far back as 1825, Mr. Pomeroy, in an essay before the Maryland Agricultural Society, says: "So much have been the ravages of war and anarchy in Spain for a long time past, that the fine race of jacks that country once possessed have become almost extinct. In Majorca, however, and probably some parts of the coast opposite, the large breed may yet be obtained in its purity." Mr. Pomeroy had not discovered that they were a distinct race from those found on the mainland, but his remark illustrates the fame of the island for a large breed of jacks at even this early day.

They are possibly the largest jacks ever imported, certainly the tallest, and have been much sought after for jennet purposes. Their bone is exceedingly large with a body to correspond. While they are black, they rarely have that glossy color so admired in the Catalonian, but those brought to this country will average almost a hand taller than the latter. In Europe, they rank about the same, both being regarded as superior to the Andalusian. But they are not destined to cut any great figure in this country; their number is too limited, and there is no way in which to greatly augment it. The island from which they are imported is small, and has been literally stripped of its most meritorious animals. What few have been brought to this country, have been scattered to the four quarters of the earth. No jennets have been imported, and under the present tariff, none are likely to be, so that in a few years, there will not be a pure bred Majorca in the country.

They have not been here long enough to fully demonstrate their value as a cross on the native stock, but in Europe, for a large, heavy class of mules, they outrank the other Spanish breeds, but are inferior for the propagation of the smaller and more stylish animal. The Spanish government obtians a large part of her artillery mules from Majorca, and the English government have been importing them for the transport service in Egypt and elsewhere.

As to height, those brought to this country will average about fifteen and a half hands, and are more uniform in size than the Catalonian. A good many have been exported to South America, and at prices that are astonishing. Two sold there a few years ago, are reported to have gone at $900.00 each, which, if all expenses are added, makes a pretty good figure for a country considered by us so far in the rear of North American civilization.

Their heads are enormous, and are inclined to a bulky appearance. While they have the longest and largest ears of any race in existence, they are not so erect and piercing as some others, nor have they the style and action; in fact, they may be said to incline to sluggishness. Judge Goodpasture imported a sixteen hand jack of this breed, and a two year old colt fifteen and one half hands, but as the former was sold to Georgia and the latter to Texas, he never knew anything as to the value of their progeny.

The Poitou. Judge Goodpasture was not only the first to import and introduce the Poitou breed, but the last to try the experiment, no other importer caring to risk the amount necessary to buy and bring them over, their cost being quite double that of the other breeds.

Their early history is most interesting. They are to be found in the province of Poitou, known as the granary of France—in the richest and most fertile part of that most fertile of all countries, and are especially abundant in the departments of La Vendee and Deux-Sevres.

In 1866, Mr. Eugene Ayrault, of Niort, France, published a volume on the Piotou jack. It is a book of a high order of merit, and was awarded a gold medal by the Society of Agriculture in France, is the only book known to the writer published on jacks, and is confined to a single breed. We give his description of these jacks. He says:

"His head is enormous in size, and is very much larger than that of any other race in existence. His mouth is smaller than that of the horse; teeth small, but the enamel exceedingly hard. The opening of the nostril is narrow, the ear very long, and adorned with long curly hair, called cadanette, which is much esteemed by breeders. It is said that animals with the longest bodies produce the best mules, and this is greatly looked to. The tail is rather short, and furnished with long hair at its extremity only. The chest is very broad, and the belly voluminous. The shoulders are short; the muscles of the forearm long, but not very thick. The knees are exceedingly large, as are all the joints. The chestnuts or horny places near the knees, are large and well developed. The abundance of hair which covers the jack constitutes one of the most sought for qualities. The animals are called well taloned or well mustached when they have these qualities in a high degree.

"The mane is long and fine, the skin smooth, the hair fine and silky in texture. We give great preference to large feet, for which this breed is noted. The skin is almost universally black or dark brown. The gray jack, though seldom met, is rejected by good mule breeders. The animals which have the end of the nose black, and whose bodies are wholly of this color, are said to be lacking in breeding. The skin and coating of the jack is very important, and it is thought that the mules from a jack superior in this respect, mature earlier."

Such is Mr. Ayrault's description of them. We will add, that they are physically the most powerful of any race yet discovered; they have greater weight and more bone and substance generally. They are not exceedingly tall, their legs being very short, but in a cross with a mare of fair size the mule will be found to have all the height desired. During the Judge's visit to Paris, Marseilles and other French towns, the Poitou mules seen would average not less than sixteen hands with a size and weight never approached by those seen in America.

The first impression one gains of a Poitou is not a favorable one. They are never trimmed or groomed, and we are unaccustomed to their long hair and bulky appearance. The demand for them is such that it cannot be supplied, and even French breeders in certain parts of the country are forced to use the Catalonian and Majorca. Their price is enough to stagger one, considered from a European standpoint. Mr. Ayrault says that $1,000 to $1,200 is ordinary, while $2,000 for a single animal is not uncommon.

Large numbers of Poitou mules are imported into Spain for draft purposes, and especially by the large firm of San Marti and son of Barcelona, who supply mules both to the government and to individuals. In Spain, their price is very much higher than that of the native stock. The province from which they come is hardly larger than one of our ordinary counties, yet in 1866, the latest statistics at hand, fifty thousand mares were bred to jacks, and the yearly export of young mules amounted to between two and three millions of dollars. Mule breeding there, for profit, is without a parallel in agriculture.

Judge Goodpasture imported quite a large number of both jacks and jennets from Poitou. It was in vain that he called attention to the many conclusive facts establishing the superiority of the breed. It was impossible to overcome the antiphathy of American breeders to a coat of hair six or eight inches long, and their enormous bulk of body. The best price he received for one of these jacks was fifteen hundred dollars. It may be, however, that the seed was planted, and that the progeny of this importation will, in time, prove to the progressive breeder their value to the farmer. The Poitou is the only jack that has been bred for any length of time upon the highest scientific principles.

What Was Accomplished. The firm, in addition to bringing about a new birth to the importation business, publishing the first jack cut ever to appear in a paper, importing the best jack ever brought to America, conducting the business on a scale never before approached, and introducing to the public new and better breeds, inaugurated other reforms of the greatest importance to the jack producing sections. .

In every census previous to 1890, mules and jacks had been enumerated together under the general designa-tion of mules and asses. This was very misleading. For instance, it is notorious that there are few jacks and jennets in Shelby County, Tennessee, yet it was broadly put down in the census as having more mules and asses than any county in the United States. Again, Davidson County, Tennessee, having more jacks than any other county in the State, ranks comparatively low in number of mules and asses when enumerated together. Hence, before the census of 1890 was taken, the firm wrote Superintendent Porter, giving all the facts, and calling attention to the misleading character of all previous censuses. They likewise wrote and obtained the active assistance of the senators and congressmen from the jack breeding states, and an order was obtained, having the census of 1890 taken separately, thus giving the jack sections proper credit for that year.

The firm also assisted in the organization of the American Breededs' Association of Jacks and Jennets. An elaborate article was published by them in the

Farmer's Home Journal, of Louisville, Kentucky, advocating strongly such an association, and several letters were received by the firm asking them to inaugurate the enterprise. Afterwards Mr. Chas. F. Mills, of Springfield, Ill., who was not a jack man but an official in the state agricultural department, undertook and carried through the preliminary organization. Subsequently permanent organization was effected at Chicago, of which Hon. Chas. E. Leonard, a prominent breeder of Missouri, was made president, and W. H. Goodpasture, secretary. Mr. Goodpasture, as secretary, wrote a great deal on the subject of jacks and the stud-book to the agricultural press of the country, and in 1890, he issued a valuable annual in behalf of the association. In 1891, volume one of the American Jack Stock Stud-Book was published by him and it, together with the Annual, constituted the first distinctive jack literature to make its appearance in America.

Judge Goodpasture, being a member of the association, attended its meetings and greatly aided in the success it attained. The firm labored incessantly for its advancement, and raised the jack business to a commanding position never before occupied by it.

As noted in the earlier pages of this book, Judge Goodpasture also made the first direct importation of Cleveland Bay horses to the South. They were a most superior lot, and added much to the breeding interests of the country.

CHAPTER XXI.

Sickness and Death. This practically ended the active and business career of Judge Goodpasture. About this time A. V. Goodpasture was appointed Clerk of the Supreme Court, and W. H. Goodpasture entered the office as deputy. This broke up the firm, and Judge Goodpasture devoted some time to selling the stock on hand, collecting the debts and closing out the multifarious business that accumulates in every venture of importance.

For a while, he still dealt some in real estate, but for the last three years of his life he was in bad health and did little. In 1893, accompanied by one of his daughters. he visited the World's Fair at Chicago, and wrote up some of his observations on that great exposition, but never had the article published.

He took few cases in the courts after this, and what he did have were before the Supreme Court. He spent a good deal of his time in the clerk's office, not only because his sons were there, but because he met lawyers and friends from all over Middle Tennessee. It was a good place to smoke and talk. His sons kept a box of smoking tobacco always on hand for the use of themselves and the bar, but found it difficult to keep pipes. The Judge bought a half bushel of his favorite hickory pipes with cane stems, and sent them up. After this, there was little trouble on the pipe question.

He took a severe case of the grip in the winter of 1892-3. For a time afterwards, he would get better in summer and then worse in winter. It is a disease sufficiently bad for the young and robust, but with a man of his age, it seems almost impossible to get entirely rid of it. It sapped his great energy, and gave him a disinclination to carry on business of consequence.

His mind ran much on the past, on the struggles of his early life, on the people he had known and met, and personal reminisences. No matter how much conversation lagged, it was never much trouble to arouse his interest by an inquiry as to some odd character he had known many years before, or ask him to relate one of his favorite anecdotes. These were never second hand, but always an occurrence happening under his own observation.

But disease had begun to undermine his powerful frame and constitution. His family could see it, but as he retained his flesh, it was not so apparent to his friends. He grew to have a disinclination to go out in town, and spent most of his time at home. On Sunday afternoon, their only leisure time, one or both his sons living in Nashville, would go out and see him. These were always delightful occasions to them.

He never lost interest in the general public, and carefully read the daily papers. One of his last attempts at going out was to hear Mr. Bryan speak, and he came home that night thoroughly exhausted.

He was at last taken down, though he would not go to bed, occupying a big, roomy, office chair. He had never believed in sending for doctors except in extreme cases, and never felt that he himself needed one. But Dr. Ewing was summoned. The patient grew steadily worse, and the illness was pronounced that dread disease,

Bright's. The fact was not disclosed to him, and it is not certain that he knew that his sickness was to be fatal. If so, he never disclosed it. The absent son, Rev. J. R. Goodpasture, was sent for, and arrived at the bedside in time to help nurse and minister to his wants. His suffering for some days was extreme. The devotion of his wife was intense and untiring. She was present with him day and night, and watched with an unflagging zeal to allay some pain or gratify some desire. She relinquished sleep and refused rest, and nursed him as only a wife can. Dr. John G. Goodpasture, his brother, came from his home at Carthage, Tennessee, to see him, but was never fully recognized by him. On November 2, 1896, he died, and, according to his own often expressed wish, his funeral, like the life he had lived, was simple and unostentatious.

Little need be said of Judge Goodpasture's character beyond what is developd in these pages. He lived an uncommonly busy life, and never knew an idle period. He has been heard to say that in early life he had some temper, but he had gained a complete mastery over it, and had one of the gentlest and most lovable natures imaginable. He had a great deal of charity for the short comings and faults of others, more than almost anyone. If an individual deeply wronged him, he would feel hurt and provoked for a time, but we have never known any one who could so quickly forget and forgive. The occurrence was completely effaced, and did not leave even a scar. And he would take the first opportunity to show it to him who had committed it.

He was a philosopher. If things occurred, as they do in all active careers almost constantly, that were calculated to worry and annoy, he would study and reflect over it, try to see the good in it, and never take his mind from it until he had reached a satisfactory conclusion. This philosophical habit of treating all the unpleasant happenings of life, was a prominent and valuable feature of his character that was very striking to those who knew him intimately enough to observe it.

He loved his family with an intense and sacrificing devotion, and was always ready to kindly aid, console or advise. Thus died a busy man, who never intentionally wronged a human being in his life. He was a member of the Cumberland Presbyterian Church, and his funeral was conducted by Rev. Ira Landrith assisted by Rev. Angus McDonald.

16

APPENDIX.

THE FAMILY OF

CAPTAIN JAMES GOODPASTURE.

—

FIRST GENERATION.

No. 1.

James Goodpasture was one of the pioneers of the Wolf's Hill, or Abingdon settlement, in Virginia, where all his children were born except the youngest. He emigrated to Tennessee in the latter part of the eighteenth century. and located, first, near Southwest Point, a Federal fort on the Indian line. But in 1800 he moved west, across the Indian territory, called the wilderness, and made a permanent settlement on Flat Creek, then in Smith, but now in Overton County. When the Indian title to the wilderness was extinguished, and Overton County erected, he was elected captain in its first military organization. He was a great admirer and partisan of President Jefferson, for whom his youngest son, born two months after his inauguration, was named. He married a Miss Hamilton in 1776, and had eight children. He died about 1820.

2. William, born June 4, 1777; died March 15, 1848.

3. John, born November 4, 1778; died July 28, 1864.

4. James.

5. Martha.

6. Arthur.

7. Margaret.

8. Abraham.

9. Jefferson, born May 13, 1801; died in September, 1857.

SECOND GENERATION.

No. 2.

William Goodpasture, son of James and ———— (Hamilton) Goodpasture, was born in Washington County, Virginia. He did not go West with the other members of his father's family, but remained on the old homestead, where he died. He married Sarah Lockhart (1778-1840) and had seven children.

10. Wm. Lockhart, born May 14, 1803; died Sept. 22, 1889.

11. Martha Hamilton, born Nov. 7, 1805; died Sept. 4, 1854.

12. Mary Campbell, born Jan. 25, 1808; died July 15, 1872.

13. Abraham Hamilton, born July 10, 1810; died September 8, 1854.

14. Elizabeth Lockhart, born May 12, 1813; died January 19, 1882.

15. Margaret B., born Dec. 6. 1815; died March 15, 1885.

16. Jane Campbell, born Jan. 4, 1817; died June 14, 1848.

No. 3.

John Goodpasture, son of James and ———— (Hamilton) Goodpasture, was a native of Virginia, who emigrated to Tennessee in the latter part of the eighteenth century, and settled near Hilham, in Overton County, in 1800. He was a Justice of the Peace, and a leading citizen in his community. He married Margery (1786-1864), daughter of William Bryan, in 1803, and had fourteen children.

17. Mary R., born January 24, 1805; died April 20, 1893.

18. Martha H., born Dec. 28, 1806; died August 1, 1876.

19. Nancy B., born December 25, 1807; died July 12, 1891.

20. Levina, born October 27, 1808; died August 20, 1885.

21. William B., born August 25, 1810; died April 4, 1893.

22. Abraham H., born June 21, 1812; died Sept. 21, 1885.

23. Elizabeth B., born May 27, 1814: died January 1, 1897.

24. Esther A., born August 26, 1816; died February 15, 1896.

25. Andrew B., born July 16, 1818; died April 17, 1842.

26. Margaret Ann, born March 21, 1820; died Dec. 25, 1890.

27. John G., born April 21, 1822.
28. Jefferson D., born August 3, 1824; died Nov. 2, 1896.
29. James McD., born April 17, 1827; died August 11, 1876.
30. Winburn W., born October 20, 1828.

No. 4.

James Goodpasture, son of James and ——— (Hamilton)
Goodpasture, was born in Virginia, and emigrated with his
father to Tennessee. He married in Overton County, Tennessee, where he died in early manhood, leaving two sons,
the elder of whom was raised by his brother Abraham, and
the younger by his brother John.
31. Madison.
32. Jefferson.

No. 5.

Martha Goodpasture, daughter of James and ———
(Hamilton) Goodpasture, married a Mr. Willard and moved
to Illinois, many years ago. No other information.

No. 6.

Arthur Goodpasture, son of James and ——— (Hamil
ton) Goodpasture, was born in Virginia and died in Overton County, Tennessee. He has many descendants in Ten
nessee and Illinois, but we have not been able to get any
information from them in time for this publication. We
give the names of such of his children as are known to us.
33. Robert M.
34. William I., born Sept. 29, 1815; died August 23, 1891.
35. Abraham H.
36. Malinda.
37. Sarah.
38. A daughter.

No. 7.

Margaret Goodpasture, daughter of James and ———
(Hamilton) Goodpasture, married Andrew McClain, and
lived in Knox County, Tennessee. No other information.

No. 8.

Abraham Goodpasture, son of James and ———— (Hamilton) Goodpasture, was born in Virginia and moved with his father to Overton County, Tennessee, whence he subsequently moved to Morgan County, Illinois. He had nine children.

39. William.
40. Abraham.
41. Alexander.
42. Hamilton, born in 1808.
43. Jane.
44. John.
45. Hannah.
46. Martha.
47. Elizabeth.

No. 9.

Jefferson Goodpasture, son of James and ———— (Hamilton) Goodpasture, was the only one of his father's children born after he settled in the present county of Overton, in Tennessee. He married Nancy Allen (1805-1864) in 1827, and had nine children.

48. Mary M., born December 7, 1828; died August, 1857.
49. Francis M., born May 10, 1830.
50. James H., born December 11, 1831; died June, 1854.
51. Marena, born March 16, 1833; died, 1890.
52. Thomas C., born October 28, 1834; died January 8, 1862.
53. Melinda E., born September 23, 1837.
54. Eliza E., born August 23, 1841; died, 1865.
55. Sarah C., born September, 1843; died, 1890.
56. William P., born October 26, 1845; died, 1871.

THIRD GENERATION.

No. 10.

William Lockhart Goodpasture, son of William and Sarah (Lockhart) Goodpasture, married Jane White, July 31, 1834, and had five children.

57. A. W., born June 10, 1835.

58. Hugh W., born September 25, 1837.

59. Ellen W. W., born June 11, 1839.

60. James L., born August 10, 1845.

61. Mary Campbell, born April 7, 1849.

No. 11.

Martha Hamilton Goodpasture, daughter of William and Sarah (Lockhart) Goodpasture, married John T. Sprinkle, October 27, 1825, and had ten children.

62. Mary Terrel, born November 20, 1826.

63. Charles Henry, born Nov. 1, 1830; died Jan. 8, 1857.

64. William Emlar, born June 31, 1832; died April 16, 1863.

65. Sarah Elizabeth, born May 5, 1834.

66. Naomi, born Sept. 25,1836; died Jan. 22, 1845.

67. Ferdinand Archibald, born December 11, 1838; died November 23, 1860.

68. Susana Jane Ganaway, born February 5, 1841.

69. Levicie Bowen, born Jan. 28, 1843; died Sept. 2, 1854.

70. Narcissa Cecil, born December 21, 1844.

71. Virginia Graves, born August 20, 1850; died September 13, 1854.

No. 12.

Mary Campbell Goodpasture, daughter of William and Sarah (Lockhart) Goodpasture, married James Fleming, and had children.

72. William.

No. 13.

Abraham Hamilton Goodpasture, son of William and Sarah (Lochart) Goodpasture, married Sarah M. Humphrey (1814-   ), November 28, 1833, and had eleven children.

73. William Hamilton, born September 5, 1834.

74. Sarah Margaret, born February 3, 1836.

75. David Washington, born September 29, 1837; died August, 1863.

76. Ellen Virginia, born August 7, 1839.

77. S. F., born May 31, 1841; died in infancy.

78. E. A., born October 24, 1843.

79. Elizabeth St. Clair, born October 18, 1845; died September 7, 1854.

80. Jane Lockhart, born October 28, 1847.

81. John Henry, born Jan. 18, 1850; died Sept. 12, 1854.

82. Casper Winton, born January 25, 1852; died January 14, 1854.

83. Abraham Hamilton, born October 4, 1854.

No. 14.

Elizabeth Lockhart Goodpasture, daughter of William and Sarah (Lockhart) Goodpasture, married Roland Wolfe, September 21, 1848, and had five children.

84. Ellen V., born April 21, 1850; died May 15, 1884.

85. Sarah M., born October 29, 1851.

86. Maggie F., born March 26, 1854.

87. Melissa F., born April 12, 1856; died December 22, 1860.

88. Emma C., born November 6, 1857.

No. 15.

Margaret B. Goodpasture, daughter of William and Sarah (Lockhart) Goodpasture, married William Rector, and had children.

89. James.

No. 17.

Mary R. (Polly) Goodpasture, daughter of John and Margery (Bryan) Goodpasture, was born in Overton County, Tennessee. She married Abraham W. Carlock (1800-1884), April 10, 1825, and settled near Bloomington, in McLean County, Illinois, where she died. She had twelve children.

90. John G., born January 28, 1826; died April 25, 1888.

91. Martha, born June 21, 1827; died August 25, 1828.

92. Madison P., born April 16, 1829.

93. Nancy J., born January 9, 1831; died March 5, 1868.

94. Sarah, born January 9, 1833.

95. Mahala, born January 9, 1835.

96. Reuben, born June 17, 1837.

97. Levina, born December 17, 1839.

98. William B., born March 15, 1842.

99. Mary, born April 5, 1844; died March 25, 1869.

100. Abraham H., born August 21, 1846.

101. Margery, born October 20, 1849; died August 6, 1889.

No. 18.

Martha H. (Patsy) Goodpasture, daughter of John and Margery (Bryan) Goodpasture, was born in Overton County, Tennessee. She married William Dale (1806-1877) in 1827, and settled on Cumberland River, in Clay County, Tennessee, where she died. She had eleven children.

102. Levina, born October, 1828; died November 6, 1854.

103. John Dillard, born in 1829; died in infancy.

104. William Jackson, born December, 1831; died September 20, 1863.

105. Elizabeth, born October, 1833.

106. Wilburn Hamilton, born October, 1835.

107. Cleon Easallus, born December 31, 1837.

108. Alfred Lafayette (twin), born November 30, 1840.

109. Andrew Columbus (twin), born November 30, 1840.

110. John Francis, born October 31, 1842.

111. Dulcena, born July, 1846; died in 1882.

112. Dillard Goodpasture, born July 12, 1848; died October 18, 1854.

No. 19.

Nancy B .Goodpasture, daughter of John and Margery (Bryan) Goodpasture, was born in Overton County, Tennessee, and married Rev. Joseph H. Bates (1806-1888), March 11, 1828; moved to Illionis in 1830, and died at Lincoln, in that State. She had fourteen children.

113. William Iredell (twin), born December 15, 1828.

114. Mary Elzada (twin), born December 15, 1828.

115. John Russell, born January 22, 1830.

116. Hettie Elizabeth, died in infancy.

117. Thomas Jefferson, born February 21, 1833.

118. Permelia Jane, born October 11, 1854; died July 25, 1882.

119. Madison Canby, born July 7, 1836.

120. Margery Josephine, born January 30, 1839.

121. Joseph Baxter, born January 11, 1841.

122. Abraham Henderson (twin), born December 30, 1812.

123. Dulcena (twin), born December 30, 1842; died in infancy.

124. Marquis Jerome, born April 23, 1845; died December 28, 1872.

125. Margaret Ann, born July 20, 1847.

126. Harriet Rosanna, born March 17, 1850; died July 29, 1876.

No. 20.

Levina Goodpasture, daughter of John and Margery (Bryan) Goodpasture, was born in Overton County, Tennessee. In 1830, she married Thomas Dale, now in the eighty-seventh year of his age, and moved to Illinois. Returning, they subsequently moved to Dade County, Missouri, where she died. She had nine children.

127. Marrillena, born in 1831; died May, 1855.

128. Margery, born in 1832; died in infancy.

129. Edward, born 1834; died in infancy.

130. W. A., born January 17, 1836.

131. John W., born July 17, 1837; died September, 1870.

132. Abraham B., born May 22, 1839; died in 1862.

133. Tennessee, born 1841; died 1861.

134. Thomas A., born 1843; died 1867.

135. Mary M., born 1845.

No. 21.

William B. Goodpasture, son of John and Margery (Bryan) Goodpasture, was born in Overton County, Tennessee, and was married four times. First, to Jane A. ————— (-1835), June 29, 1830; second, to Martha Ann Harville (-1855), September 21, 1836; third, to Adelphia Smith, December 20, 1855; and, fourth, to —————————, January 15, 1885. He settled in Sangamon County, Illinois, where he died. He had twelve children.

BY HIS FIRST WIFE.

136. John F., born September 26, 1832; died September 26, 1836.

BY HIS SECOND WIFF.

137. Azariah Thomas, born September 17, 1837; died October 15, 1863.

138. Mary Margery, born January 12, 1839; died July, 1863.

139. James Harden, born May 4, 1840; died in infancy.

140. Andrew Seymour, born March 9, 1842.

141. Lucy Dulcena, born January 25, 1844.

142. William Erastus, born November 25, 1845.

143. Philander Cass, born June 9, 1848.

144. McGrady, born September 20, 1850; died July 30, 1851.

145. Martha Ann, born April 7, 1853; died June 26, 1873.

146. Levi Dodds, born January 28, 1855.

BY HIS THIRD WIFE.

147. Jesse Fletcher, born September 25, 1856.

No. 22.

Abraham H. Goodpasture, son of John and Margery (Bryan) Goodpasture, was born in Overton County, Tennessee, and died in Petersburg, Illinois. He professed religion October 17, 1833, and in November of the same year, became a candidate for the ministry, under the care of the Elyton (Alabama) Presbytery, of the Cumberland Presbyterian Church; was licensed April 25, and preached his first sermon May 3, 1835; moved to Illinois, and became a member of Sangamon Presbytery, and was very active in the work of the ministry. From the journal, which he kept during the first forty years of his ministerial life, it appears that he preached 4,320 sermons, durng that time. He had an appointment for the Sunday succeeding his death. He was a man of sublime faith, a joyous and cheerful disposition, and a charming social nature. He married Dulcena B. Williams (1819-   ), the daughter of James (-1834) and Hannah (Maupin) Williams, January 10, 1843, who still

survives him, in the 79th year of her age. They had three
children.
148. J. Dillard, born May 9, 1846.
149. Hattie E., born March 5, 1855.
150. Jacob Ridley, born May 10, 1860.

No. 23.

Elizabeth B. (Betsy) Goodpasture, daughter of John and
Margery (Bryan) Goodpasture, was born in Overton County,
Tennessee; married Claiborne Hinds (-1872), October
11, 1846, and settled in Guntown, Mississippi, where she died.
She had five children.
151. Tennessee G., born Aug. 28, 1847; died April 22, 1879.
152. John S., born January 6, 1849.
153. Martha F., born December 6, 1850.
154. Mary A. E., born March 20, 1854; died March 12, 1875.
155. Ova C., born December 22, 1859.

No. 24.

Esther A. (Hettie) Goodpasture, daughter of John and
Margery (Bryan) Goodpasture, was born in Overton County,
Tennessee, where she died, greatly beloved by all who knew
her. She was twice married; first, to James Maxwell, Clerk
of the County Court of Overton County; second, to Lemuel
Gustin Rose, a prosperous farmer, who survives her, now
in the 87th year of his age. She never had any children.

No. 25.

Andrew B. Goodpasture, son of John and Margery (Bryan)
Goodpasture, was born in Overton County, Tennessee.
Soon after reaching his majority, he emigrated to Illinois,
where he died not long afterwards. His was the only death
in the family during the lifetime of his parents. He was
never married.

No. 26.

Margaret Ann (Peggy) Goodpasture, daughter of John
and Margery (Bryan) Goodpasture, was born in Overton

County, Tennessee, where, also she died, surviving the last of her two children only a week. She married Dennis C. Mitchell, September 13, 1848. Her two children were,

156. Isaiah Winburn, born June 25, 1849; died December 18, 1890.

157. John M. D., born April 12, 1851, died June 18, 1854.

No. 27.

John G. Goodpasture, son of John and Margery (Bryan) Goodpasture, was born in Overton County, Tennessee; served as a volunteer in the Mexican war; is a practicing physician, and resides at Algood, in Putnam County. He has been married twice: first, to Catherine M. Atkinson (1830-1896), July 14, 1850; second, to Maybelle Mills (1874-) on the eleventh day of March, 1897. He has four children, all by the first wife.

158. Winburn A., born in 1851.

159. Sallie M., born in 1853.

160. Josie, born in 1855.

161. Hettie, born April 21, 1872.

No. 28.

Jefferson Dillard Goodpasture, son of John and Margery (Bryan) Goodpasture, was a native of Overton County. Tennessee, where he obtained a common school education. He attended the law school at Cumberland University in 1848-9; in 1847, before he ever appeared in a lawsuit, he was appointed Clerk and Master, at Livingston, and was re-appointed at the expiration of his term, in 1853. In 1856. he was a delegate to the National Democratic Convention, at Cincinnati; resigned the office of Clerk and Master, in 1857, to accept a seat in the State Senate. After the expiration of his term in the Senate, devoted himself wholly to the law, in which he achieved eminent success. In 1872, was one of the Presidential electors, elected on the Greeley and Brown ticket. Moved to Nashville in 1879, and traded largely in real estate, and later engaged extensively in the importation of live stock. He died in Nashville. He was twice married: first, to Sarah Jane (1835-1868), daughter of Jacob and Jane C. (Marchbanks) Dillen, May 15, 1852, second, to Nannie, daughter of Austin C. and Lucette (Clark) Young, June 17, 1869. He had nine children.

BY HIS FIRST WIFE.

162. John Ridley, born March 5, 1854.
163. Albert Virgil, born November 19, 1855.
164. William Henry, born November 28, 1859.
165. Harvey Dillard, born July 27, 1864; died June 8, 1867.
166. Jacob Dillen, born August 27, 1867; died Feb. 20, 1868.

BY HIS SECOND WIFE.

167. Lucette Margery, born May 15, 1870.
168. Austin Young, born August 26, 1872.
169. Mona Clark, born April 1, 1874.
170. Jefferson Dillard, born April 13, 1877.

No. 29.

James McDonnold Goodpasture, son of John and Margery (Bryan) Goodpasture, was born in Overton County, Tennessee, and died in Putnam County. He was a physician by profession, and was for six years Clerk and Master, at Cookeville. He married Ova Arnold (1839-   ), December 5, 1854, and had four children.
171. Avo, born September 27, 1855.
172. Mary Hettie, born September 23, 1858.
173. John Bryan, born July 15, 1864.
174. Sarah Margery, born March 13, 1868.

No. 30.

Winburn W. Goodpasture, son of John and Margery (Bryan) Goodpasture, was born and still lives in Overton County, Tennessee. He is a prominent lawyer, and has been both Circuit Judge and Chancellor. He married Martha Ann Capps (1836-   ), daughter of Doak H. Capps, long a successful merchant of Livingston, Tennessee, January 17, 1854, and has had five children.

175. Eugene, born September 13, 1856; died February 3, 1858.

176. Lou G., born April 4, 1857.

177. Ala May, born March 5, 1859; died August 4, 1891.

178. Maggie L., born December 28, 1863.

179. Elmo C., born March 12, 1867.

No. 31.

Madison Goodpasture, son of James Goodpasture, Jr., moved with his uncle Abraham Goodpasture to Morgan County, Illinois. Subsequently he lived at Louisiana, Missouri. He was twice married and had children.

180. James.

No. 32.

Jefferson Goodpasture, son of James Goodpasture, Jr., soon after reaching manhood moved to the State of Illinois, where he has descendants, but we have not been able to get particular information with reference to them.

No. 33.

Robert M. Goodpasture, son of Arthur Goodpasture, married and had children.

181. Milton.

182. Dillard.

183. Martha.

No. 35.

Abraham H. Goodpasture, son of Arthur Goodpasture, moved to Illinois, and had children. No other information.

No. 36.

Malinda Goodpasture, daughter of Arthur Goodpasture, married Thos. J. Murphy, and lived at Hilham, Tennessee. She died several years ago. No children.

No. 37.

Sarah Goodpasture, daughter of Arthur Goodpasture, married Hiram Hembree and lived in Overton County, Tennessee. She had children.

184. Campbell.
185. Joseph Robert.

No. 38.

———— Goodpasture, daughter of Arthur Goodpasture, married Arthur Garrett, of Overton County, Tennessee. No other information.

No. 41.

Alexander Goodpasture, son of Abraham Goodpasture, of Morgan County, Illinois, married and had children. After his death his widow married Jacob Gillespie, and the family lived near Eugene City, Oregon. No other information.

No. 42.

Hamilton Goodpasture, son of Abraham Goodpasture, of Morgan County, Illinois, was born in Overton County, Tennessee. He married Eleanor Ellyson, in 1836, and had eight children.

186. Elizabeth, born November 9, 1836.
187. Andrew Jackson, born August 18, 1840.
188. William Hamilton, born in 1841; died August 9, 1865.
189. Abraham, born in 1843.
190. John Ellyson, born October 7, 1847.
191. James P., born March 19, 1848.
192. Martha Jane, born June 7, 1850; died Jan. 17, 1893.
193. Thomas B., born July 1, 1852.

No. 43.

Jane Goodpasture, daughter of Abraham Goodpasture, of Morgan County, Illinois, married a Mr. Deaton, and had seven children.

194. Bounaparte.
195. Alexander.
196. Simpson, drowned in Missouri River.
197. James (twin).
198. Thomas (twin).
199. Hannah.
200. Margarette.

No. 45.

Hannah Goodpasture, daughter of Abraham Goodpasture, of Morgan County, Illinois, married a Mr. Long, and lived near Concord, Illinois. No other information.

No. 46.

Martha Goodpasture, daughter of Abraham Goodpasture, of Morgan County, Illinois, married a Mr. Smith, and lived near Concord, Illinois. No other information.

No. 47.

Elizabeth Goodpasture, daughter of Abraham Goodpasture, of Morgan County, Illinois, married a Mr. Taylor, and lived near Concord, Illinois. No other information.

No. 48.

Mary M. Goodpasture, daughter of Jefferson and Nancy (Allen) Goodpasture, died unmarried.

No. 49.

Francis M. Goodpasture, son of Jefferson and Nancy (Allen) Goodpasture, is one of the substantial citizens of Overton County, Tennessee; did much to preserve the county records, during the war, and has since been one of its leading magistrates. He married Lydia L. Thomas (1842-   ), July 28, 1868, and has had five children.

201. James T., born May 5, 1869.
202. Florence, born March 14, 1871.
203. John J., born October 12, 1873.
204. Flora A., born November 6, 1876; died August 19, 1887.
205. Albert B., born May 14, 1881; died September 3, 1885.

No. 50.

James H. Goodpasture, son of Jefferson and Nancy (Allen) Goodpasture, died unmarried.

No. 51.

Marena Goodpasture, daughter of Jefferson and Nancy

(Allen) Goodpasture, married Clinton Masters (-1861), in 1855. She had no children.

No. 52.

Thomas C. Goodpasture, son of Jefferson and Nancy (Allen) Goodpasture, married Adelade Smith, in 1859, and had one child.

206. James J., born in 1860.

No. 53.

Malinda E. Goodpasture, daughter of Jefferson and Nancy (Allen) Goodpasture, married Porter Winton, in 1859, and has seven children.

206. William.
207. Robert.
208. Nancy.
209. Ann.
210. Belle.
211. Ferdinand, deceased.
212. Quitman.

No. 54.

Eliza E. Goodpasture, daughter of Jefferson and Nancy (Allen) Goodpasture, married John Tays (-1864), in 1863, and had one child.

213. John W., born in 1865.

No. 55.

Sarah C. Goodpasture, daughter of Jefferson and Nancy (Allen) Goodpasture, married James Cooper (-1870), in 1868, and after his death, married Richard Hamilton. She had four children. The names of the last two not known.

BY HER FIRST HUSBAND.

214. Lillie May, born August 22, 1869.

BY HER SECOND HUSBAND.

215. Albert, born in June, 1874.

No. 56.

William P. Goodpasture, son of Jefferson and Nancy (Allen) Goodpasture, married Bethier Lee, in 1870, and had one child.

216. Willie Ann, born in June, 1871.

FOURTH GENERATION.

No. 57.

A. W. Goodpasture, son of William Lockhart and Jane (White) Goodpasture, married Minnie Rhudy, January 19, 1870.

No. 58.

Ellen W. W. Goodpasture, daughter of William Lockhart and Jane (White) Goodpasture, married Rev. John M. Scott (-1891), April 11, 1867, and had eight children.

217. Bertie J., born February 14, 1868; died March 5, 1869.
218. Milton, born May 31, 1870.
219. Mary Ellen, born February 14, 1872.
220. J. Walter, born April 25, 1874.
221. Josephine Cleo, born October 20, 1876.
222. William Trigg, born August 25, 1878.
223. Conley S., born July 23, 1881.
224. Wilson White, born November 13, 1888.

No. 60.

James L. Goodpasture, son of William Lockhart and Jane (White) Goodpasture, married Mary Hoofnagle, January 12, 1869, and has two children.

225. Clarence, born April 3, 1870.
226. Anna Clyde, born April 3, 1874.

No. 61.

Mary Campbell Goodpasture, daughter of William Lockhart and Jane (White) Goodpasture, married Prof. H. C. Clutsam (-1887), June 10, 1868.

No. 62.

Mary Terrel Sprinkle, daughter of John T. and Martha Hamilton (Goodpasture) Sprinkle, married Wm. Snider, May 24, 1845, and had twelve children.

227. John Henry, born July 7, 1846.
228. William Hamilton, born February 13, 1848.
229. Peter Terrel, born June 1, 1850.
230. George Washington, born July 7, 1852.
231. Charles Sylvester, born July 16, 1854.
232. Martha E. C., born Nov. 25, 1856; died Sept. 30, 1890.
233. Lafayette McMullen, born December 2, 1858.
234. Sarah Emma Jane, born July 22, 1861.
235. A. R. F., born April 23, 1863.
236. Archibald S., born May 18, 1866; died Dec. 7, 1872.
237. Mary Susana Levisa, born January 5, 1868.
238. Alice Virginia, born March 30, 1870.

No. 73.

William Hamilton Goodpasture, son of Abraham Hamilton, and Sarah M. (Humphrey) Goodpasture, was married three times—first, to Mary E. Curren, September 22, 1859; second, to Margaret E. Winbarger, September 18, 1866; and, third, to Mary J. Pafford, January 25, 1894. He has nine children.

BY HIS FIRST WIFE.

239. Albert S., born November 21, 1860.

BY HIS SECOND WIFE.

240. David W., born July 29, 1868.
241. Charles H., born July 10, 1870.
242. Sarah E., born December 27, 1872; died July 23, 1851.
243. James Glenn, born July 17, 1875.
244. Everett Hamilton, born March 19, 1878.
245. Livonia V., born June 19, 1880.

BY HIS THIRD WIFE.

246. Robert Lee, born December 27, 1894.
247. Milton W., born March 17, 1896.

No. 74.

Sarah Margaret Goodpasture, daughter of Abraham Hamilton and Sarah M. (Humphrey) Goodpasture married L. R. Colley.

No. 75.

David Washington Goodpasture, son of Abraham Hamilton and Sarah M. (Humphrey) Goodpasture, enlisted in the Confederate Army, and was killed in battle in 1863.

No. 76.

Ellen Virginia Goodpasture, daughter of Abraham Hamilton and Sarah M. (Humphrey) Goodpasture, married Samuel Farris.

No. 78.

E. A. Goodpasture, daughter of Abraham Hamilton and Sarah M. (Humphrey) Goodpasture, married John V. Musser.

No. 80.

Jane Lockhart Goodpasture, daughter of Abraham Hamilton and Sarah M. (Humphrey) Goodpasture, married C. R. Johnston, November 19, 1869, and has had ten children.

248. Minnie Jane, born August 30, 1870.
249. Lizzie Bickle, born May 21, 1872.
250. John Abraham, born August 31, 1874.
251. Walter Enos, born August 14, 1876.
252. George Washington, born February 7, 1878.
253. Charles Worley, born Sept. 27, 1880; died July 4, 1881.
254. Joseph Keller, born December 31, 1883.
255. Henry Clay, born October 7, 1886.
256. Clara Belle, born January 26, 1888.
257. Ella Blanche, born October 1, 1891.

No. 83.

Abraham Hamiltin Goodpasture, son of Abraham Hamilton and Sarah M. (Humphrey) Goodpasture, married Kate Moore.

No. 84.

Ellen V. Wolfe, daughter of Roland and Elizabeth Lockhart (Goodpasture) Wolfe, married William A. Winbarger, December 17, 1872.

No. 85.

Sarah M. Wolfe, daughter of Roland and Elizabeth Lockhart (Goodpasture) Wolfe, married Ephraim Six, February 17, 1887.

No. 86.

Maggie F. Wolfe, daughter of Roland and Elizabeth Lockhart (Goodpasture) Wolfe, married John A. Corrico, October 23, 1883, and has three children.

258. Andrew Blain, born November 10, 1884.
259. Lutie Estelle, born April 24, 1886.
260. Ella May, born May 12, 1891.

No. 88.

Emma C. Wolfe, daughter of Roland and Elizabeth Lockhart (Goodpasture) Wolfe, married H. C. Defreese, May 6, 1880.

No. 90.

John G. Carlock, son of Abraham W. and Mary R. (Goodpasture) Carlock, was born in McLean County, Illinois, where he died. He married Lucinda Musick, September 5, 1850, and had eight children.

261. Dillard H., born October 15, 1851; died young.
262. George M., born December 10, 1852; died young.
263. Mary L., born January 1, 1854.
264. Richard L., born July 1, 1856.
265. Hester E., born August 2, 1858; died April 1, 1864.
266. S. Gertrude, born March 16, 1860.
267. John G., born February 14, 1863; died in 1868.
268. Lorin A., born December 8, 1867; died in 1870.

No. 92.

Madison P. Carlock, son of Abraham W. and Mary R. (Goodpasture) Carlock, was born in McLean County,

Illinois. He was twice married. First to Elizabeth Ewing (-1858), June 20, 1853, and, second, to Nancy E. Judy, June 14, 1860. He was the father of fifteen children.

BY HIS FIRST WIFE.

269. Arabelle, born September 28, 1854; died September 27, 1855.

270. James Howard, born September 1, 1856.

271. Isaac, who died in infancy.

BY HIS SECOND WIFE.

272. Rosalie, born March 17, 1861; died February 20, 1883.

273. George W., born June 4, 1862.

274. John A., born September 1, 1863.

275. Ida M., born April 8, 1865.

276. Horace L., born January 3, 1867.

277. Lyman J., born January 26, 1868.

278. Madison B., born January 4, 1870; died April 29, 1871.

279. Lina Gennette, born January 23, 1873.

280. Roy R., born June 29, 1875.

281. Wayne B., born March 17, 1877.

282. Marion P., born December 25, 1880.

283. Grace Lenore, born March 23, 1882.

No. 93.

Nancy J. Carlock, daughter of Abraham W. and Mary R. (Goodpasture) Carlock, was born in McLean County, Illinois; married Thomas Brown, October 1, 1858; moved to the State of Nebraska, where they now reside. They have four children.

284. Jacob M., born December 12, 1859.

285. Hattie, born January 5, 1861.

286. Abraham C., born April 17, 1862.

287. Cora, born June 10, 1865.

No. 94.

Sarah Carlock, daughter of Abraham W. and Mary R. (Goodpasture) Carlock, was born in McLean County,

Illinois, and now resides in Santa Cruz, Cal. She was
twice married; to William Allen, March 15, 1850; and to
William P. Marley (-1860), March 2, 1858. She had two
children.

BY HER FIRST HUSBAND.

288. Zepheniah, born April 22, 1851.

BY HER SECOND HUSBAND.

289. William P., born January 22, 1859.

No. 95.

Mahala Carlock, daughter of Abraham W. and Mary R.
(Goodpasture) Carlock, was born in McLean County,
Illinois, where she still resides. She married Benjamin
Gaddis (-1895), September 22, 1853, and had eleven chil-
dren.

290. Madison W., born July 4, 1854; died May 18, 1876.
291. Albert W., born October 9, 1855.
292. Cassius M., born November 18, 1857.
293. Mary F., born December 28, 1859.
294. Florence L., born March 30, 1862; died Jan. 10, 1863.
295. James A., born October 16, 1863; died March 30, 1864.
296. Silas M., born April 30, 1865.
297. George E., born September 1, 1867.
298. Luella, born September 13, 1870.
299. Rosa B., born Sept. 14, 1875; died Sept. 8, 1882.
300. Gertrude, born September 7, 1878.

No. 97.

Levina Carlock, daughter of Abraham W. and Mary R.
(Goodpasture) Carlock, was born, and still resides in
McLean County, Illinois. She married Ira Rowell, Novem-
ber 16, 1869, and has had five children.

301. Lillie, born September 27, 1870.
302. Laura B., born December 20, 1871; died June 15, 1890.
303. Lula J., born Nov. 21, 1875; died Feb. 18, 1895.
304. Edith J., born June 30, 1879.
305. Ira, born October 10, 1885.

No. 98.

William B. Carlock, son of Abraham W. and Mary R. (Goodpasture) Carlock, was born in McLean County, Illionis, and is now a prominent lawyer at Bloomington. He married Missouri McCart, October 6, 1870, and has three children.

306. Leslie Bryan, born September 14, 1871.
307. William C., born July 15, 1877.
308. Madeline (adopted), born August 15, 1892.

No. 100.

Abraham H. Carlock, son of Abraham W. and Mary R. (Goodpasture) Carlock, was born in McLean County, Illinois, and now resides at Carlock, in that county. He married Ida I. Edwards, January 9, 1879, and has three children.

309. Lula E., born October 25, 1879.
310. Pearl L., born August 3, 1881.
311. Celia W., born April 14, 1884.

No. 101.

Margery Carlock, daughter of Abraham W. and Mary R. (Goodpasture) Carlock, was born in McLean County, Illinois, where she died. She married William Pusey, October 10, 1881, and had four children.

312. William.
313. Mary.
314. Lucretia.
315. Parker Elmo.

No. 102.

Levina Dale, daughter of William and Martha H. (Goodpasture) Dale, married G. W. Parrish, in 1852, and died childless.

No. 104.

William Jackson Dale, son of William and Martha H. (Goodpasture) Dale, married Leanna Butler (1840-1890), in March, 1854. He was a captain in the Confederate Army, and was killed at the battle of Chickamauga, September 20, 1863. He left four children.

316. William Thomas, born in 1856.

317. Martha, born in January, 1858.

318. James, born in 1860.

319. Jennie Lee, born April 27, 1861.

No. 105.

Elizabeth Dale, daughter of William and Martha H. (Goodpasture) Dale, married L. B. (Tuck) Butler, in April, 1851, and has had six children.

320. Martha, born in February, 1852; died about 1880.

321. Louisa, born in 1854.

322. Marcella, born about 1856.

323. Jane Ann, born about 1858.

324. Dulcena, born about 1860.

325. John, born about 1867.

No. 106.

Wilburn Hamilton Dale, son of William and Martha H. (Goodpasture) Dale, lives at Butler's Landing, Tennessee, and has been married three times—first to Catherine Maberry (-1874), in August, 1854; second, to widow Hampton (-1878), about 1876; and, third, to ————. He has a large family.

No. 107.

Cleon Easailus Dale, son of William and Martha H. (Goodpasture) Dale, married Frances P. Chism (-1894), in January, 1858, and has had ten children.

326. Bettie, born December 11, 1859.

327. Ann, born in 1861.

328. Andrew, born in 1863.

329. Bennett, born in 1865.

330. William, born in 1867.

331. Sallie, born in 1868.

332. Jennie, born in 1872; died in 1877.

333. Nettie, born in 1874.

334. John, born in 1876.
335. Ada, born in 1878.

No. 108.

Alfred Lafayette Dale, son of William and Martha H. (Goodpasture) Dale, resides in Livingston, Tennessee, and has been married twice. His first wife was Sallie Butler, whom he married in 1864. After her death, he married her sister, Lucette Butler, December 10, 1884. He has had nine children.

BY HIS FIRST WIFE.

336. Russell Aubry, born in 1865.
337. Jake Bennett, born about 1866.
338. Butler, born in 1868; died in childhood.
339. Lura, born in 1870.
340. Lizzie, born in 1872.

BY HIS SECOND WIFE.

341. A son, died in infancy.
342. Perry.
343. Lillie.
344. Pauline.

No. 109.

Andrew Columbus Dale, son of William and Martha H. (Goodpasture) Dale, was a Lieutenant in the Confederate Army and is now a prominent citizen of Davidson County, Tennessee. He has been married twice—first to Jane Ann Chowning (-1883), January 23, 1868, and, second, to Mary Kyle, December 10, 1884. He has had ten children.

BY HIS FIRST WIFE.

345. Marcellus C., born March 2, 1869.
346. Etta, born March 17, 1872.
347. James C., born December 10, 1875.
348. William R., born in February, 1880; died in infancy.

BY HIS SECOND WIFE.

349. Dillard Y. (twin), born November 4, 1885.

350. Nellie (twin), born November 4, 1885; died November 14, 1886.

351. Rebecca, born December 13, 1887.

352. Andrew C., born September 7, 1889.

353. Paul, born April 21, 1894.

354. Hugh, born April 23, 1897.

No. 110.

John Francis Dale, son of William and Martha H. (Goodpasture) Dale, lives at Bennett's Ferry, Tennessee, and has been twice married—first, to Margaret Dervin (-1886), in 1872, and, second, to ——————. He has children.

BY HIS FIRST WIFE.

355. Stone Plumlee.

No. 111.

Dulcena Dale, daughter of William and Martha H. (Goodpasture) Dale, married Capt. Jacob C. Bennett, of Morgan's Confederate Cavalry, in June, 1863. Her husband was one of the six officers who escaped with General Morgan from the Ohio Penitentiary. She had ten children.

356. Lizzie, born in February, 1866.

357. Mattie, born in 1867.

358. John, born in 1869; died in 1878.

359. William, born in 1871; died in 1878.

360. Ida (twin), born in 1873; died in 1878.

361. Edgar (twin), born in 1873.

362. Albert Ridley, born in 1876; died in 1876.

363. A son, died in infancy.

364. Jackson, born in 1878; died in 1887.

365. Fannie, born in 1879.

No. 113.

William Iredell Bates, son of Joseph H. and Nancy B. (Goodpasture) Bates, is a farmer, living near Columbus,

Adams County, Illinois, but has, for several years, been superintendent of Adams County Alms House and Farm, a position requiring special skill and tact. He was married to Mary Ann Robertson, June 27, 1851, and has had nine children.

366. Martha Dulcena, born May 7, 1854; died May 17, 1854.
367. Amos Dillard, born September 3, 1855.
368. Myra Josephine, born March 26, 1858.
369. Ida Frances, born July 25, 1861.
370. Mary Effie, born November 25, 1863.
371. William Eddy, born Junary 20, 1866.
372. Hattie Loas, born January 4, 1868; died December 12, 1870.
373. Joseph Marcus, born April 18, 1870.
374. Orval Lee, born December 13, 1874.

No. 114.

Mary Elzada Bates, daughter of Joseph H. and Nancy B. (Goodpasture) Bates, married William Downing, May 28, 1850, and lives in Camp Point, Illinois. She has five children.

375. John Franklin, born in May, 1851.
376. Joseph Henry, born in 1856.
377. Albert Rezin, born in 1859.
378. Jessie Viola, born in 1864.
379. Harriet E., born in 1867.

No. 115.

John Russell Bates, son of Joseph H. and Nancy B. (Goodpasture) Bates, is married, but has no children. He lives at Republic, Greene County, Missouri. When a young man, he went to Oregon, and was, at one time, a member of the legislature of that State.

No. 117.

Thomas Jefferson Bates, son of Joseph H. and Nancy B. (Goodpasture) Bates, is a retired farmer, living in Galesburg, Illinois. He has represented Adams County in the Illinois Legislature, and served many years on supervisor's board of that county.   He married Leonora Wilson, November 6, 1859, and has had seven children.

380. Melgar McClellan, born August 18, 1860; died August 25, 1862.

381. John Emmett, born August 17, 1862.

382. Henson Everett, born March 8, 1864.

383. Henry Malcolm, born December 20, 1865.

384. Carrie Geneva, born December 19, 1867.

385. Leonora Wilson, born September 27, 1869.

386. Mary Emma, born August 13, 1871.

No. 118.

Permelia Jane Bates, daughter of Joseph H. and Nancy B. (Goodpasture) Bates, married James Sharp, a prosperous farmer of Camp Point, Illinois, April 21, 1864. She had three children, two of whom survived her.

387. Fletcher.

No. 119.

Madison Canby Bates, son of Joseph H. and Nancy B. (Goodpasture) Bates, lives in Oberlin, Ohio. He was married to Emma Latimer, May 16, 1861, and has five children.

388. George Latimer.

389. Eula Goodpasture.

390. Mary Drumon.

391. Harriet Myrtle.

392. Madison Clair.

No. 120.

Margery Josephine Bates, daughter of Joseph H. and Nancy B. (Goodpasture) Bates, married David R. Thomas, a farmer and trader of Augusta, Hancock County, Illinois, November 22, 1860, and has had eight children.

393. Lizzie May, born September 15, 1861.

394. Nancy Josephine, born August 19, 1863; died February 25, 1887.

395. Edith Allegra, born October 21, 1865.

396. Arthur Reed, born June 18, 1868.

397. Augusta Bates, born July 2, 1871; died September 1, 1872.

398. Lottie Maud, born October 11, 1873.
399. Freddie, born July 17, 1876; died February 17, 1877.
400. Madison C., born December 19, 1879.

No. 121.

Joseph Baxter Bates, son of Joseph H. and Nancy B. (Goodpasture) Bates, received a college education. Taught school and raised cotton in Alabama. Was admitted to the bar. Was a Republican candidate for the legislature, and for Presidential elector. Returned to Illinois in 1877, and entered the field of journalism. Has been, for many years, political editor of the Bloomington, Illinois, Daily Pantagraph, the most widely circulated paper in Illinois, outside of Chicago. He married Sophie Harrison Rucker, of Bedford County, Tennessee, June 23, 1870, and has six children.

401. Lucy Ragsdale, born March 20, 1873.
402. Annie Rucker, born November 13, 1874.
403. Jerome Lowell, born January 30, 1877.
404. Robert Paul, born July 16, 1879.
405. Ralph Dwight, born November 7, 1882.
406. Irene Huron, born September 25, 1888.

No. 122.

Abraham Henderson Bates, son of Joseph and Nancy B. (Goodpasture) Bates, of Springfield, Illinois, received a college education, and entered the ministry of the Presbyterian Church. Has had charge of churches at Empire City, Oregon, and Mawa and Springfield, Illinois. He married Lydia E. Parker, June 17, 1880, but has no chidren.

No. 124.

Marquis Jerome Bates, son of Joseph H. and Nancy B. (Goodpasture) Bates, was a greatly beloved and highly respected business man. He was never married.

No. 125.

Margaret Ann Bates, daughter of Joseph H. and Nancy B. (Goodpasture) Bates, married Leland S. Breese, a business

18

man of Wilmette, Illinois, August 22, 1869, and has had six children.

    407. Margaret Josephine, born February 20, 1871.

    408. Bessie Maybelle, born August 31, 1872.

    409. Harriet Isabelle, born August 9, 1875.

    410. Paul Leland, born January 14, 1883.

    411. Niles Sidney Sumner, born June 15, 1886.

    412. Beulah Nancy, born June 5, 1888; died April 27, 1889.

No. 126.

Harriet Rosanna Bates, daughter of Joseph H. and Nancy B. (Goodpasture) Bates, married David M. Harris, a minister, teacher and editor, of the Cumberland Presbyterian Church, August 25, 1869, but had no children.

No. 127.

Morillena Dale, daughter of Thomas and Levina (Good pasture) Dale, married Thomas Brown, at Melville, Dade County, Missouri, in 1854. She had no children.

No. 130.

W. A. Dale, son of Thomas and Levina (Goodpasture) Dale, a merchant at Cane Hill, Missouri, is a permanent cripple from service in the Confederate Army. He married Rebecca Lewis, of Dade County, Missouri ,in 1860, and has had six children.

    413. A daughter, born February 4, 1861; died in infancy.

    414. Alpha, born June 22, 1862.

    415. Cora, born August 27, 1866.

    416. Levina, born May 7, 1869.

    417. Thomas A., born September 4, 1872.

    418. Willie Lewis, born January 31, 1885; died in infancy.

No. 131.

John W. Dale, son of Thomas and Levina (Goodpasture) Dale, married Martha Rountree, in December, 1867, and had two children.

    419. Loney, who died at the age of six years.

    420. Flora.

No. 132.

Abraham B. Dale, son of Thomas and Levina (Goodpasture) Dale, was born in Overton County, Tennessee, and died in the Confederate service, at Little Rock, Arkansas, He was never married.

No. 135.

Mary M. Dale, daughter of Thomas and Levina (Goodpasture) Dale, married J. M. Rountree, in 1868, and has had seven children, five of whom are living, to-wit:

421. John T.
422. Clyde.
423. Charles.
424. Lee.
425. Lula.

No. 137.

Azariah Thomas Goodpasture, son of William B. and Martha Ann (Harville) Goodpasture, joined the Union Army in Illinois, and died in the service, unmarried.

No. 138.

Mary Margery Goodpasture, daughter of William B. and Martha Ann(Harville) Goodpasture, married Charles Jones, in 1863, and had six children. Three died young. The others are:

426. Fanny.
427. Ida.
428. Nettie.

No. 140.

Andrew Seymour Goodpasture, of Auburn, Illinois, son cf William B. and Martha Ann (Harville) Goodpasture, married mary Jane Fletcher, April 2, 1868, and has three children.

429. Nettie, born December 17, 1868.
430. Henry Fletcher, born December 15, 1870.
431. Andrew Ward, born August 6, 1874.

No. 141.

Lucy Dulcena Goodpasture, daughter of William B. and Martha Ann (Harville) Goodpasture, married Jacob Walters, in 1863 or 4, and lives in California. She has six childrer. The names of two of them are not known.

432. Willis.
433. Effie.
434. Nola.
435. Willia.

No. 142.

William Erastus Goodpasture, son of William B. and Martha Ann (Harville) Goodpasture, was twice married. By his second wife he had one child.

436. Marshall, born in 1871.

No. 143.

Philander Cass Goodpasture, son of William B. and Martha Ann (Harville) Goodpasture, married Ella Lowdermilk, in 1877, and has seven children living.

437. Lloyd.
438. Edith.
439. Curtis.
440. Minnie.
441. Bessie.
442. Effle.
443. Walter DeWitt Talmage.

No. 146.

Levi Dodds Goodspasture, son of William B. and Martha Ann (Harville) Goodpasture, married Martha Fletcher, in 1874, and has four living children.

444. Ida Pearl.
445. Della Maud.
446. Nathan Clyde.
447. Beulah Myrle.

No. 147.

Jesse Fletcher Goodpasture, son of William B. and Adelphia (Smith) Goodpasture, married Matilda Porterfield, in 1876, and has four children.

448. Byron May, born in 1877.
449. Lena, born in 1880.
450. Francis Liddell, born in 1881.
451. Jesse Lea, born in 1886.

No. 148.

J. Dillard Goodpasture, son of Abraham H. and Dulcena
B. (Williams) Goodpasture, was born in Petersburg,
Illinois. After attending the common schools, he spent a
year at North Sangamon Academy, and six months at
Lincoln University. In 1869 he moved to Holt County,
Missouri, and settled on the wild prairie, hauling the lumber
to build his house a distance of 23 miles. The soil proved
productive, and he now has one of the best grain and stock
farms in the county. He moved to Maitland in 1893. Is
a member of the school board, and of the County Court.
He assisted in organizing the Nodaway Valley District Fair,
for the counties of Nodaway, Andrew, Atchison and Holt,
and served one year as its President. He is a director in
the Farmer's Bank, of Maitland; a Mason and a member
of the Methodist Church. He married Frances H. (1848-
    ), daughter of George M. (1827-1853), and Mariam A.
(Flinn) Obanion (1827-1897), September 1, 1868, and has
seven children.
452. Edwin R., born July 26, 1869.
453. Abraham H., born May 20, 1871.
454. Deedie A., born January 17, 1873.
455. Mary E. C., born July 31, 1875.
456. George B., born October 5, 1877.
457. Vrenna J., born August 31, 1881.
458. Ethel Frances, born January 26, 1885.

No. 149.

Hattie E. Goodpasture, daughter of Abraham H. and Dulcena B. (Williams) Goodpasture, was born in Sangamon
County, Illinois. She has been twice married, and has had
four children. She married her first husband, W. G. Web
ster, August 17, 1875; and her second, James M. (1845-   ),

son of Rufus H. and Angeline F. (Matthews) Walker, September 6, 1892.

BY HER FIRST HUSBAND.

459. A son, born June 29, 1876; died in infancy.
460. Isabelle, born September 18, 1877.

BY HER SECOND HUSBAND.

461. Rupert S., born September 11, 1893.
462. Frank L., born January 23, 1895.

No. 150.

Jacob Ridley Goodpasture, son of Abraham H. and Dulcena B. (Williams) Goodpasture, was born in Sangamon County, Illinois, and moved thence to Hebron, Nebraska. He was twice married: first to Hannah Quaintance (- 1893), in December, 1884; and second, to Lizzie Gordon, seventh daughter of Joseph and Ruth A. Combs, July 21, 1896. He has had four children.

BY HIS FIRST WIFE

463. Lee, born in September, 1885.
464. Gertrude, born in October, 1886.
465. Dillard, born in 1887.
466. George, born in 1890.

No. 151.

Tennessee G. Hinds, daughter of Claiborne and Elizabeth B. (Goodpasture) Hinds, married L. A. Mitchell, January 30, 1866, and had seven children.

467. Ollie, born December 22, 1866; died September 17, 1879.
468. Ella, born September 26, 1868.
469. Dillard C., born March 12, 1870.
470. Elbert A., born January 1, 1872.
471. Nancy E., born August 2, 1874.
472. John C., born September 19, 1876.
473. Allen L., born February 21, 1879; died October 6, 1879.

No. 152.

John S. Hinds, son of Claiborne and Elizabeth B. (Goodpasture) Hinds, married T. A. Jones, January 24, 1872, and has ten children.

474. Luvada, born February 11, 1873.
475. Mollie, born November 24, 1874.
476. Katie, born January 22, 1876.
477. Anna, born December, 16, 1880.
478. William, born December 9, 1882; died July 3, 1884.
479. Mary, born May 22, 1884.
480. Porter, born August 27, 1886.
481. Curtis, born November 16, 1888.
482. Bessie, born December 16, 1890.
483. Ruth, born December 28, 1892.

No. 153.

Martha F. Hinds, daughter of Claiborne and Elizabeth B. (Goodpasture) Hinds, married J. D. Johnson, July 10, 1865, and has five children.

484. Dillard, born July 4, 1869; died February 8, 1870.
485. Ollie, born February 26, 1870.·
486. Cora, born February 5, 1872.
487. Edward, born February 10, 1874.
488. Fletcher, born March 6, 1876.

No. 155.

Ova C. Hinds, daughter of Claiborne and Elizabeth B. (Goodpasture) Hinds, married L. A. Mitchell, the husband of her deceased sister, Tennessee, May 16, 1880, and has seven children.

489. William G., born February 22, 1881.
490. Emma D., born February 8, 1883.
491. Clara B., born January 1, 1885.
492. Lois E., born February 4, 1887.
493. Chester, born April 30, 1889.
494. Mabel, born February 21, 1892.
495. Baby, born July 10, 1897.

No. 156.

Isaiah Winburn Mitchell, son of Dennis C. and Margaret Ann (Goodpasture) Mitchell, was a successful farmer, near Livingston, Tennessee. He married Sophronie C. Winton, October 2, 1873, and had four children.

496. Mary Hettie, born August 11, 1874.
497. John Ridley, born September 26, 1877.
498. William Walter, born August 29, 1881.
499. Winburn Elmo, born July 28, 1884.

No. 157.

John M. D. Mitchell, son of Dennis C. and Margaret Ann (Goodpasture) Mitchell, of Livingston, Tennessee, though he died in early manhood, achieved distinction at the bar, and was twice Attorney General of his district. He was never married.

No. 158.

Winburn A. Goodpasture, son of John G. and Catherine M. (Atkinson) Goodpasture, married Sue Keeton, of Overton County, Tennessee, October 28, 1873, and is now living in Gainesville, Texas. He has seven children.

500. Lizzie, born July 30, 1875.
501. Alvin Cullom, born August 24, 1877.
502. Kate, born September 18, 1879.
503. Albert Virgil, born September 19, 1881.
504. Nettie Lea, born August 28, 1883.
505. John, born September 14, 1887.
506. Alfred M. Keeton, born August 19, 1891.

No. 159.

Sallie M. Goodpasture, daughter of John G. and Catherine M. (Atkinson) Goodpasture, married Dr. Henry E. Hart (1852-   ), son of H. W. and Laura (Young) Hart, a leading physician of Carthage, Tennessee, October 18, 1874, and has three children.

507. Lucy Harris, born July 20, 1875.
508. Alexander Selkirk, born September 3, 1876.
509. Dewees Berry, born June 2, 1892.

No. 160.

Josie Goodpasture, daughter of John G. and Catherine
M. (Atkinson) Goodpasture, married John Sanford, of
Carthage, Tennessee, in December, 1881, and subsequently
moved to Paul's Valley, I. T., where they now reside. She
has had two children.

510. Grace, born May 12, 1887; died in infancy.
510. Eva, born October 31, 1894.

No. 161.

Hettie Goodpasture, daughter of John G. and Catherine
M. (Atkinson) Goodpasture, married B. F. Sanders, of Carthage, Tennessee, in September, 1896, and now resides in
that town.

No. 162.

John Ridley Goodpasture, son of Jefferson Dillard and
Sarah Jane (Dillen) Goodpasture, was born in Livingston,
Tennessee; graduated at East Tennessee University in 1875,
from which school he received the degree of Master of Arts
in 1882. While here he projected, and was one of the first
editors of the University monthly, the first periodical ever
published by the students of the University. In 1876, he
was elected a member of the State Legislature, where he
made much reputation as a State credit Democrat. In a
public address in Columbia, in 1878, Hon. Wm. J. Sykes
said of him: "Permit me to say that the speeches made
in the last Legislature by two of the rising young men of
Tennessee, R. P. Frierson, of Bedford, and J. R. Goodpasture, have not and cannot be answered by any of the
opponents of State credit, no matter how venerable in
age or how experienced in debate." In 1878, he was elected
a member of the committee on resolutions in the Democratic State Convention, over Judge Jo. C. Guild, after both
had been called upon, and publicly expressed their views on
the issues of the campaign. He entered upon the practice
of the law, at Clarksville, in 1877, in partnership with his
brother, A. V. Goodpasture, but in November, 1878, he
yielded to an inexorable impression to preach, and aban-

doning all purpose of achieving professional as well as
political preferment, he entered the ministry of the Cumberland Presbyterian, in which he has now labored for nearly
twenty years. He has lately moved from Overton to Davidson County, and is now living at Shwab, in that county,
and is giving all his time to evangelistic work. He married
Sallie A., daughter of Rev. John Lansden, on the 28th day
of December, 1880, and has had eight children.

    512. Ruth, born January 13, 1882; died April 30, 1890.

    513. John Albert, born August 8, 1883.

    514. William Dillard, born October 23, 1885.

    515. James Ridley, born September 16, 1887.

    516. Hugh Lansden, born October 26, 1889.

    517. Lurton, born December 24, 1891.

    518. Frank, born July 15, 1893.

    519. Hettie Rose, born June 9, 1895.

No. 163.

Albert Virgil Goodpasture, son of Jefferson Dillard and
Sarah Jane (Dillen) Goodpasture, was born in Livingston,
Tennessee; attended preparatory schools at Cookeville and
New Middleton, and graduated at East Tennessee University (University of Tennessee) in 1875, from which school
he received the degree of Master of Arts, in 1882. In 1877,
he graduated in the law department of Vanderbilt University, and commenced the practice of his profession in Clarksville, Tennessee, July, 1877, in partnership with his brother,
J. R. Goodpasture. His brother having abandoned the bar
for the pulpit, in 1879 he became associated with Gen. Wm.
A. Quarles and Hon. Wm. M. Daniel, in the well known
law firm of Quarles, Daniel and Goodpasture. In 1884 and
1885, in connection with his brother, W. H. Goodpasture, he
made two importations of Holstein-Friesian cattle from
Holland. In 1888, he was elected a member of the House
of Representatives in the General Assembly of Tennessee,
and in 1890, a member of the Senate. He served on the
Ways and Means Committee, in both of these bodies. In
1891, he resigned his seat in the Senate to accept the posi-

tion of Clerk of the Supreme Court, at Nashville, which position he held until 1897. He married Jennie Wilson, daughter of Stephen W. (1822-1887) and Martha L. (Wilson) Dawson (1825-1864). November 16, 1880, and has had six children.

520.Mattie Madge, born June 2, 1882.

521. William Dillard (twin), born May 21, 1884; died May 24, 1884.

522. Ridley Rose (twin), born May 21, 1884.

523. Ernest, born October 17, 1886.

524. Sarah Jane, born September 15, 1890.

525. Albert Virgil, born April 2, 1893.

No. 164.

William Henry Goodpasture, son of Jefferson Dillard and Sarah Jane (Dillen) Goodpasture, was born in Livingston, Tennessee. He received his literary education at Burritt College and Vanderbilt University, and graduated in the law department of the latter institution. He ranked high in his college career, representing his society in the annual debate and oratorical contest, and also represented the Phi Delta Theta fraternity at the biennial meeting at Richmond, Virginia, in 1882. He visited all the countries of Europe, except Turkey and Russia, in 1883, and in 1884 and 1885, made two importations of Holstein-Fresian cattle from Holland, for the firm of A. V. & W. H. Goodpasture. He then joined his father in the importation of jack stock and Cleveland Bay horses, making eight trips to Europe for that purpose. He projected, assisted in the organization, and became the first Secretary of the American Breeders' Association of Jacks and Jennets, and to his careful and intelligent work the success of this organization is mainly due. He published a valuable pamphlet on jack stock, and edited the first volume of the American Jack Stock Stud-Book. In 1891, his brother, A. V. Goodpasture, was appointed Clerk of the Supreme Court, at Nashville, and he retired from the stock business to accept the place of Deputy Clerk, in his office, which position he held until 1897. He has never married.

No. 167.

Lucette Margery Goodpasture, daughter of Jefferson Dillard and Nannie (Young) Goodpasture, was born in Overton County, Tennessee, and moved with her parents to Nashville in 1879. She was educated at Ward's Seminary. She married Joe M. Stewart, November 10, 1896. Her husband is the proprietor of the Stewart Pants Co., and Stewart Book and Music Co., of Nashville. They have one child.

526. Marjorie Goodpasture, born October 10, 1897.

No. 168.

Austin Young Goodpasture, son of Jefferson Dillard and Nannie (Young) Goodpasture, was born in Overton County, Tennessee, and moved with his parents to Nashville, in 1879, where he now resides, unmarried.

No. 169.

Mona Clark Goodpasture, daughter of Jefferson Dillard and Nannie (Young) Goodpasture, was born in Overton County, Tennessee, and moved with her parents to Nashville, in 1879. She was educated at the Nashville College for Young Ladies. She married Alexander R., son of Rev. Joseph B. Erwin, on the 29th day of April, 1896. Her husband is employed in the main office of the N., C. & St. L. Ry. They have one child.

527. Tennie Marie, born February 8, 1897.

No. 170.

Jefferson Dillard Goodpasture, was born in Overton County, Tennessee, and moved with his parents to Nashville, in 1879, where he now resides, engaged in the real estate business.

No. 171.

Avo Goodpasture, daughter of James M. and Ova (Arnold) Goodpasture, married Dr. J. F. Dyer, a leading physician of Cookeville, Tennessee, June 10, 1894. No children.

No. 172.

Mary Hettie Goodpasture, daughter of James M. and Ova (Arnold) Goodpasture, married A. W. Boyd, a prominent lawyer, formerly Clerk and Master, and at present State Senator, of Cookeville. Tennessee, December 15, 1878, and has had nine children.

528. Ernest Houston, born October 1, 1879.

529. Ova, born October 17, 1881.

530. Vallie, born May 31, 1883.

531. Allie, born December 26, 1884.

532. McDonnold Jefferson, born November 25, 1887; died September 11, 1888.

533. Margery, born February 22, 1890.

534. Grover Cleveland, born September 30, 1891.

535. Gretchen, born March 3, 1894.

536. Alvin Goodpasture, born October 16, 1895; died October 10, 1896.

No. 173.

John Bryan Goodpasture, son of James M. and Ova (Arnold) Goodpasture, lives in Cookeville, Tennessee, and is unmarried.

No. 174.

Sarah Margery Goodpasture, daughter of James M. and Ova (Arnold) Goodpasture, married E. H. Jared (-1896), a most promising young lawyer of Cookeville, December 3, 1891, and has one child.

537. Eugene Franklin, born December 12, 1895.

No. 176.

Lou G. Goodpasture, daughter of Winburn W. and Martha Ann (Capps) Goodpasture, married C. M. Hensley, a minister in the Methodist Church, about 1880. They now live in Birmingham, Alabama, and have two children.

538. Ala M., born in 1882.

539. Ethel, born in 1883.

No. 177.

Ala May Goodpasture, daughter of Winburn W. and Martha Ann (Capps) Goodpasture, was never married.

No. 178.

Maggie L. Goodpasture, daughter of Winburn W. and Martha Ann (Capps) Goodpasture, married William G. Currie, an estimable gentleman and an excellent lawyer, formerly of Brownsville, but now of Cookeville, Tennessee, about 1884. They have three children.

540. Loula May, born January 27, 1887.
541. Mattie Capps, born November 6, 1889.
542. Winburn Goodpasture, born July 21, 1893.

No. 179.

Elmo C. Goodpasture, son of Winburn W. and Martha Ann (Capps) Goodpasture, is a merchant in Chattanooga, Tennessee. He has never married.

No. 186.

Elizabeth Goodpasture, daughter of Hamilton and Eleanor (Ellyson) Goodpasture, married John Ford (-1857), in 1852, and had one child. She was married again to Samuel M. Fancher (-1863), March 3, 1858, and had two children. She was married a third time, to George W. Wilson, in January, 1873, and had three children. She lives in Pacific County, Washington.

BY HER FIRST HUSBAND.

543. A son, who died at the age of two years.

BY HER SECOND HUSBAND.

544. Loyd Watson, born December, 1859.
545. Kate, born June 1, 1861; died June 7, 1872.

BY HER THIRD HUSBAND.

546. Emerson J., born March 31, 1875.
547. Howard M., born July 29, 1878.
548. Olive Eleanor, born September 24, 1880.

No. 187.

Andrew Jackson Goodpasture, of Bay Centre, Washington, son of Hamilton and Eleanor (Ellyson) Goodpasture, married Rebecca Scanlan, at Indianola, Warren County, Iowa, in 1866, and died in 1888, from lung disease contracted in the war. No children.

No. 188.

William Hamilton Goodpasture, son of Hamilton and Eleanor (Ellyson) Goodpasture, enlisted in the 13th Iowa Infantry Volunteers, in 1861, and was killed in front of Atlanta, Ga., August 9, 1864.

No. 189.

Abraham Goodpasture, son of Hamilton and Eleanor (Ellyson) Goodpasture, was born in Morgan County, Illinois; at the age of sixteen, moved to Kansas, and lived there two years; moved to Iowa, and in 1878, settled at Anita, Cass County; is a contractor and builder. He married Arazona Almira Bidlake, March 24, 1868, and has eight children.

549. Susan, born in 1869; died in September, 1878.
550. Myra, born in 1872; died in October, 1878.
551. Mary A., born in 1874.
552. Charles H., born in 1876.
553. Leonard R., born in 1882.
554. Theodore B., born in 1884.
555. Mildred A., born in 1886.
556. Ellen G., born in 1892.

No. 190.

John Ellyson Goodpasture, of Bay Centre, Washington, son of Hamilton and Eleanor (Ellyson) Goodpasture, married Sarah Ann Shockley, at Summerset, Warren County, Iowa, in 1870, and has had four children—one boy and three girls.

557. G. Frank, born April 21, 1872.
558. Minnie Alma, born March 21, 1876; died June 13, 1895.

559. Alice May, born March 3, 1882.
560. Edith Madge, born May 5, 1888.

No. 191.

James P. Goodpasture, son of Hamilton and Eleanor (Ellyson) Goodpasture, was born in Hamilton County, Illinois; lived a while in Kansas; moved to Iowa in 1860; thence to Oregon in 1870; and thence to Bay Centre, Washington, in 1876. He has been twice married, first, to Edith R. Matthews (-1885), in 1883; and, second, to Mrs. Delphia C. Sparks, in 1895. No children.

No. 192.

Martha Jane Goodpasture, daughter of Hamilton and Eleanor (Ellyson) Goodpasture, married Leonard M. Rhodes of Pacific County, Washington, in 1874, and died at Bay Centre, Washington, leaving two children.

561. Carl, born in 1875.
562. Elsie, born in 1879.

No. 193.

Thomas B. Goodpasture, of Sam's Valley, Jackson County, Oregon, son of Hamilton and Eleanor (Ellyson) Goodpasture is a Methodist minister; married in 1876, and has had eight children.

563. A daughter, died at the age of ten years.
564. DeWitt, born in 1879.
565. Ernest, born in 1882.
566. Lloyd, born in 1884.
567. Waine, born in 1886.
568. Victor, born in 1890.
569. Ira, born in 1892.
570. John, born in 1894.

No. 201.

John J. Goodpasture, son of Francis M. and Lydia L. (Thomas) Goodpasture, married Lora Thompson, January 21, 1894, and has two children.

571. Benton Cordell, born April 9, 1895.
572. Ethel, born January 30, 1897.

No. 214.

Lillie May Cooper, daughter of James and Sarah C. (Goodpasture) Cooper, married Charles Cooper, in September, 1895.

FIFTH GENERATION.

No. 217.

Bertie J. Scott, daughter of John M. and Ellen W. W. (Goodpasture) Scott, married W. G. Pannil, February 14, 1888, and had one child.

573. Hallie Bell, born December 15, 1888.

No. 218.

Milton Scott, son of Jno. M. and Ellen W. W. (Goodpasture) Scott, married Libbie Smith, February 21, 1894, and has one child.

574. Walter Ralph.

No. 219.

Mary Ellen Scott, daughter of John M. and Ellen W. W. (Goodpasture) Scott, married C. C. Killinger, February 2S, 1894, and has one child.

575. Hugh W.

No. 225.

Clarence Goodpasture, son of James L. and Mary (Hoofnagle) Goodpasture, married Cordelia Akers, and has one child.

576. Josphine.

No. 226.

Anna Clyde Goodpasture, daughter of James L. and Mary (Hoofnagle) Goodpasture, married George Vandergrift, and has two children.

577. Glenna Lee, born January 22, 1892.
578. James Thomas, born December 26, 1895.

19

No. 227.

John Henry Snider, son of William and Mary Terrel (Sprinkle) Snider, married Mary E. Wolfe, November 22, 1866, and has one child.

579. Josephine, born September 15, 1871.

No. 228.

William Hamilton Snider, son of William and Mary Terrel (Sprinkle) Snider, married Ann Eliza Oakes, February 13, 1872.

No. 229.

Peter Terrel Snider, son of William and Mary Terrel (Sprinkle) Snider, married M. C. A. Killinger, February 11, 1872.

No. 232.

Martha E. C. Snider, daughter of William and Mary Terrel (Sprinkle) Snider, married George A. Groseclose, in January, 1874, and has three children.

580. Charles P., born October 26, 1875.

581. Mary E., born September 27, 1878.

582. Emma E., born September 20, 1881.

No. 233.

Lafayette McMullen Snider, son of William and Mary Terrel (Sprinkle) Snider, is married and has three children.

583. Bertha Lee, born May 26, 1885.

584. Gracie Blanche, born February 23, 1889.

585. Maud May, November 15, 1890.

No. 235.

A. R. F. Snider, son of William and Mary Terrel (Sprinkle) Snider, married Cora V. Hankle, December 21, 1887, and has four children.

586. Gracie Pearl, born February 10, 1889.

587. Mattie E., born October 4, 1890.

588. Lettie May, born May 28, 1893.

589. Alma Gay, born April 3, 1897.

No. 237.

Mary Susana Levisa Snider, daughter of William and Mary Terrel (Sprinkle) Snider, married Albert S. Goodpasture, September 1, 1887. See No. 239.

No. 238.

Alice Virginia Snider, daughter of William and Mary Terrel (Sprinkle) Snider, married William P. Falke, February 17, 1897.

No. 239.

Albert S. Goodpasture, son of William Hamilton and Mary E. (Curren) Goodpasture, married Mary Susana Levisa Snider, September 1, 1887, and has four children.

590. Leonia May, born September 23, 1888.

591. Archie S., born August 30, 1891.

592. Florence Alberta, born April 12, 1893.

593. Early Page, born February 8, 1895.

No. 240.

David W. Goodpasture, son of William Hamilton and Margaret E. (Winbarger) Goodpasture, married Dora Kegley, and 'has three children.

594. Conley.

595. Everett.

596. Mary Gay.

No. 241.

Charles H. Goodpasture, son of William Hamilton and Margaret E. (Winbarger) Goodpasture, married Gay Snider, and has had two children.

597. Selma Gay, born June 5, 1895; died June 14, 1896.

598. Hilda V., born in May, 1897.

No. 263.

Mary L. Carlock, daughter of John G. and Lucinda (Musick) Carlock, married Robert L. Sabin, June 20, 1877, and resides at Beatrice, Nebraska. She has five children, but the names of the youngest two are not known.

599. Ralph M., born in 1878.
600. Robert L., born in 1880.
601. Mary Louise, born in 1883.

No. 264.

Richard L. Carlock, son of John G. and Lucinda (Musick) Carlock, married Sallie M. Dunlap, January 15, 1879, and has one child.

602. Claud, born in 1881.

No. 266.

S. Gertrude Carlock, daughter of John G. and Lucinda (Musick) Carlock, married Harvey L. Hart, June 15, 1888, and resides in Bloomington, Illinois. She has two children.

603. Harvey L., born in 1891.
604. Alfred T., born in 1894.

No. 272.

Rosalie Carlock, daughter of Madison P. and Nancy E. (Judy) Carlock, married Thomas J. Mountjoy, and left two children.

605. Holton C.
606. Wayne B.

No. 273.

George W. Carlock, son of Madison P. and Nancy E. (Judy) Carlock, married Ella Martin, February 28, 1884, and resides in Omaha, Nebraska. He has four children.

607. Frederick, born in 1884.
608. Maggie, born in 1886.
609. Clinton, born in 1889.
610. Helen, born in 1895.

No. 274.

John A. Carlock, son of Madison P. and Nancy E. (Judy) Carlock, married Clara Gordon, June 15, 1890, and has one child.

611. Colby C., born in 1892.

No. 275.

Ida M. Carlock, daughter of Madison P. and Nancy E. (Judy) Carlock, married Jesse B. Jordan, October 2, 1891, and has had two children.

612. Cecil Marie, who died in infancy.

613. Jessie Hellene, born in 1894.

No. 276.

Horace L. Carlock, son of Madison P. and Nancy E. (Judy) Carlock, married Ollie Thompson, January 1, 1886, and has four children.

614. Ralph T.

615. Neva.

616. Cleon.

617. Holton.

No. 277.

Lyman J. Carlock, son of Madison P. and Nancy E. (Judy) Carlock, married Mabelle Riddle, September 1, 1893, and has one child.

618. Lael Marie, born in 1895.

No. 279.

Lina Gennette Carlock, daughter of Madison P. and Nancy E. (Judy) Carlock, married John W. Applegate, March 10, 1894, and has one child.

619. Grace Modelle, born in 1896.

No. 285.

Hattie Brown, daughter of Jacob M. and Nancy J. (Carlock) Brown, married William Taylor, May 16, 1873, and resides in or near Little Rock, Arkansas. She has several children, whose names are not known.

No. 287.

Cora Brown, daughter of Jacob M. and Nancy J. (Carlock) Brown, married James Bacon, June 16, 1892. N further information.

No. 288.

Zepheniah Allen, son of William and Sarah (Carlock)
Allen, married Belle Center, October 10, 1891, and resides at
Normal, Illinois. He has two children.
620. Lucille, born in 1893.
621. Mildred, born in 1895.

No. 289.

William P. Marley, son of William P. and Sarah (Carlock)
Marley, married Nellie Bergen, November 15, 1890, and
resides at Peoria, Illinois. He has two children.
622. Robert Cedric, born in 1891.
623. Lucette Marjorie, born in 1893.

No. 291.

Albert W. Gaddis, son of Benjamin and Mahala (Carlock)
Gaddis, is married and has four children. No other information.

No. 316.

William Thomas Dale, son of William Jackson and
Leanna (Butler) Dale, lives in Clay County, Tennessee.
He married Mollie Quarles (-1897), in 1879, and has four
children.
624. Robert.
625. Walter.
626. James.
627. A girl.

No. 317.

Martha Dale, daughter of William Jackson and Leanna
(Butler) Dale, married Hugh Kyle, of Clay County, Tennessee, February 22, 1874, and has had five children.
628. Millard Jackson, born December 10, 1875.
629. Floyd, born August 30, 1877; died in 1880 or 1881.
630. Charles Lee, born April 30, 1880.
631. Frank, born in May, 1882.
632. Lizzie, born in July, 1887.

No. 318.

James Dale, son of William Jackson and Leanna (Butler) Dale, married Mollie Chandler, about 1887, and has children.

No. 319.

Jennie Lee Dale, daughter of William Jackson and Leanna (Butler) Dale, married Stephen S. Kirk (1852-   ) July 28, 1878. They live in Dallas, Texas, and have four children.

633. Eula Dale, born July 13, 1881.

634. Annie Lola, born January 1, 1883.

635. Ralph Carl, born December 4, 1885.

636. Paul Toof, born January 14, 1888.

No. 320.

Martha Butler, daughter of L. B. and Elizabeth (Dale) Butler, married W. C. Bailey, about 1869, and has had six children.

637. A daughter.

638. Lizzie.

639. Benjamin.

640. Jennie, now dead.

641. James.

642. Allie.

No. 321.

Louisa Butler, daughter of L. B. and Elizabeth (Dale) Butler married Reuben Beck, of Butler's Landing, Tennessee, and has children.

No. 323.

Jane Ann Butler, daughter of L. B. and Elizabeth (Dale) Butler, married Amonett Kirkpatrick, in 1874, and has had one child.

643. Bedford, born in 1876; died in December, 1884.

No. 325.

John Butler, son of L. B. and Elizabeth (Dale) Butler, married a Miss Hampton, and resides at Butler's Landing, Tennessee.

No. 326.

Bettie Dale, daughter of Cleon E. and Frances P. (Chism) Dale, married R. T. Peterman, of Celina, Tennessee, October 4, 1880, and has had nine boys.

644. J. H., born August 11, 1881.
645. W. R., born February 4, 1883.
646. C. E., born November 26, 1885.
647. A. C., born April 8, 1887.
648. R. V., born March 27, 1889.
649. S. F., born January 6, 1891.
650. J. I., born February 18, 1893.
651. G. B., born December 22, 1894.
652. H. B., born September 10, 1896.

No. 327.

Ann Dale, daughter of Cleon E. and Frances P. (Chism) Dale, married T. L. Meadows, in January, 1894, and has one child.

653. Inez.

No. 328.

Andrew Dale, son of Cleon E. and Frances P. (Chism) Dale, married Lizzie Peterman, in 1882, and has seven children.

654. Tennie, born in 1883.
655. Cheatham.
656. R. T.

No. 329.

Bennett Dale, son of Cleon E. and Frances P. (Chism) Dale, married a Miss Moore, about 1889 or 1890, and has one child.

657. A girl.

No. 335.

Ada Dale, daughter of Cleon E. and Frances P. (Chism) Dale, married —————, December 25, 1896.

No. 336.

Russell Aubry Dale, son of Alfred Lafayette and Sallie (Butler) Dale, married a Miss Hinton.

No. 337.

Jake Bennett Dale, son of Alfred Lafayette and Sallie (Butler) Dale, is married.

No. 345.

Marcellus C. Dale, son of Andrew C. and Jane Ann (Chowning) Dale, married Ollie Carter, February 22, 1892, and has had three children.

658. Elsie, born in December, 1892; died in August, 1893.
659. Ernestine, born December 23, 1893.
660. Gertrude, born in March, 1894.

No. 346.

Etta Dale, daughter of Andrew C. and Jane Ann (Chowning) Dale, married John E. Binns, of Davidson County, Tennessee, January 28, 1895, and has one child.

661. Andrew Dale, born May 23, 1897.

No. 356.

Lizzie Bennett, daughter of Jake C. and Dulcena (Dale) Bennett, married James Speck, in 1893, and has one child.

662. A daughter.

No. 357.

Mattie Dale, daughter of Jake C. and Dulcena (Dale) Bennett, married Dr. J. E. Sidwell, in 1890, and has two children.

663. A son.
664. A son.

No. 361.

Edgar Bennett, son of Jake C. and Dulcena (Dale) Bennett, married a Miss Maxwell, in 1895.

No. 367.

Amos Dillard Bates, son of William Iredell, and Mary Ann (Robertson) Bates, married Florena Irene Seaton, September 20, 1882, and has one child.

665. Charles R., born April 15, 1884.

No. 368.

Myra Josephine Bates, daughter of William Iredell and Mary Ann (Robertson) Bates, married James R. Guthrie September 27, 1882, and has four children.

666. Maude M., born July 29, 1883.
667. Myrtle Irene, born January 12, 1885.
668. Ethel Reaugh, born December 2, 1886.
669. James Ralph, born June 9, 1890.

No. 369.

Ida Frances Bates, daughter of William Iredell and Mary Ann (Robertson) Bates, married David Lee Meyers, February 6, 1889, and has two children.

670. Harry Robertson, born March 28, 1893.
671. Justin Tinsmore, born November 14, 1895.

No. 370.

Mary Effie Bates, daughter of William Iredell and Mary Ann (Robertson) Bates, married James Anderson McAnulty, April 16, 1885, and has two children.

672. Arthur Dean, born January 10, 1886.
673. Grace Irene, born April 8, 1888.

No. 371.

William Eddy Bates, son of William Iredell and Mary Ann (Robertson) Bates, married Lillie Marshall, January 10, 1889, and has four children.

674. Bessie, born September 2, 1889.
675. Neva Don, born October 27, 1893.
676. Clarence Dillard, born May 3, 1895.
677. William Eddy, born February 4, 1897.

No. 373.

Joseph Marcus Bates, son of William Iredell and Mary Ann (Robertson) Bates, married Nora Earl, December 20, 1893. No children.

No. 375.

John Franklin Downing, son of William and Mary Elzada (Bates) Downing, was twice married, first, to Selina Lowrey,

September 12, 1872; second, to Lillie M. Elliot, May 3, 1892. He has one child.

BY HIS FIRST WIFE.

678. Albert W., born September 19, 1875.

No. 376.

Joseph Henry Downing, son of William and Mary Elzada (Bates) Downing, married Anna Tipton, June 16, 1880, and has had two children.

679. Jessie, born August 2, 1893.

680. Robert, born August 8, 1896; died September 30, 1897.

No. 377.

Albert Rezin Downing, son of William and Mary Elzada (Bates) Downing, married Emma Strickler, April 11, 1888, and has one child.

681. William Strickler, born March 6, 1896.

No. 378.

Jessie Viola Downing, daughter of William and Mary Elzada (Bates) Downing, married Mathew F. Smith, April 7, 1887, and has two children.

682. Ray Franklin, born January 14, 1889.

683. Henry Mathew, born January 18, 1895.

No. 381.

John E. Bates, son of Thomas J. and Leonora (Wilson) Bates, married Clara White, February 13, 1889, and has two children.

684. Harry W., born October 3, 1891.

685. J. Russell, born December 12, 1894.

No. 382.

Henson E. Bates, son of Thomas J. and Leonora (Wilson) Bates, married Hattie Sawyer, June 6, 1890, and has two children.

686. Floyd Bailey, born March 8, 1891.

687. Esther Sawyer, born May 3, 1893.

No. 383.

Henry M. Bates, son of Thomas J. and Leonora (Wilson) Bates, married Mary Adams, November 28, 1888, and has two children.

688. Myrl Meron, born December 5, 1889.
689. Charles Emmett, born October 20, 1891.

No. 384.

Carrie G. Bates, daughter of Thomas J. and Leonora (Wilson) Bates, married Samuel McClintock, April 15, 1891, and has two children.

690. Carl Everett, born August 29, 1892.
691. Forrest Bates, born August 9, 1896.

No. 388.

George Latimer Bates, son of Madison C. and Emma (Latimer) Bates, is in West Central Africa, making scientific collections of birds, animals, flowers, and plants.

No. 389.

Eula Goodpasture Bates, daughter of Madison C. and Emma (Latimer) Bates, is a missionary in Hadgin, Turkey.

No. 390.

Mary Drumon Bates, daughter of Madison C. and Emma (Latimer) Bates, married A. I. Sargent, a dentist, of Huntington, West Virginia, June 24, 1896, and has one child.

692. Constance, born September 29, 1897.

No. 393.

Lizzie May Thomas, daughter of David R. and Margery Josephine (Bates) Thomas, married Dr. H. H. Littlefield, November 24, 1887, and has one child.

693. Eula Belle, born September 27, 1888.

No. 394.

Nancy Josephine Thomas, daughter of David R. and Margery Josephine (Bates) Thomas, married Z. H. Sexton, September 23, 1885, and had one child.

694. Josephine, died May 7, 1887.

No. 395.

Edith Allegra Thomas, daughter of David R. and Margery Josephine (Bates) Thomas, married H. C. Smith December 7, 1892, and has one child.

695. Ethel Z., born September 30, 1893.

No. 398.

Lottie Maud Thomas, daughter of David R. and Margery Josephine (Bates) Thomas, married D. H. Flickwis, March 8, 1891, and has three children.

696. Jcsephine, born November 26, 1891.

697. Helen, born December 8, 1892.

698. Hallie N., born March 29, 1894.

No. 407.

Margaret Josephine Breese, daughter of Leland S. and Margaret Ann (Bates) Breese, married William Hugh Olm-sted, August 8, 1894, and has one child.

699. Cordelia Browne, born May 12, 1895.

No. 414.

Alpha Dale, daughter of W. A. and Rebecca (Lewis) Dale, married L. K. Edge, in 1881, and has four children.

700. Howard.

701. Loy.

702. Ova.

703. Glaidest.

No. 415.

Cora Dale, daughter of W. A. and Rebecca (Lewis) Dale, married M. M. Martin, in 1884, and has four children.

704. Winburn.

705. Raymond.

706. Oliver.

707. A girl.

No. 416.

Levina Dale, daughter of W. A. and Rebecca (Lewis) Dale, married E. E. Rountree, in 1888, and has four children—three girls and a boy.

708. Jewell.
709. Willie.
710. Lucy.
711. Ward L.

No. 417.

Thomas A. Dale, son of W. A. and Rebecca (Lewis) Dale, married Josephine Emerson, in February, 1895, and has one child.

712. Irene.

No. 420.

Flora Dale, daughter of John W. and Martha (Rountree) Dale, married a Mr. Ingram, and lives at Black Jack Grove, Texas. They have three children.

No. 421.

John T. Rountree, son of J. M. and Martha M. (Dale) Rountree, married Myrtle Pyle, and has one child.

713. Lawrence.

No. 429.

Nettie Goodpasture, daughter of Andrew S. and Mary Jane (Fletcher) Goodpasture, married William Foster, and has one child.

714. Ivan.

No. 430.

Henry Fletcher Goodpasture, son of Andrew S. and Mary Jane (Fletcher) Goodpasture, married Amy Caldwell, December 25, 1894, and has one child.

715. Gladys Marie, born September 10, 1896.

No. 413.

Andrew Ward Goodpasture, son of Andrew S. and Mary Jane (Fletcher) Goodpasture, married Claudia Williamson, June 20, 1895.

No. 436.

Marshall Goodpasture, son of William E. Goodpasture, married Pheby Chenney.

No. 452.

Edwin R. Goodpasture, son of J. Dillard and Frances H.
(Obanion) Goodpasture, was born in Morgan County,
Illinois, and moved with his father to Holt County, Missouri,
where he is a progressive farmer, and an extensive breeder
and feeder of live stock.   He married Cora (1872-   ),
daughter of William and Elizabeth Shields. September 20,
1893, and has one child.

716. Clyde M., born June 20, 1894.

No. 453.

Abraham H. Goodpasture, son of J. Dillard and Frances
H. (Obanion) Goodpasture, was born in Holt County, Missouri, where he is an energetic and successful young farmer,
a school director, and member of the Methodist Church.   He
married Josephine (1871-   ), daughter of Robert and
Lucinda Medsker, December 2, 1891.

No. 454.

Deedie A. Goodpasture, daughter of J. Dillard and Frances
H. (Obanion) Goodpasture, was born in Holt County, Mis-
souri, and educated at Cameron and St. Joseph.   She mar-
ried James E. Weller, son of Ernest F. and Ruth Weller,
September 16,1896.   Her husband is cashier of the Farmers
Bank, of Maitland, where they have a beautiful home.
They have one child.

717. Hiram Dillard, born September 22, 1897.

No. 455.

Mary E. C. Goodpasture, daughter of J. Dillard and
Frances H. (Obanion) Goodpasture, was born in Holt
County, Missouri, and was educated in the Maitland High
School, where she graduated in 1895, and was valedictorian
of her class.   She is a member of the Methodist Church, in
Maitland, Assistant Superintendent of its Sunday School,
and President of its Epworth League.

No. 456.

George B. Goodpasture, son of J. Dillard and Frances H. (Obanion) Goodpasture, was born in Holt County, Missouri, where he is engaged in farming and stock raising. He married Grace M. (1876-   ), daughter of William and Alice Nute, February 12, 1896.

No. 457.

Vrenna J. Goodpasture, daughter of J. Dillard and Frances H. (Obanion) Goodpasture, was born in Holt County, Missouri, and is now in school at Maitland.

No. 458.

Ethel Frances Goodpasture, daughter of J. Dillard and Frances H. (Obanion) Goodpasture, was born in Holt County, Missouri, and is now in school at Maitland.

No. 460.

Isabelle Webster, daughter of W. G. and Hattie E. (Goodpasture) Webster, was born in Sangamon County, Illinois, and graduated in the High School, at Petersburg, in 1895.

No. 468.

Ella Mitchell, daughter of L. A. and Tennessee G. (Hinds) Mitchell married F. C. Freeman, of Weakley County, Tennessee.

No. 469.

Dillard C. Mitchell, son of L. A. and Tennessee G. (Hinds) Mitchell, married Addie L. Long, of Robertson County, Tennessee.

No. 471.

Nancy E. Mitchell, daughter of L. A. and Tennessee G. (Hinds) Mitchell, married a Mr. Brown, of Texas.

No. 474.

Luvada Hinds, daughter of John S. and T. A. (Jones) Hinds, married D. W. Higginbotham, of Mississippi.

No. 475.

Mollie Hinds, daughter of John S. and T. A. (Jones) Hinds, married M. M. Davie, of Mississippi.

No. 496.

Mary Hettie Mitchell, daughter of Isaiah W. and Sophronie C. (Winton) Mitchell, married B. L. Speck, of Livingston, Tennessee. January 10, 1895.

20

INDEX.